THE HIGHLANDER'S UNTAMED TEMPEST

BROTHERS OF WOLF ISLE

The Highlander's Untamed Tempest

BROTHERS OF WOLF ISLE

Heather McCollum

USA TODAY BESTSELLING AUTHOR

This book is a work of fiction. Names, characters, places, and incidents are the product of the author's imagination or are used fictitiously. Any resemblance to actual events, locales, or persons, living or dead, is coincidental.

Copyright © 2024 by Heather McCollum. All rights reserved, including the right to reproduce, distribute, or transmit in any form or by any means. For information regarding subsidiary rights, please contact the Publisher.

Entangled Publishing, LLC
644 Shrewsbury Commons Ave
STE 181
Shrewsbury, PA 17361
rights@entangledpublishing.com

Scandalous is an imprint of Entangled Publishing, LLC.

Edited by Alethea Spiridon
Cover design by LJ Anderson, Mayhem Cover Creations
Cover photography by FXQuadro/GettyImages and TomasSereda/GettyImages
Interior design by Britt Marczak

Manufactured in the United States of America
First Edition September 2024

SCANDALOUS

The Highlander's Untamed Tempest is the fifth Brothers of Wolf Isle book from *USA Today* bestselling author Heather McCollum. The story includes elements that might not be suitable for all readers. Threat of rape, threat of children being harmed, abduction, and threat of drowning are mentioned in the novel. Readers who may be sensitive to these elements, please take note.

*To Rachel, my dear high school friend, (1972–2024)
and all those who fight so incredibly hard to live.*

Foreign Words

French (F) and Scots Gaelic (SG)

Amenez le chat – Bring the Cat (F)

bébé – baby (F)

dieu merci – Thank God (F)

garçon – lad (F)

Je suis français – I am French (F)

leis an diabhal – by the devil (SG)

ma fille – my daughter (F)

mo Dhia – my God (SG)

mon cœur – my heart (F)

mon Dieu – my God (F)

mon père– my father (F)

putain – whore but used like the F word (F)

rapidement – quickly (F)

taing Dhia – Thank God (SG)

verge – old slang for penis (F)

Chapter One

Isle of Mull, Scotland
31 October 1550

"'Tis Samhain," Eagan Macquarie's brother, Drostan, said. "Perhaps ye can find the headless Lady Gwyn to marry." Shrouded in white, the ghost was said to roam the moors on the night of Samhain with her black pig.

Eagan frowned down into his mug of honey mead. The lowering sun cast his shadow across the wooden table set in the meadow above Aros Castle as they celebrated with the Maclean Clan on the Isle of Mull. The familiar discussion about who Eagan should wed began once again, making his stomach twist and his mood blacken.

I'm leaving in the morning. The thought sat on his tongue, ready to stop all the nagging. But if he voiced his plans, the night would erupt into another turmoil as his family ordered him to stay. And he was resolute.

"I still say that Anna's sister, Kat, is bonny and old enough to wed now," Callum, Drostan's twin, said. He clamped his meaty paw down on Eagan's shoulder and moved it back and forth without Eagan resisting. "She's twenty."

Lark, Eagan's sister-by-marriage, tapped her fingernail on the rough table. "Meg Maclean would be the perfect addition to our clan."

Her husband, Adam, who was the oldest of the five brothers and the Macquarie chief, took Lark's hand and kissed it before saying, "Tor won't allow his daughter to wed a Macquarie. At least not until the curse is truly broken."

"Meg marrying Eagan will break the curse," Drostan said, lifting his tankard in salute.

Beck, the second oldest, snorted. "Meg and Eagan are practically sister and brother anyway. No bairns would come from that union."

His family threw names of potential brides about Eagan as if he weren't there. As if he had no say in the matter, a political bride locked away from any decisions regarding her life.

Eliza, Beck's pirate wife, sat with their two-year-old son on her knee. "If he weds Cecilia Maclean, he'll have an instant family." Her knee rose up and down, making Richard giggle, his blond curls dancing about his cherubic face.

Eagan frowned at Eliza, and she grinned back. His ire was licking up inside him like a fire gathering strength. 'Twas good it was Samhain, or he'd leave that minute. His bag was already packed and sitting in Gylin Castle.

"Cecilia's bairn will be a bastard," Rabbie MacDougall, their father's old friend, mumbled.

"Not Eagan's bastard," Adam was quick to add. "So it doesn't matter." He pulled Lark in toward him and squeezed her.

"Tor's niece is coming over from Barra Isle with Mairi and Alec MacNeil this week," Beck said. "I'm talking with Alec about shipping routes, and Eagan can talk to him about his sweet daughter, Brenna."

Bang! Eagan's tight fist hit the table, making all the wooden bowls jump. Some of the spiced nuts and sweet treats bounced out of them, scattering along the wooden planks in a chaotic mix. Eagan stood to his full height. "I'm not marrying anyone."

"Ye must," Rabbie said, his fuzzy gray eyebrows pinching as if they were two caterpillars trying to kiss. "To break the curse."

"The willow tree is full of bright leaves, and Wolf Isle is being repopulated," Eagan said.

Adam crossed his arms over his chest. "Unnaturally green leaves in autumn."

The willow tree that sat in the bailey before Gylin Castle on their isle represented the curse brought down on Wilyam Macquarie and his clan a century ago. Wilyam, the young chief, got a local lass with child, but abandoned her and married another, driving the pregnant lass to hang herself. Her mother, after cutting the bairn from her daughter's still-warm body, had brought the curse down on the Macquaries and their isle, stabbing the bloody knife into the willow tree where it still seemed to bleed today. No one could budge it nor explain the strange life cycle of the tree, but with each Macquarie brother finding love, the tree had healed from the dead willow it had been before. But the knife wound still bled, streaking the trunk with sap that looked like fresh blood.

All eyes rested on Eagan, and he jammed his hands through his chin-length hair. "The curse won't be broken by me marrying just anyone."

"Aye," Callum said. "Love must be involved."

Eagan crossed his arms. "I don't think that exists." He looked at his four brothers, each glancing at their wives with raised brows. "Not for me anyway," Eagan said. "For the four of ye, sure, but I'm independent." From the age of ten, Eagan had decided that he would one day go his own way. "I don't need the same woman warming my bed for the rest of my life."

Beck laughed. "Ye say that like 'tis a bad thing." He wrapped his arms around his wife, Eliza, their son before her.

"Vomit true love poetry and advice all ye want," Eagan said, "but I haven't met a lass interesting enough to make me want to talk to her rather than—"

"Eagan!" Lia, Drostan's wife, and Lark yelled at the same time.

"Little ears," Lark said, nodding to the three children around the table.

"Apologies," Eagan murmured and trudged off into the shadows toward one of the bonfires lit to keep away malevolent spirits.

Children of all sizes, several of them Macquaries, joined hands to dance around the fire. Just looking at them laughing and dancing with hearty health proved his clan had recovered. And Eagan wasn't about to let his happy family force him into wedding some lass to make the bloody willow tree drop its leaves in the fall.

He recognized the slender frame of his elderly Aunt Ida too late. She stood by the bonfire watching the children and turned to see him. "Eagan," she said, nodding, and reached out to grab his arm. The usual creases in her face and her frown seemed smoother. She almost looked happy. She turned back to the children but didn't relinquish his arm. "They make a lot of noise, but they're fun to watch."

The woman, his mother's sister, was old, grumpy, and probably lonely. She isolated herself in his childhood cottage here on Mull. "Happy Samhain," Eagan said.

"I'll set a place for your father…and my sister."

"If ye don't want to, I'm sure Lark will."

Ida flapped her free hand at the notion. "I always do it.

Lark can invite the dead to eat once I'm one of them."

The gloaming slowly gave way to night as they stood. Ida's gaze moved up and down him. "You look like a lad who's tired of the world.

He snorted. "I'm tired of my clan and isle and people telling me what to do." He was the bairn of the five brothers and had been told what to do by someone all his life, but now he was a man, larger in stature than all of them, and he'd decided he wanted to be free. He crossed his arms over his chest, bracing his hands in his armpits. "I'm going to journey to the mainland." The idea had taken shape into a solid plan over the last year, as his family's suggestions for brides became more forceful.

"Does Adam know?" she asked.

"He will tomorrow when I tell him." Eagan had supplies and coins to take him to the northern isles, where he could live alone for some time before continuing to wherever his feet took him. "I want to be left alone."

"You were a twin in the womb. You've never been alone."

She repeated what he'd been told his whole life. But Eagan had never felt a connection with a sister who died at birth. From the time he'd convinced himself that monsters didn't hide in the shadows, he'd fought to be by himself, which was nearly impossible in a home with four older brothers who were always tasked with watching out for him.

"You're part of the Macquarie pack of Wolf Isle," Aunt Ida said, and he heard the smile in her voice.

"I'll go as a lone wolf," Eagan said, liking the sound of that. No one telling him he had to wed. No lectures about working with a life partner to make things easier. No reminders that he was now responsible for ending the bloody curse.

"And leave your clan cursed?"

He inhaled long and full. "I'll return someday or maybe I'll marry somewhere else, and ye'll know it when the willow tree behaves like a tree and the dagger just falls out of the trunk one day." The point was he was tired of people telling him what he must do and when he must do it.

Fast footfalls crunched on the broken shells scattered on the path through the village before Aros Castle, and Eagan turned, releasing his aunt's arm. Meg Maclean, the Maclean Chief's daughter, ran toward him, a frantic look on her pale face.

"Meg?" he asked and recognized that Beck was right. Eagan only felt sisterly affection toward the bonny lass catching her breath before him. She would never be his second half, as Beck called his wife, someone who fit against him, making him whole. For fok's sake, Eagan felt whole all by himself even if he was at one time a twin.

Meg tried to catch her breath. "Row me over...to Wolf Isle. My mother and Aunt Grace... They're having trouble with Cecilia's birth." Meg blinked back tears. "I must fetch Grissell to save Cecilia and her bairn."

"Pardon, Aunt Ida." Eagan grabbed Meg's arm, and the two ran toward the dock. Cecilia had always been a prickly thorn, but when she'd found herself pregnant and her beau died before he could wed her, they'd all tried to be kinder toward her. Even Eliza who'd taken great offense of her interest in Beck.

Meg was too frantic for Eagan to stop to tell Adam, so they hurried on. "Grissell may not come. I've never known her to leave Wolf Isle," Eagan said.

"She said she'd help." They stopped by the ferry that his large family had poled over, but Meg pointed to a rowboat. "Take that one."

Out in the slip of water between the isles, Meg's breath finally calmed enough to speak in full sentences. "Grace said Grissell met with her the last time she visited your isle." Meg sat facing him, looking forward as Eagan put his shoulders into rowing them easily through the calm water.

"She said she'd come to Cecilia's birthing?" he asked. "She doesn't even like the woman."

"Grissell said she would help, because Cecilia would need it. 'Twas as if she knew the birth would be troublesome."

As Eagan watched the lights from Mull grow distant, he heard Meg gasp softly. "She's there on the shore. She knows," she whispered, passing the sign of the cross before her.

A glance over his shoulder showed a figure in white standing at the dock next to the lantern Adam left burning. If the circumstances weren't dire, he'd have asked if it was headless Lady Gwyn with her pig. He pulled the small craft up to the floating wooden dock and tied the boat's rope to iron loops in the wood. "'Tis safe," he said and felt the boat rock as Meg clambered out. He followed her up the wooden pier.

"Mistress Grissell, did you know I'd come tonight?" Meg spoke to the hunched form of Grissell, the elderly woman who took in women and children with nowhere else to go. She kept a series of cottages on the south side of the isle. One of her ancestors had cursed the Macquaries and sunk the knife into the willow tree a century ago.

"'Tis a dangerous night for those caught between life and death," Grissell said, her voice strong even if her body seemed weak.

"'Tis Cecilia," Meg said. "The bairn won't come. She needs you."

Grissell stared back while two white cats slid along her white petticoat. "I'm not going across."

"My Aunt Grace said you would give aid." Meg's voice held a note of pleading.

Grissell turned to the trees where a second figure in white walked out. The woman seemed to glide down the slope to the bank. Her petticoat, bodice, and shawl were white, giving her a ghostlike appearance. Meg took a step closer to Eagan. The woman stopped by Grissell, and the crone's gnarled fingers caught the woman's arm. "Tessa will go in my place."

The woman slid the shawl off her hair, revealing dark, wavy tresses that ended somewhere around her waist. Her face was pale in the darkness, standing out like the white of her clothing. She carried a bag. "I have cures and knowledge," she said, and her voice glided evenly like her walk. Graceful and serene. 'Twas almost like a song, and Eagan had the sudden yearning to hear her sing.

"Won't you come, Mistress?" Meg inspected Tessa with obvious unease.

Grissell was already turning away. "Tessa will take the place of me. I've prepared her." A darkly spotted cat, Sia, trotted out from the woods to join the two white ones flitting about the old woman, as she walked toward the woods without looking back.

Tessa stepped easily into the boat and sat, holding the satchel in her lap as Meg climbed in, followed by Eagan.

"I'm Meg Maclean. Thank you for coming to help my friend."

Tessa nodded and looked at Eagan.

"I'm Eagan. How long have ye been on Wolf Isle?" He hadn't heard anything about a beautiful dark-haired woman living with Grissell.

"One year."

Had she been hiding? "And yer name is Tessa?"

"I am Claudette Tempest Ainsworth, but I'm called Tessa."

Her accent was mixed and melodic. It seemed English on the surface but with French undertones.

"Hurry," Meg said, her fingers curled into the lip of her seat. Eagan used his oar to push off and turned them back the way they'd come.

"Ye're English?" Eagan asked, his arms working hard, bringing the familiar burn of training into his shoulders.

"I'm of Wolf Isle," Tessa said, meeting his gaze calmly. The light from Meg's lantern made Tessa's eyelashes seem even longer over her large eyes, eyes turned black in the shadows.

"Then you must know Gaelic," he said in the language.

Staring at him, her lips opened, and a string of French came out. He was only able to catch a few words and one sentence. "Je suis français."

"Ye're French," he said.

"I'm now Scottish," she said in English, a calm sternness over her smooth features. Her voice held serene conviction, daring him to contradict what she'd thrown out as absolute truth. He felt his mouth relax. If he had that quality, that inner determination, he'd have walked away from Wolf Isle years ago.

Eagan curbed his last stroke through the gently lapping water. The rowboat bumped up to the dock along the edge of Mull. "I'll help ye learn some Scots Gaelic," he said, and a prickle itched along the skin of his back.

Hadn't he just told Aunt Ida he was leaving Wolf Isle after tonight? And yet Claudette Tempest Ainsworth, with her fathomless eyes and gracefully retained strength, threatened to push him off course in the time it took to row across the strait.

Chapter Two

Tessa kept her eyes forward as they walked along the dark, winding path through the village. Raucous singing ebbed and flowed from the meadow off to the right, where two bonfires were lit for Samhain. The Scottish accents sounded harsh to her ears, so different from the flow of French, the sound of her true home.

Even after a year of living with the wild wind and sea around her, she didn't belong.

She never would.

The slicing edge of the coming winter cut along her cheeks with the wind, and she clutched her shawl closed. Tessa's heart thrummed in her chest, a cadence to the music and singing and the light fall of her thin boots on the crushed shells and pebbles making up the road.

The young woman who'd introduced herself as Meg Maclean talked continuously between sucking in gulps of air. The tethered panic in her voice made Tessa's feet move faster until she felt almost like she was floating. Grissell said it was one of her better qualities, how silently she could move.

There was safety in being silent.

"Her waters came this morn, and…the bairn is not… breaching," Meg said. "Cecilia is strong, but she's growing tired." Meg broke into a jog to keep up. "Aunt Grace thought Grissell would come."

"I have all her knowledge," Tessa said, her voice even. *And some of my own.* She was no longer an apprentice, not after helping her mother for twenty years before she died.

The man who'd rowed them across kept up easily on her other side, remaining slightly ahead to lead the way. Light-colored hair hung to his even cheekbones, sometimes covering his eyes. His beard was trimmed and neat, and his clothes draped him in the Highland style. Was Cecilia his wife? He was like a dutiful sentry, watching for anything that would slow their hastening. He was tall and broad across the back and shoulders. How he'd rowed proved no padding was needed to fill out his jacket. He was a warrior, not a courtier.

He'd looked at her with intensity on the boat, and she'd met his gaze. Tessa wasn't one to look away first when being pierced by sharp eyes. Her mother had said she reminded her of her father when she stared so intently.

"If you're the father, you may be of use inside the cottage," Tessa said.

"I'm no relation to Cecilia Maclean."

"You aren't a Maclean?" she asked. Candlelight from a few windows splashed dim light onto the dark path.

"I'm Eagan Macquarie, and I happened to be available to row Meg across."

Her heart quavered. *A Macquarie. Eagan Macquarie.* Grissell had kept her hidden from the Macquaries for the last year, teaching her in secret about her cures and meditations and how to run the orphanage and women's home. 'Twas as if she was protecting Tessa from them, but Eagan Macquarie didn't look like a monster. Grissell had seen him at the rowboat but had beckoned Tessa forward anyway. Was the birthing woman and her babe worth letting the Macquaries know Tessa was on their isle?

Meg ran ahead, rapping on a door before throwing it open. The loud keening of a woman in labor cracked out into the night. Tessa glanced at Eagan before entering. "Relation or not, I may need you to lift her, so don't go anywhere."

"Lift her? Where?" His eyes grew large as if she expected him to carry the woman all the way to Paris. *Mon Dieu.*

"Up toward the rafters," Tessa said.

"I don't th—"

"If I had your strength, I wouldn't ask. Stay here."

Tessa ducked around the door into the dimly lit room. The birthing scene was organized. The windows across the cottage were open just enough to allow air to move, but the hearth kept the temperature warm. Two middle-aged women stood on either side of the dark-haired woman on the bed. Sweat and tears wet her pinched face.

"Grissell sent Tessa," Meg said, gesturing toward her. "Tessa Ainsworth, who has been learning from Grissell over the last year."

"Good that old crone didn't come." The mother-to-be spat. "I don't want a witch touching my bairn."

Tessa's brows rose. *Witch?* Anger rose in her, but she pushed aside her want to defend her benefactress. The babe needed a calm world, and she wouldn't add to the angst swelling in the room.

A handsome older woman with a large bosom smiled at her, tilting her head, which held a bun of twisted braids. "A year. And we haven't met?"

"Perhaps witches are keeping my bairn from coming into the world," the straining woman said, her face flushed and splotchy.

"Hush now," soothed the woman with a long braid.

"There are no witches about. Tessa has come to help." The woman looked at Tessa. "I'm Ava Maclean, lady of Aros Castle. This is my sister, Grace Mackinnon." Ava nodded to Meg. "You've met my daughter, Meg."

Grace walked closer to Tessa, lowering her voice. "Grissell sensed this birth would be difficult and said she would help."

Tessa met Grace's sharp stare. "She is helping by sending me. I know everything she knows, and I apprenticed for twenty years with a midwife in France." Even though her words were firm, Tessa's stomach tightened. She'd helped her mother and she'd seen much, but childbirth was dangerous. Both mother and bébé could die even with the best care.

"Twenty years?" Grace asked. "You barely look twenty."

"I began with my mother when I was five. I am eight and twenty now."

Grace blinked and then turned toward Cecilia, her skirts flaring with the force. "Mistress Tessa is a renowned midwife, Cecilia," she called over the woman's groan. "She'll bring your bairn into the world and keep you in it."

Lord, please let it be true.

Tessa walked up to the straining lady, removing her shawl. "I will check your progress and devise a plan to help you labor easier."

The woman didn't answer, which indicated she was weakened. Tessa wanted to help her rest as much as she could between pains. She set her satchel near a table and pulled out her supplies, laying them out in an orderly fashion. Tansy root decoction, two knives, string, three clean cloths, a tray, and the Eagle's Stone Grissell had given her. It was a hard nut that rattled when one shook it, but it was known by midwives to ease the pain of childbirth, especially if the woman laboring believed in it. Same with a knife placed under the bed.

Tessa took one knife and the Eagle's Stone to the side

of the bed. She held up the knife. "This goes under the bed to cut the pain." She slid it under the bed, hearing it coming to rest on the wooden floorboards. "And here is the Eagle's Stone from Afrika that Grissell is letting you borrow." She slid it over Cecilia's head and lowered it to rest on her chest. "It protects the babe and the mother from death."

"I've heard of this," Grace said, fingering the stone. "It rattles." She shook it gently and looked at Cecilia. "Hear it? 'Tis a real Eagle's Stone."

"I'll check your progress," Tessa said but waited until Cecilia nodded. Tessa slid back the bottom sheet, which was wet with urine and birthing fluids. "We need to change these linens."

Grace hurried to find more in the corner. Tessa looked under for a long moment and came up, keeping her face serene despite the worry coursing through her. The woman's body wasn't opening enough to allow passage.

"Rest," she said, smiling at Cecilia before turning to Ava. "We need a warm bath in here. I want her in it. We must relax the body so it will open farther. Plus, my herbs."

Ava didn't question her but strode to the door, throwing it open as if to charge out. Tessa saw Eagan standing there. "Oh," Ava said. "Good. We need a bath brought here immediately and buckets of water from the caldrons up at Aros. There is a large bathing tub there, too."

Eagan's gaze slid into the room, and Tessa felt it connect with hers. Then he turned and jogged off into the darkness.

Tessa brought Cecilia the tansy root decoction. "Two spoonsful to strengthen you and your babe, Cecilia." The tired woman took it down without hesitation. Good. She had hope. 'Twas the most important contribution to a successful birth.

"We will have a warm bath for you to soak in." Tessa spoke evenly when Cecilia shook her head. "Warm water will keep you and the babe clean of this foulness. My herbs will soothe it and help your body open."

"It will drown," she said.

"No, the babe gets its air from you until I cut the cord that binds you together."

"You've seen this done?" Grace asked. "A birth in water?"

Tessa nodded. "I assisted my mother three times this way." She looked back at Cecilia. "But 'tis up to the mother, of course."

"Bloody foking hell," Cecilia cursed. "I don't know what to do."

Tessa took her hand, which was balled tightly. She stroked the fingers open one by one. "Then trust me." She looked into Cecilia's eyes. The young woman was terrified. *Soothe her.* Tessa could almost hear her mother's whisper. "Trust me." And then Tessa began to sing.

Her voice flowed out from her middle as if she'd opened an aqueduct, the higher-pitched notes rising and falling with the words of her mother's favorite lullaby about a bird learning to fly. Tessa sang in French, but it wasn't the words that soothed. It was the melody. She closed her eyes, releasing the emotions of worry, hope, and then triumph as the bird joined its mother in a tall oak tree.

"Little bird, little bird, do not fear the ground. Look upon the sky above and soar toward Heaven..."

When Tessa sang, she imagined the sound ribboning out of her to swirl about those nearby. She inhaled, taking the air from her lungs and turning it into beauty, like a mosaic or tapestry of colors. Orderly but beautifully woven.

When the song finished, Tessa opened her eyes to find everyone in the room staring at her. The exhausted woman's face had warmed with color, and she breathed easier.

Meg sat holding Cecilia's hand but stared at Tessa as if in

a trance. Ava spoke first. "That was…" She shook her head. "The most beautiful song I've ever heard. A bird struggling to fly."

Tessa looked at her. "You know French?"

"Oui," Ava said and took a breath. "You are most talented, Mistress Tessa."

"'Twas a song my mother taught me." Tessa nodded to Cecilia. "It calms."

A breeze blew around them, and Tessa looked at the door, which was open. Eagan Macquarie stood there with a large wooden tub sitting on its end. He cleared his throat. "I brought the tub." Had he heard her sing or was he just shocked to be this close to a birthing woman?

Grace draped Cecilia with a clean sheet, and Eagan brought the tub in. Several other men followed. "Two steaming buckets," a brawny man with graying hair said. "And two boiled and cooled earlier."

"Good, the water is clean," Tessa said, nodding and pointing to a spot near the hearth to set the tub.

The man poured his bucket in the tub and walked to Grace, tipping her chin to bring her eyes up to his. "Usually 'tis I who makes ye dumbfounded by my kisses." He leaned in and kissed her mouth.

When he backed up, Grace's cheeks were stained red. "Her song," Grace said. "'Twas mesmerizing."

As the men filed out, they glanced at Tessa, mild suspicion in their eyes. "I'll stay outside in case ye need me," Eagan said and closed the door behind him.

The men walked off, along with Keir and Tor, toward the bonfires. Eagan knew he could call on them if more help was needed.

"Who is she?"

Eagan turned to the shadows next to the house where he spotted a short, stout man he didn't know. Father Timothy, the traveling priest, stood with him. Were they hiding there?

"A midwife," Eagan said, his instincts making his blood rush. "From Wolf Isle."

The man wore a cape over a tunic and breeches tucked into tall black boots. His tall rectangular hat sat over hair that fell to his shoulders. He carried a staff.

"Her singing mesmerized everyone who walked within hearing," the man said, using his upright staff to indicate a wide circle before the cottage.

Eagan glanced at the silent priest and then back at the man. "Who are ye, and what's yer business here on Mull?"

A cold smile spread over the man's clean-shaven face, giving him a devilish look in the flicker of Father Timothy's lantern. "I am Walter Gleeb, and my business is witches."

Instant dislike licked up inside Eagan. He'd heard how people on the mainland and all throughout Europe were being judged and executed as witches without proof except for their confessions under torture.

"There are no witches on Mull or Wolf Isle, Master Gleeb," Eagan said and nodded to the priest. "As I'm certain Father Timothy has told ye."

"'Tis a fearful business," the young priest said, crossing himself. "The church has asked us to hunt out any heretics worshipping Lucifer and"—he looked at Eagan with widening eyes—"and who cast curses on good Christian peoples."

"Good Christian peoples?" Eagan asked, letting his disregard float on his words. "How about terrible Christian peoples?" He spoke of his ancestor Wilyam Macquarie who brought the curse onto his clan a century ago.

Gleeb frowned, the harsh lines of his face more cutting in the flickering light. "'Tis not humorous, lad."

The term 'lad' made Eagan's hands ball into fists. As the youngest Macquarie, he'd fought all his life to be seen as older. Now that he was twenty-six and the tallest of his brothers, the term didn't fit him.

"There are witches all over Scotland," Gleeb continued. "And I'm paid by the crown to find and punish them."

"I've seen no evidence of witchcraft, Master Gleeb," Father Timothy said, which was probably true. He'd rarely come to Wolf Isle, and as far as Eagan knew, he'd never actually seen Grissell, who looked very much like the proverbial witch with her long white hair and gnarled features.

Gleeb nodded at the cottage, where the faint melody of another song began. "Open your eyes, Father. Witches are walking amongst you. They're especially active tonight when the veil between the living and dead is thin."

"Samhain is a night to honor our dead," Eagan said. "There's nothing evil about it."

"True, true," Father Timothy said, nodding his head rapidly. "'Tis All Saints Day on the morrow. We celebrate the saints." Pope Gregory renamed the pagan day in the ninth century, making it Christian.

Gleeb pointed at the bonfire on the hill, around which people clasped hands and danced in a circle. They laughed, and several people were passing along bottles of spirits. "I don't think your flock is praying to saints, Father."

Inside the cottage, the singing had stopped. The stilted cries of a newborn bairn trickled out to announce a new life into the world.

And what a dangerous world it had come into.

・・・

Tessa worked with Cecilia in the warm tub, helping her purge the afterbirth into the now murky water. The bath had worked wonderfully to calm the mother, helping her body to open and pulse the baby down the channel into the warm embrace of water. Water births helped clean the newborn, providing a calm, warm environment not unlike the womb.

"We'll get you out soon," Tessa said. "And give you a bath in clean water." There were still two buckets left and one was being reheated over the hearth flames.

Cecilia nodded, but her head lulled back with her exhaustion. "Sing to me again," she whispered. "'Tis calming."

Tessa was tired, too, but not as tired as this woman. She began a lullaby she used to sing to the young Prince Francis II of France, although his father, King Henri, paid her to continue even after his son had fallen asleep each night. The memories tightened her stomach, but the fluid sound of her voice slid through her, untangling the knots wrought by memories of her past.

The babe was surrounded by experienced midwives, so Tessa kept her attention on Cecilia.

"And the nightingale sings to the princess and prince, floating them off to the lake of dreams…" she sang in French.

Meg and Ava came over. "We will help her out if you think 'tis time."

The evidence of the placenta was in the tub, so she nodded. "Then we will change the water and let her bathe again."

"Lady Grace wishes you to see the bairn," Meg whispered near her ear. Tessa frowned, glancing toward the woman as she examined the newborn.

"I want to hold Lydia," Cecilia said.

"Soon," Ava answered, gathering dry linens that were warming by the fire.

Tessa turned to Grace, who held Lydia near the hearth. "Is there an issue?" Tessa whispered.

Grace slid the blanket down to expose the child's left

arm, where a one-inch irregular circle of bright red sat. Tessa had seen small bright red birthmarks, but this one was large and raised. She rubbed her thumb over it. "I've seen these before. So has Grissell. She says they fade away."

Grace lifted the babe up to lie across her ample bosom and slid the blanket down. "There's a second mark here."

Tessa touched it. "It doesn't seem to pain her."

Ava came over. "I worry about Cecilia's reaction." She glanced over to the bed where Cecilia was covered in linen, while Meg lifted buckets of water out of the tub, tossing it out the window.

"They'll fade," Tessa said with a confident nod.

"I have ointments that will help," Ava said, sighing. "With varying success."

Ava took the babe from Grace and carried her over to Cecilia, who waited for clean water to be added to the now empty tub. Meg had done all the heavy lifting and stood panting, wiping an arm over her damp forehead.

"Here is Lydia," Ava said, smiling, and laid the babe in Cecilia's open arms.

"She's beautiful." Tears sprang to Cecilia's dark eyes.

Tessa's mother had told her to watch new mothers meet their babes.

'Tis when the mother's heart, which was selfishly inside her all her life, is born into another. It now lives outside her in that little person she will do anything to protect.

"She has a special mark," Ava said. "Two actually. They will fade as she gets—"

"A mark?" Cecilia's eyes widened. "What type of mark?" She began to pull the babe's swaddling loose, and Ava reached to help her pull the arm from the blanket. Cecilia gasped as she saw the bright red circle raised on Lydia's arm.

"I didn't do anything wrong." Cecilia shook her head. It was believed that mothers could inadvertently harm their growing babe by doing random acts of living like seeing a hare, or having intercourse, or even burning their tongues on soup. Tessa thought it was all flim-flam.

Cecilia's wide gaze snapped to Tessa. "You did something," she whispered. "You made me get in the tub, and my bairn has a burn on her."

"'Tis a birthmark that will fade," Tessa assured her. "I've seen both marks before, and they disappeared before the child was grown."

Cecilia shook her head as if not taking in anything Tessa said. "Stay away from me and my Lydia," Cecilia yelled. "Your singing and your touch. You cursed her!"

A wise person knew when to leave, and Tessa had learned to be wise. As Cecilia began to cry, Tessa gathered her herbs and instruments. She fished among the pillows under Cecilia's head to find the Eagle's Stone.

"Stay away from me!" Cecilia yelled, but Tessa wasn't about to leave Grissell's stone.

Her fingers closed around it, and she spun away from the crying woman to grab up her satchel. "Your babe will be hale and hearty," Tessa said. Let the other ladies take care of Cecilia now. Tessa flung open the door, rushing out.

She stopped short, hand flattening against her heart. Eagan Macquarie stood taller than the two other men, one of them a priest and the other with a tall hat and a thin staff. A whirl of dizziness swamped Tessa, and she staggered.

Eagan's hands shot out to support her shoulders. "Tessa?"

"The babe is healthy. A girl." She looked to the priest. "There's no immediate need for christening, Father. She seems hearty."

Eagan guided her to lean onto his outstretched arm. Muscles lay over bone under his tunic, feeling unbreakable no matter her weight. "I will take ye up to Aros to rest," he said. Exhaustion and the warmth of him stopped her from pulling away even though he was a Macquarie.

"Mistress Ainsworth," the tall-hatted man said. Something in his smile sent another shiver through her. Eagan drew her closer as if trying to clothe her in his heat.

"I am Master Gleeb, and I will speak with ye in the morn."

It wasn't a request. It was an order.

Chapter Three

Eagan kept her arm tucked into his. Even though she seemed tired, her steps were light as if she'd been born part fairy and hovered with supernatural grace. "Meg told me ye're invited to stay the night at Aros Castle. Lady Ava probably wants ye to check in on Cecilia before ye leave for Wolf Isle."

Tessa remained silent throughout his speech. He listened for the slight crunch of her feet on the ground, as if that would prove she was a lass and not some ethereal fae roaming the night of Samhain. "Did ye celebrate Samhain in France or England or wherever you came from?"

"No," she said, glancing beside him where long tables had been set for the dead. "Is there a big feast to come?"

He hadn't even thought about her being hungry. "We already feasted but there's still food. Let's find ye something." He veered them toward the tables.

"But the tables are dressed as if no one has eaten."

"'Tis for the dead." They walked to a table with the remaining food. "'Tis tradition that we celebrate those who have died on Samhain night," he explained. "We set a place for each person we mourn, so they feel welcome and remembered."

She turned large, dark eyes up to him. "Do you think the dead feel anything?" Light from the torches set up around the feast tables showed the pinch in her brows.

"I don't know," he said, "but 'tis a tradition, more for the living than the dead."

Her attention shifted to the tables. "Does it help?"

"Help?"

"Do you mourn less by doing it?"

Did he? Eagan obviously didn't remember his mother since she'd died soon after he was born, along with his twin sister. He mourned his father when he died years ago. Would the pain of losing him linger more if he hadn't set a place for him at the Samhain table?

"I don't know," Eagan answered.

"You don't know a lot," she murmured, but her tone was teasing.

He snorted softly and handed her a bun and knife smeared with butter. "I don't think about the dead much."

Her small grin slid away. "Then you've not lost someone you love." Tessa slathered the butter on the bun and walked along the table, bending to peer at some of the dolls that were set to represent people. "Are there plates set for your family?" she asked.

He strode halfway along the far table. "My mother, Hilda Gunn Macquarie…" He touched a doll of braided hay. "My father, John Macquarie…" He pointed to the next plate where a jagged rock sat. "'Tis a rock from Wolf Isle." He moved to the small plate next to his mother. "And this is for my twin sister, Felicia." A woven doll, the size of his thumb, lay swaddled on the plate.

"Your twin? How terrible. You must mourn them, and

your father."

"Felicia died at birth, and my mother shortly after. I didn't know them, and my father seemed...content to move on."

Tessa laid her hand on his arm. The simple gesture, so light and gentle, dispelled the twinge of sadness like a wave washing away a line in the sand. "But to lose your twin... You must have a sense of loneliness."

Eagan felt his face tighten. "I'm never alone with a large family around me. I am actually searching for some loneliness." He grinned, but it was forced.

"I have been alone more times than not."

"I'm sorry."

Her smile seemed filled with memories. "Doing things alone can be satisfying but doing things with another pulls on two sets of strengths. My mother and I made a great team, but now she is gone."

Eagan supposed he and his brothers were a team of sorts, protecting their home against the pirate, Jandeau, and any Englishmen who came to cause trouble.

They were silent for a long moment, the evening breeze crisp. "Would ye like to add a place for her?"

She nodded, her dark hair moving about her beautiful pale face. "Oui." He retrieved a plate from the stack provided by Tor and Ava and made room next to Felicia. "Do ye have something of hers to put on it? If not—"

"I have this," she said, pulling a locket from her bodice. It hung on a golden chain and was shaped like a birdcage. "'Twas my mother's, but I never take it off." Before he could study it, she tucked it away. "But I have a ribbon we shared." She pulled a blue ribbon from a pocket in her white petticoat, which was stained with water from the bathing birth. Her fingers worked to tie it in a little bow, and she placed it on the plate. "Will I get it back?"

"No one dares touch the items to call the dead," he said, and placed a small rock on one end of the ribbon. "So it won't blow away."

A smile curved her lips. "Merci," she whispered.

The word made her lips touch together before parting, and like a spell, the movement and lyrical sound seemed to pull him closer to her. *Soft lips. Kissable lips.* Eagan wanted to do more than kiss her. He wanted to wrap her in his arms, protecting and warming her on every side.

It was more than a mere carnal reaction to being in the presence of a beautiful woman. He'd lusted before. Lust was like a tickling throb through his body, a hardening, preparing it for action. This feeling was like a languid flow of heat spreading across his chest. Perhaps it was her delicate form or that she'd no one besides Grissell to protect her. Her mother was dead, and she hadn't mentioned a father.

Tessa's full inhale made her breasts rise, swelling a bit above the embroidered neckline of her bodice. He blinked, bringing his gaze back to her face. Her mouth quirked up on one side as if she'd caught him looking at her breasts. Her cool fingers found his hand, and she tugged him toward the meadow where people still laughed and danced.

"Now show me the fires."

. . .

Tessa was tired, but the revelry called to her. After a year at Grissell's orphanage on Wolf Isle, the isolation, so different from the courts of Paris, had begun to weigh on her spirit. Perhaps she should suggest Eagan change places with her so he could relax in some loneliness, because Tessa surely missed the laughter and celebration found in a crowd.

When her mother, Rebecca, lived, she'd taken Tessa to

all the festivals in Paris and the surrounding countryside, following the court of King Francis I. The colors and music, the luster and laughter had mesmerized Tessa, and in turn she had mesmerized the court with her voice.

"We walk between the fires to be blessed for the coming year," Eagan said. As they walked across the uneven ground, he offered her his arm, and she took it. She prided herself in her grace but liked the feel of him under her hand. And despite his gaze momentarily taking in her body, he'd only looked into her eyes. What an unusual man.

He led her up to the fire, heat billowing out as the bright flames reached for the inky sky above. They stood before the larger one where the dancing had stopped, the children being rounded up by several young women who looked over at her with Eagan. They were curious, but Tessa saw no venom in their faces. Her mother had taught her long ago how to spot treachery behind bland smiles and plotting eyes.

Three girls skipped over toward them, holding hands. One was nearly a woman, one about ten years old, and the last, with blond braids, was not older than five years. "Uncle Eagan," the middle child called. "'Tis time to go home." All three smiled, curtseying before Tessa.

"My lady," the oldest said.

"Milady," the littlest repeated, holding her dress wide as she sunk again.

Tessa smiled in return. Such good manners. She dipped into a deep curtsy. "My ladies," she said.

They stared wide-eyed at her, the youngest giggling.

"I'm Pip," said the middle child. "And this is my sister, Hester." She squeezed the little girl to her.

"And I'm Aggie," the oldest said. "Two of my sisters are married to two of Eagan's brothers." She nodded to him.

"I'm Tessa."

"You're lovely," Hester whispered, and Tessa felt the

girl's sweetness flow through her as if she'd been infused with honey.

She lowered so she came even with the youngest. "And you are précieux, precious." She caught one of the curls spinning out from her braid to curve along her flushed cheek.

"Tessa can come home with us," Aggie said, looking at Eagan. "Meg told Lark and Anna that she lives with Grissell." Aggie looked embarrassed and turned her gaze to Tessa. "That you, milady, live on Wolf Isle." There was a question in her tone.

Tessa looped her arm through Eagan's again. All three girls watched with curiosity. "I do," Tessa said, "but tonight I must remain to check on the wee babe and mother in the morn."

"I'll stay with her," Eagan said, placing her hand on his arm. "I mean…I'll stay at Aunt Ida's and bring Tessa over in the morn when she's done."

Tessa liked the warmth of his large palm over the back of her hand. She could feel the roughness of callouses, proving that his muscles were built from hard work.

"Aunt Kat said you'd stay here with her," Hester said in her little-girl voice and giggled.

Pip whispered something in the child's ear, and Hester covered her mouth with both hands, one on top of the other.

"When you do come over," Aggie said, looking at Tessa, "my sister and the other wives of the Macquarie brothers invite you to visit Gylin Castle. We would like to know you." She tipped her head to one side. "I can't believe you've been on Wolf Isle for a year, and we've never met."

Ye should stay hidden from them.

Grissell's warning nagged at Tessa, but she nodded at the girls and raised her gaze to the women standing beyond in a cluster. There were at least six adult women and four children, two boys and two girls chasing around each other. She gave the curious ladies a nod, and they smiled back.

"I would be pleased to visit," Tessa said, and Hester clapped her hands.

The three bobbed another curtsy and ran back to the group. Several large men nodded toward Eagan and herded the children toward the dock. An older man with a thick beard trotted after them as if worried he'd be forgotten.

"You have a large family," she said as she watched.

"Aye," he said, sounding almost sullen. "And there are few secrets with the littles being sent off to discover information."

Tessa laughed softly. "They're good at finding things out."

"Ye have no idea," he murmured.

Her smile faded, and she turned back to the flames. "Having a family is a blessing." She dropped his arm and walked toward the fire.

He caught up in two strides. "Apologies, Tessa."

"For what?"

He frowned down at her. "For whatever I said that took the smile from yer lips."

He'd been watching her lips? She sniffed, looking back at the fire. "I have no siblings," she said, "and my mother died two years ago. So…having a large family seems wonderful to me."

"I'm sorry about yer mother." After a long pause, he asked, "Ye don't know yer father?"

"I do," she said, her mind going to the imposing figure of the man who'd brought her to Wolf Isle. "My father is Captain Lemaire, who sails for the French Navy." She looked at him. "They were married, but he was unable to live with us due to his station."

She looked back at the flames lest he see the disappointment in her eyes. "He rescued me from the Paris streets after my mother died. I had nowhere to go unless it was to some man's bed as a mistress. My father dropped me off at Ulva Isle, or Wolf Isle as you call it. He promised to return for me when he could." She nodded, clutching her hands together into a fist to rest against her chest. "I know he will, and I wait for him." She could feel the outline of her locket beneath the white bodice Grissell had given her to wear since it was Samhain.

So the spirits will think of ye as one of their own and leave ye be.

"How did he even know about Grissell's home or our little isle?" Eagan asked.

She shouldn't give too much information out to near strangers. "Captain Lemaire is knowledgeable about the isles around Scotland and England. King Henri is most interested in places he could land troops to invade England."

Eagan rubbed the back of his neck. "'Twould be nice to have England on the defensive. Now that Scotland's wee Queen Mary is in France to wed the dauphin, some think the French should help defend us from the bloody English."

"A drink for ye." A woman's voice made them both turn from the fire.

"Ah," Eagan said, "good eve, Greta."

"I know ye were helping birth a bairn," the curvaceous woman in an apron said, handing cups to her and Eagan. "I saved ye both a cup of my latest whisky batch, and 'tis a good thing, too, for this rowdy group has left barely a drop."

"Ye make the smoothest spirits, Greta."

With a quick perusal of Eagan, and a smile for them both that looked genuine, she turned and walked off, her hips swaying like a pendulum. Tessa glanced at Eagan, but he'd turned back to the fire, missing the display.

"She wants you in her bed."

Eagan spit out the sip he'd taken, his gaze going to her

and then to Greta walking down the hill.

"What?"

"The woman, Greta, she'd welcome you to her bed."

"I...I'm not interested in her bed."

Tessa took a sip of the whisky, letting it slide down her throat. It was smooth.

Eagan watched her. "Ye're experienced with drinking whisky then?"

She took a bigger sip and breathed out the fiery fumes. "My mother felt I should keep my wits when men ply me with drink."

He swallowed, watching her as the liquid slid down his throat. "Have men plied ye with drink?"

Tessa felt the fiery brew begin to release the tension in her shoulders. "Oui, they did try, but..." She looked mischievously over the rim of her cup at him. "They were not successful."

They both took a drink while staring at one another, and Tessa felt a stirring coil down inside her to her loins. Since coming to Scotland, she'd only felt cold inside and out, but the heat from the fire, whisky, and the magnificently brawny Highlander began to thaw her.

She certainly hadn't been promiscuous before, her mother watching her like a mother should at the French court, but Tessa wasn't a virgin, either. Her mother, wanting to make sure her daughter experienced pleasure before being caught up in the whirlwind of living, hired a talented man to show Tessa what should happen between a man and a woman. Rebecca had explained how bodies came together in words, and Tessa had agreed to the one-night liaison with the man who had pulled pleasure from her and taught her the ways to give pleasure.

I won't leave your education up to some rutting incompetent, her mother had said.

Tessa watched Eagan Macquarie. What would Rebecca Ainsworth think of the tall, muscular man drinking whisky with her? She opened her mouth to ask him if he was a rutting incompetent.

"Would ye like to walk between the fires for the blessing?" he asked, and she pulled her question back inside. Maybe she'd just have to discover if he were incompetent or not.

"I could always use a blessing," she said and took his offered arm again. As they walked across the uneven ground, Tessa noticed many young and older ladies watching them. "There will be talk tomorrow."

"Talk?" He looked around and then said something low and in Gaelic that sounded like a curse. "Those are lasses who want to wed and their scheming mothers."

"You don't want to wed one of them?" There were some women with light hair, dark hair, tall stature, curvaceous softness…every type of woman.

"Nay," he said, guiding her around fresh cow dung from the parade of animals.

"Tell them we're courting then," she said, her heart picking up speed despite her uncaring tone.

He chuckled. "Thank ye, but they won't believe it. I've tried to start a rumor that I was interested in a lass, and it didn't work."

"Did she not play the part?" Tessa asked. The flames chased away the chill in the autumn air as they slowly walked between the two bonfires.

"She didn't exist, so nay, she didn't play her part. I couldn't ask a real lass to act like we were courting. 'Twould lead her to believe we would eventually wed."

"And you don't want to wed?"

He exhaled. "I've been trying to escape the wedding noose my whole life. I have other plans that will take me exploring. First the rest of Scotland and then farther reaches of the world."

"And the mamas want you to stay and wed their daughters, tie you here, trap you."

"Ye can see why 'tis too risky to pretend with a lass here."

Perhaps it was the whisky relaxing her, or the loneliness that had plagued her, but Tessa made up her mind quickly. As they walked out from between the fires, she pulled Eagan to stand before her and planted her hands on his chest. The muscles beneath the tunic were hard, and she slid upward to capture the back of his neck, pulling his face down to hers. He let her, and before she could worry, Tessa planted her lips on Eagan's.

The stiffness in his form dissolved, and his arms came up around her. Heat hit Tessa from all sides, but the warmth that drew her was from Eagan. Without releasing his neck, she slanted her mouth against his, deepening the kiss. He tasted of whisky, and his kiss held barely restrained passion. One of his hands came up to thread into her hair, climbing to cup her head, allowing him to bend her into his body.

Tessa had the urge to get closer to Eagan, to feel his skin on her skin. His verge was hard enough that she could feel it through his plaid and her single petticoat. This wasn't the response her sexual tutor had exhibited when they'd kissed. His touch had been precise, slow, meticulous whereas Eagan was fierce and almost rough. It was as if he wished to shred her clothing right off her. The thought scattered through her like falling sparks, unleashing her own passion.

"Tessa?"

The woman's voice was far off. She wouldn't have noticed it except that Eagan stiffened and cold replaced the warmth of his mouth on her damp lips. He stepped back, and she made to follow.

"Meg is coming," Eagan said, and it took a moment for Tessa's thoughts to solidify enough for her to remember who this interfering Meg was. Eagan glanced around. "And everyone is watching."

Tessa stared up into his frowning face and released a slow breath. "Now they'll believe we're courting."

Chapter Four

Eagan walked through the morning mist toward the cottage at the edge of Aros Village. 'Twas where he and his father and brothers had lived with their mother's sister, Ida, soon after he was born.

The fifty-five-year-old woman went by Ida Macquarie, adopting the last name when her sister married John Macquarie. Even though she was only a bit older than the chief's wife, Ava, she acted like an old woman. Perhaps it was her grumpy nature that aged her.

Eagan shook the water droplets from his hair. The dip in the loch north of the village had helped cool his blood after a night of stimulating dreams about Tessa. Even the scent of his aunt's cottage, lavender and mugwort, hadn't been enough to quell his jack. Luckily, Aunt Ida had been asleep when he'd come in from the fire after Meg had led Tessa away to the castle. He'd left the festival right afterward, not wanting to answer questions from the lads. And he had no desire to find a willing lass after Tessa's kiss.

That one kiss had ensnared his mind like her song had

earlier in the evening.

By the devil! He'd wanted to dive into her soft, sweet body right there. Eagan had kissed his fair share of lasses on Mull and at fairs on the mainland, but he'd never been kissed like that. 'Twas as if liquid fire had infused him. Even though it had just been a kiss, he felt like they'd tupped. No, not tupped. That sounded too casual, too light. What occurred between them was more primal, more all-consuming.

And they'd been right out there where everyone could see.

He knocked. "Aunt Ida?" Heaven forbid he walked in on Ida getting dressed. "'Tis Eagan."

"Come inside," she called.

He hadn't wanted to wake her before dawn when he rose to bathe, but she was up now, dressed and spooning out porridge from a small pot sitting in the coals from last night.

Her hard eyes turned on him. "You were off to the loch?"

"Aye."

"Want to smell nice for the new lass?"

"New lass?"

"Aye, the one everyone's talking about. The one you were practically getting with child by the fires last eve."

Eagan's face warmed. She snorted softly, and her frown relaxed into something close to a grin. "Rabbie's going to warn you about not begetting a bastard." That was Ida's way of warning him, too.

Eagan had heard about the curse of Wolf Isle from the moment his eldest brother, Adam, noticed that lasses were more interesting than their male friends. An ancestor of Grissell's, a known witch, had rescued her granddaughter from her daughter's still-warm body after the girl hanged herself in grief. Wilyam Macquarie, the chief, had gotten the girl pregnant but then wed another. Grissell's great-grandmother had cursed the clan, stabbing the willow tree with the knife coated in her own daughter's blood, the knife she'd used to cut the bairn free so it wouldn't die with her. The knife was still embedded in the trunk of the willow tree standing in the bailey of Gylin Castle, unable to be removed.

Eagan sat down, pulling the bowl before himself. The steam rose up from the creamy texture dotted with dark currants. "Thank ye for this."

"You should marry her now. 'Twill stop the town from gossiping and your brothers and their wives from nagging you."

"Tessa won't want to marry me," he said, blowing on the hot porridge. *And I'm leaving.*

"I hear she's agreed to let you court her." Ida sat down with her own bowl. "I thought you were leaving, going to the northern isles or some such nonsense."

"I'm still planning to go." A pretty lass and a kiss weren't changing his course. "Just not today. I need to take her back to Wolf Isle."

He felt Ida's sharp stare. The woman used a needle-like intensity to wheedle out the truth.

"Or you could stay and marry her," Ida said. "Then the damn curse will be fully broken."

Grissell had told them that the Macquarie curse could only be broken if all five Macquarie brothers learned the truths about love, finding it in another person. That love must be secured with marriage vows so a bastard couldn't be born between them. A bastard would doom the clan again.

"You were all on the brink of dying out," Ida continued. "That bloody willow tree standing barren and dripping blood from the dagger. Now the village of Ormaig on Wolf Isle is filling up with settlers, and the tree has green leaves. 'Tis up to you now to fully break the curse."

"Bloody hell," he whispered and spooned another mouthful. He followed it with a swig of weak ale to save his tongue from burning. The pressure to finish breaking the curse was heavy and made it hard to breathe, which was another reason to leave. Now he understood Drostan's foolish attempt to cut down the willow tree as a lad, how he'd been desperate not to be the one to curse the clan.

'Twas said one couldn't father a child if he touched the dagger or tree. So far, even after three years wed, Drostan hadn't gotten Lia with child. Although they seemed plenty happy trying while tucked away in Drostan's cabin on the far side of Wolf Isle.

Eagan almost jumped when Ida's hand fell on his. It was a solid hold, belying the weakened state she portrayed. "Whatever you decide to do," she said, "you're welcome here, Eagan. Since my sister died soon after birthing you, I've felt like you're my son."

Eagan was aghast at the softness in Ida's tone, and she chuckled, releasing his hand and standing. "Don't look so surprised," she said, going to stir the pot on the coals. "I fed you pap, changed your swaddling, bathed you, and rocked you to sleep. Did everything except nurse you."

She turned and smiled tightly at Eagan. "You're John's son." She nodded. "Yes, I always felt you were mine."

"Thank ye…for all that," Eagan said and stood. "But I don't plan to stay long."

He carried the bowl up to the bucket of wash water and walked back to kiss her soft cheek. "And if ye decide ye don't like aloneness here, ye're also welcome to come to Wolf Isle."

She blinked at him, and he realized when she wasn't squinting, her eyes were a pretty shade of green. "Now why would I move to a cursed isle?" she asked, using the voice he knew so well.

"Because that's where yer clan lives, Ida Macquarie." His smile was as bright as her frown was grim.

"Not if you move away."

He exhaled through his nose. "The rest of yer clan."

"I know." Her face pinched. "Go on now," she said, shooing him away. "But come by here before you leave for good."

"I promise." Eagan marched out of the cottage to find the sun had fully risen. The two bonfires smoldered on the hill, sending up puffs of smoke that seemed to add to the gray clouds gathering in from the sea. He headed toward the castle, nodding to villagers as they hurried to the fields or wharf or stood sweeping their stoops. Most of the women frowned at him. Had they heard he'd decided to court the new lass and would have to leave him alone? The thought floated like a buoy in his chest, making him whistle a light tune.

He rounded the corner and saw Walter Gleeb resting his well-padded arse on a low stone wall outside Cecilia Maclean's cottage.

Eagan's whistling halted. "Loitering outside a new mother's cottage, Gleeb?" he said. "'Tis not seemly."

Gleeb offered a cold smile. "I'm merely making certain no witchery is about."

"There's no witchery about."

"You did something to her." Cecilia's angry voice rose behind the door of the cottage. "The marks! What did you do to her?"

Gleeb's bushy eyebrows rose high on his forehead. "Is that so?"

A quieter voice answered in a calm cadence. *Tessa.* Eagan recognized the smooth rise and fall of her words.

Cecilia's sharp voice cut through the stone and daub of the walls containing her. "The marks are unnatural."

"Unnatural?" Gleeb said beside him. "Sounds like witchery."

Without knowing more, Eagan couldn't argue with the man. He crossed his arms and leaned against the wall waiting next to Gleeb.

"Loitering?" Gleeb asked Eagan. "How unseemly."

Eagan ignored him, focusing on the cottage, where more female voices talked in hushed tones.

The door opened, and Tessa walked out. She wore a practical wool gown in gray and green hues instead of the white she'd come in the evening before.

"I blame you, Tessa Ainsworth," Cecilia called after her.

"Nonsense," Ava replied from back inside the cottage.

Tessa closed the door without looking back. Eagan came forward, worry congealing in his gut. "Are ye well?" he asked, wanting to reach out to her but unsure in the light of day. Her dark hair was pulled back into a loose braid, leaving shorter waves to frame her oval face. She looked up at him, and he saw that her eyes were a soft gray-green color. Tessa was even more beautiful in the morning sunlight, but she didn't smile. Her lips, so soft the night before, pinched.

"Is the child well?" Gleeb asked from behind. His boots crunched on the pebbles as he came even with them.

"The bairn is hearty and suckling," Tessa said.

"What about the unnatural marks?" Gleeb asked.

Tessa glanced at him. "They are birthmarks that will fade. The mother is...not a kind person and given to hysterics."

"I can vouch for that," Eagan said, and held his arm out to Tessa.

"Is it time to leave the isle?" she asked, accepting his arm.

"If ye're ready." Eagan escorted her around the witch hunter.

"I'll see you again on Wolf Isle," Gleeb said.

"Ye'll need permission from the chief, Adam Macquarie, to visit," Eagan said as they walked away. He wouldn't leave for the mainland until Gleeb and his accusations were gone. The delay was necessary, but then he'd escape as he'd been planning.

Gleeb followed. "I'm under royal orders to search all of the Highlands."

"Wee Queen Mary sent ye orders from France?" Eagan asked merely to irritate the man.

"James Hamilton, the Earl of Arran, is her regent and has tasked me to find, judge, and execute those wicked creatures corrupted by Satan."

"Ye can mark Mull and Wolf Isle off yer list then," Eagan said, guiding them around horse shite. Hopefully, Gleeb would walk through it. "We have no wicked creatures corrupted by Satan here."

"They're everywhere, Macquarie. Some of them right under your nose." Gleeb called this last from behind where he stopped in the road.

"He'll be trouble," Tessa said, her voice soft. "Especially if he meets Grissell. She'll fit his description and will never hide."

"Is she a witch?" Eagan asked, something they'd all wondered.

"She worships nature, not Satan," Tessa said, her steps nimble over the rutted lane. "That doesn't make her a wicked, corrupted creature."

They continued down toward the docks, receiving nods from the men and frowns from the lasses. "It seems," Tessa said, "I'm not liked by the female population of Mull." Laughter tinged her tone, showing she didn't care. Tessa was unique, free to think and do what she wanted. Would she want to kiss him again?

"'Tis better than being liked too much by the female population," he murmured.

Her laughter was a beautiful pitch, almost like a song. It wrapped around him like a spell.

Chapter Five

Tessa sat in the same rowboat Eagan had ferried her across last evening. She breathed in the breeze sliding over the sea, trying to rid herself of the taint from Cecilia's accusations.

Her mother had dealt with new mothers like Cecilia. The best way to deal with them was to reassure them and leave. One wasn't likely to turn a woman's mind when she'd already decided there must be someone to blame if her babe wasn't perfect. And the midwife was a reasonable target since she wasn't a family member or friend.

She'd been glad to see Eagan outside the door when she emerged, leaving the fretful mother with Lady Ava and her daughter, Meg. As far as Tessa could tell, Cecilia and her babe were strong and healthy. There was no further need for her to remain, especially when her only role now was as a whipping post.

Eagan pulled easily on the oars as they faced one another. His muscles strained against his tunic as they bulged in his arms, and his shoulders moved with confidence and strength. Tessa hadn't been able to stop thinking about those arms wrapping around her last night. Had he been affected by their brief encounter by the fires?

"Did you sleep well last night?" she asked.

He pulled several more strokes. "Nay."

Her hands gripped the sides of the boat, and her brows rose. "Why not?"

"Do ye want the truth or the polite response?"

Tessa smiled. "Save polite responses for court. I'd rather have the truth."

His brow rose to match hers. "Even if the truth is bawdy?"

"Bawdy is my favorite," she said, her smile authentic.

He leaned forward, pausing in his rowing. "I couldn't sleep with my jack wishing for another kiss from ye."

She laughed. "Your jack wants a kiss, too?" She laughed harder at his surprised look.

"I suppose he does," he finally said and began rowing again.

The journey across the strait to Wolf Isle was choppier than the smooth passage the night before. Tessa steadied herself in the middle, and Eagan put more power into cutting through the growing whitecaps. Tessa turned her face toward the open sea beyond the coast of Wolf Isle. 'Twas habit after a year of looking for her father's return, but the horizon remained unbroken.

When they reached the floating dock tied to a pier, Tessa quickly climbed out of the boat, wishing to be on dry land again.

"Throw me the rope," Eagan said, pointing to it. He tied the boat to the dock and followed her out. The tang of low tide rot wrinkled her nose, and she climbed the ladder to the long wooden pier above, seeing the barnacles and seaweed trapped around the wooden pilings set deep in the rocky bottom.

She hurried up the long pier toward the forest bordering

the rocky shore. The remaining red and gold leaves fluttered down with the wind. Most had already fallen, leaving the trees pointing to the sky like naked skeletons.

Before she could stride away, Eagan caught her wrist. For the briefest moment, her stomach tightened. "Tessa," he said, and she turned to him. He was handsome with his youthful face and rugged, muscular frame. His hair was light and would surely catch the sun when it finally came out from the heavy clouds that seemed to shroud Scotland most of the time.

"Should we..." he started, dropping her hand. "I mean, will ye...act like we are courting here on Wolf Isle? Or was that only to keep me safe from the lasses on Mull?"

She smiled. "Keep you safe? Are there hordes of females here on Wolf Isle that wish to marry you?"

He didn't blush, but his brows and tight mouth showed embarrassment. Eagan ran one of his large hands through his hair, and she wondered if it was soft. It looked clean like he'd bathed that morn.

"Nay," he said, "but my family..." He closed his eyes briefly, shaking his head. "They pester me continuously."

She looped her arm through his, enjoying the feel of his strength. "Then we are courting for as long as you like." *Or until I leave with my father.*

His body relaxed against her. "That's gracious of ye."

"Maybe in exchange, you can come to Grissell's to help me finish fixing up my cottage. Some things need repairing."

The space between his dark brows pinched. "We've told Grissell we'll help whenever she needs—"

"She hasn't wanted anyone to see me."

"Why?"

"Her thoughts are her own, but perhaps she didn't want me to interfere with the curse." She shrugged. "At first, Grissell and I thought I'd be here for a couple of months.

Maybe she worried over my becoming attached to your welcoming family." She thought of the girls who'd come to interrogate her.

"But Captain Lemaire hasn't returned?"

She shook her head, feeling the heaviness of sorrow in her chest. The one family member she had left in the world hadn't returned. Storms were frequent on the open sea, and she'd heard tales of pirates hunting for ships. Her father had survived for decades on the water, but 'twas still dangerous.

A movement along the forest caught her eye, and she dropped Eagan's arm, realizing she'd grabbed it at some point. "Orpheline," she called, running ahead to meet her bébé.

• • •

A fawn, still wearing its spots, pranced once where it waited at the forest line, its little tail waving. Tessa ran, stopping to crouch mere inches from it, and the red deer walked into her open arms. The image was startling: a raven-haired young woman hugging a spotted fawn like a woodland fairy. She stood, lifting its little body against her chest, and turned to him, her smile joyful.

"This is Orpheline. It means orphan in French, because she was left without a mother." Tessa kissed the fawn's head as it bopped her playfully with its black nose. "But I call her Orphy for short." Tessa set the fawn down, and it pranced around her while keeping a wary eye on Eagan. Tessa laughed. "I missed you, too."

He crouched down. "I have a way with animals," he whispered. "Will she come to me?"

"Wild animals distrust all humans, so don't take offense," she said, but the fawn sidled up to her.

"Are ye not human then?"

She turned her green eyes to him. There were small flecks of gray in them like splinters of granite. Her lashes were long like the fawn's, and for a moment he considered she might be the mythological Sadhbh, who was transformed into a deer to birth a fawn that could change into a lad.

She smiled. "I'm human, though I sometimes wish I were not." She turned back to the deer. "I found Orphy when someone trapped her mother, killing her."

Eagan frowned, irritation itching within him. "We don't set traps during fawning season, and we don't shoot hinds."

She shrugged. "Someone did." Tessa stood, and Orphy dodged about, running back to the forest line with the instinctual fearfulness of prey. "I should return to Grissell."

A tightness quivered within him like a plucked bowstring. He didn't want her to go yet. "If we're courting, I should take ye to Gylin to meet everyone formally." Her ethereal nature made him wonder if she'd disappear once she left his sight, like a will-o'-the-wisp vanishing in the forest.

"Uncle Eagan!" came a voice from the path. The fawn skittered away deep into the forest, blending into the dropping foliage. Laughing children surged in a little group down the path from Gylin Castle and the village of Ormaig. His nieces, younger sisters-in-law, and his five-year-old nephew, John. The little pack seemed to run everywhere together, watched over by Aggie, who had just turned thirteen. Today, Dora, the eighteen-year-old sister of Anna and Lark, carried Anna and Callum's daughter, Elizabeth. And two-year-old, Richard, toddled after them, gripping Aggie's hand.

Normally, he'd have run into them, pretending to be a bull, plucking them off the ground to toss around. But he didn't want to leave Tessa, imagining her disappearing into the forest with her fawn.

The children surrounded them like a flood released on the world. Tessa laughed. "We meet again." She curtsied, bowing her head to Pip, Aggie, and little Hester, who giggled. "And now all of you." She spread her arms in graceful arches on either side of her and turned in a circle, taking them all in. "'Tis like a fairy circle, and we're in its center." She grabbed Eagan's hand as if malicious sprites surrounded them.

The children laughed while Aggie and Dora studied Tessa more carefully. She was different from the ladies they'd encountered before, although since Eliza's pirate crew had taken up homes in Ormaig, Wolf Isle had its share of strange people.

Tessa curtsied low and rose as if greeting royalty. "I am Tempest Ainsworth, but you may call me Tessa."

"Do you cause tempests?" Pip asked, swirling her hands up above her head as if mixing the clouds into a frenzied storm.

"Only when kings and princes make me angry," she replied. Giggles rippled among the group.

"Ones that crash ships upon the rocks?" John asked, his eyes wide.

She leaned before him. "Of course, but only in my bathing tub."

"Do you cause a great wind?" Dora asked, a sly tilt to her lips.

"That would be Callum after he eats Anna's egg pie," Aggie said with a little snort.

"I will keep that in mind," Tessa said with a mock-serious frown. Then she nodded to each lass. "I know Hester, Pip, and Aggie. Now are you"—she pointed to John—"King Henry?"

John wrinkled his nose. "I'm John."

"King John," she said, bowing over an extended leg, her toe pointed in leather boots, as if she were a knight at court.

She turned to Elizabeth in Dora's arms. "And you must be Princess Elizabeth."

The little girl nodded and hid her face against Dora's

neck. "Her name is Elizabeth." The little girl peeked past Dora's red hair, and Tessa curtsied to her. Immediately, Elizabeth turned, her little hands out to Tessa, and Tessa took her from Dora, holding her on her hip as if she'd always belonged there.

Dora shook her arms. "She gets heavy." She smiled. "I'm Dora, Anna and Lark's sister."

"And my sister," Aggie said. "And that is Richard." Aggie pointed to Eagan's nephew, who was jabbing a stick in the air.

"I see he is fighting off a pirate to keep us safe," Tessa said and turned in a circle, Elizabeth in her arms. Eliza and Beck's son laughed heartily as if he were a thirty-year-old sailor instead of a lad of almost three.

And, just like that, Tessa Ainsworth had bewitched them all.

Chapter Six

"Ye're courting her?" Callum asked Eagan. "But ye've just met her."

"Better to marry her quickly," their father's old friend, Rabbie, called from the table, where he chewed one of Anna's flaky pear tarts. He pointed the tart at Eagan, who stood near the lit hearth. "Before ye get her with child."

"I hear she loves children," Lark said.

"Elizabeth is in love with her," Anna said. "Since the dock, she keeps spinning around saying she's Princess Elizabeth." She grinned. "I think the real Princess Elizabeth would like to be represented by such an angelic child."

"Too bad she had to hurry back to Grissell's," Lia said, embroidering by the hearth.

"Perhaps she's shy," Eliza said from her spot sitting on Beck's lap. "We are a lot to take in."

Eagan's brothers and their wives relaxed in the great hall in Gylin Castle. Even though Beck and Callum had cottages in the village and Drostan had built a cabin on the north side of Wolf Isle, the family gathered often, and always on

Sundays after attending the chapel in Ormaig.

"We have only recently started courting," Eagan said, the guilt of lying to his family lumping in his gut like bad cheese. "And it may not last." He still planned to leave the isle and hadn't unpacked his satchel.

With his head clear of her voice and floral scent, Eagan saw how they were on paths that led away from each other—she back to France with her father, and he on a journey to faraway, lonely places. Even if they weren't playing a part to give him some peace, they'd never end up together for long.

"Ye might scare her off if ye ask her to wed too soon," Drostan said.

"Lark didn't scare off," Adam said, pulling his wife into his arms even though she held their one-year-old daughter, Hannah. The bairn laughed as they pressed her between them.

"Lark had other circumstances," Eagan said. "Tessa is a…" He hesitated. It was hard to describe the bright lass that was a serious midwife and also a jester with children. "She's…"

"A convict?" Eliza asked.

"A pirate?" Beck added.

Drostan lifted his nephew, John, in his arms. "Will-o'-the-wisp?"

"A cat lover?" Lia asked, with a longing look.

Rabbie swallowed the tart he'd been chewing. "A witch?"

"She's none of those things," Eagan said. "Well maybe a cat lover, but I'll tell her how ye can't breathe around them, Lia."

Lia nodded. "Maybe she'll help take care of Sia." That was the kitten she'd had to give up to Grissell.

"How do ye know she's not any of those other things?" Adam asked.

Eagan huffed. His family was annoying. "She's a

personable lass whose mother has died and whose father is a French Navy captain who left her with Grissell to save her from dying in the streets of Paris. Her mother was English, but she moved to France before she had Tessa. Tessa learned to be a midwife from her mother."

"And she sings beautifully," Lia said, nodding. "Meg told me how she calmed Cecilia through the birth with her songs."

"That's quite a feat," Eliza said, "calming that banshee."

"Cecilia wasn't calm afterward," Eagan said, taking one of Anna's tarts. "The bairn has two birthmarks, and Cecilia's blaming Tessa for it."

Lark and Adam glanced at one another before Lark looked at Eagan. "There's a witch hunter on Mull."

"I've met Walter Gleeb," Eagan said, frowning. "He's a bloody fanatic sent from Edinburgh, and he wants to come search for witches on our isle."

Adam crossed his arms. "We'll let him inspect the village but not beyond. Grissell doesn't need that type of scrutiny."

"Nor does Tessa," Anna said.

"Invite her for dinner tomorrow," Lark said. "She can bring Grissell if the woman will leave her orphanage for a few hours."

The old woman cared for only three children now, one nearly a woman. Muriel and her daughter, Little Lark as they called her, had moved to the Isle of Skye when she'd met a Mackinnon and married him. Grissell had no offspring of her own. Who would take over the orphanage once she passed? Perhaps she was teaching Tessa everything she knew so she could carry on her mission to help women and children. But Tessa was hoping to leave with her father.

Eagan threw a few tarts into the basket Anna had prepared with bread, cheese, and rabbit pie for him to take to Grissell's. He'd take more blankets to her on the morrow. He had to assess what they might need for the upcoming winter.

"Ask them both for dinner anyway," Lark called out as he headed toward the door. "And the children."

He raised his hand in answer and kept walking. Eagan nodded to several of the villagers who were coming up to the castle to visit Eliza, having been her friends from her pirating youth. Scarred and permanently painted with fantastical sea creatures, the men could look as frightening as any witch. He'd like to see Gleeb try to interrogate them.

The sun was starting its descent as Eagan jogged easily along the path in the forest that led to Grissell's shoreline cottages. The run was easy, and Eagan enjoyed the quiet. Patches of sky crisscrossed by nearly bare, reaching limbs stretched overhead. The leaves crunched and fluttered as his boots disturbed them, and woodland creatures chittered and scurried from his intrusion. He'd heard there weren't trees on Orkney Isle. Would he miss the crunching, color-drenched leaves in the fall if he chose to stop there?

He smelled the smoke before he saw the four squat cottages around a clearing where a well had been dug a century ago, and which still produced fresh water from an inland stream that emptied into the sea beyond. Except for the smoke rising from two cottages, the place seemed deserted.

"Friend, not foe," he called out, stopping near the well. Grissell's home sat closest to the sea behind solid oaks that protected it from the storms that blew in. It was the other cottage with a lit chimney that drew him. It looked different from the last time he'd visited. The thatching on the slanted roof had been enhanced with soil from which grasses and a few remaining wildflowers grew. Golden leaves from a neighboring oak covered it. A porch had been added along the front so that one could sit next to the door. A colorful garland of triangles, cut from yellow, red, and green broadcloth, hung in a swoop over the door, which had been painted green.

Boxes of purple ling flowers sat on the porch.

"Tessa?" he called. There was no answer.

Crack. Pain erupted on the back of Eagan's head, and he spun around, one hand on the sore spot and the other reaching for his sword.

Grissell stood with a young boy, two white cats rubbing against her legs.

"Ye hit me with a rock?" Eagan said, rubbing his head.

"An acorn," Grissell said. She nodded to his sword. "And you pull a blade on an old woman and a child." The lad held her hand and stared out with wide eyes. A little girl came around to take her other hand, blinking blankly at him.

He re-sheathed his sword. "Bloody feisty for an old woman," he murmured. Gleeb would certainly think she was a witch, and the cats and children her minions. "Ye could have just said something."

"Such as 'she's not here'?" Grissell asked, the corner of her lips tipped slightly higher.

"Aye."

"What's the fun in that?"

Both children smiled.

"Do ye know where Tessa is?"

Grissell's smile flattened. "Looking for her father."

The little boy pointed north along the shoreline.

"She always looks for him," the girl said.

"Let's hope he doesn't come," Grissell said

"Why?" Eagan asked.

Grissell tipped her head, examining him. "She will hurt you, youngest Macquarie." Her words sent a shiver down Eagan that he ignored. "'Twould be better if you left Wolf Isle now."

He was well over six feet tall and made of thirteen stones of muscle. Lethal with a sword and sgian dubh, Eagan wasn't afraid of being hurt physically. But Grissell's warning seemed to be something other than concern over his bloodletting.

"I do not hurt easily." And how did she know he was planning to leave?

She walked over to him. In years past, she'd seemed to float. But now she walked with care, the two children flanking her. Her weathered finger poked his chest, but he stood his ground. "Inside. Your heart will bleed." She dropped her hand, and her ear dipped toward one shoulder and the other as if she were weighing the odds on some wager. "'Tis a truth about love that it can slice a person through if 'tis lost. Perhaps it will be enough to break the curse." She shrugged. "I'll watch and see." Her hazy blue eyes pinned him. "But you will hurt."

She turned, and the two children followed her back across the clearing to her cottage. The white cats, known as Saint Joan and Saint Margaret, pranced after them.

A chill slid along Eagan's bones, and his heart beat faster as if it felt the tip of a dagger against it. Maybe they should let Gleeb meet Grissell. She'd probably stop his heart with a poke of her finger.

Eagan turned west along the shoreline, which would gradually curve around to the north. He couldn't see Tessa, but then a ribbon of song reached him, ebbing and growing louder with the direction of the breeze. Climbing back to walk silently along the tree line, Eagan headed to an outcropping of rocks where waves crashed during storms. Today, the water was choppy.

Tessa stood at the end of the sloping rocks, her dark hair rising and falling with the wind. As he neared, he could hear her clear notes that rose and fell like an instrument. It reminded him of a long-ago, wordless chant produced by nuns in prayer. The notes held him captive, the song wrapping around him like tentacles from the sea. She could be a mermaiden upon the rocks, her tail hidden beneath the green gown that billowed out around her.

When she took a breath, Eagan could move again, and walked toward her on the rocks. She glanced over her shoulder, and he saw a glistening in her eyes as if they were wet with tears. He'd already seen her joyful and mischievous with the children, seductive with him, and resigned with Cecilia and her theatrics. But now she was sad, and his heart, like Grissell had predicted, hurt.

He said nothing as he stepped up beside her, the wind rushing past his ears. They stood looking out at the choppy sea, an occasional wave smashing against the jutting rock, sending up spray. But Tessa didn't back away.

"He might never come back," she said. "He promised, but the sea doesn't honor promises."

"Yer father?"

She nodded. "He's the only person I have left in this world. No siblings. No family."

"The Ainsworths in England?"

She shook her head. "My father said my mother made up the name and didn't want to take his, that she was too independent. I don't know who her family was."

Perhaps Rebecca had been running from them. Lark and Anna, along with their three sisters, had grown up in a house full of mental and physical abuse. Lark escaped by marrying Adam, and luckily, the others survived until their father died.

Tessa's eyes looked even greener bathed in unshed tears. "Grissell says she knew my mother."

The words swelled in Eagan's head, and his hands rested on Tessa's shoulders. "What?" Grissell had never left Wolf Isle as far as he knew. "Your mother lived on Wolf Isle?"

Tessa nodded. "Yes."

Chapter Seven

"Grissell sheltered yer mother here?" Eagan asked.

Tessa watched Eagan's hard face. Brows lowered with a look of confusion and concern. His hands gripped her shoulders, and he looked like he wanted to peer inside her mind. It made her words come quickly. "'Tis how my father knew to bring me here when he rescued me from Paris but couldn't take me on his ship."

"Grissell remembers her?"

Tessa nodded. "She says Rebecca was happy here, but she went with my father to France."

"Where ye were raised," Eagan finished for her.

She nodded, remembering the cryptic words from the old woman.

Your mother fell in love and lost her mind. I'm glad you've come home.

But Wolf Isle didn't feel like home to Tessa. No place did. She'd moved around with her mother, following the royal court when Rebecca was the king's mistress. Even a royal mistress that was eventually set aside was welcome as long as she was beautiful and talented. No matter the fickleness of royalty, Rebecca Ainsworth had continued to be both. Tessa attended court with her at times, singing for various groups and even the newborn Prince Francis.

"Grissell wants me to stay here, take up where my mother left off." She looked one last time at the angry sea empty of ship masts and walked toward the tree line where it was quieter. Eagan followed.

In the protection of the thick trunks, leaves fluttering down to be caught by the wind, she touched his arm. Eagan was sturdy, like the oaks around them. To Tessa, who felt adrift as if lost in the sea, his powerful body felt solid, as if he were a safe harbor, which was a ridiculous notion. Her mother had taught her no man could be trusted, except for her father.

"Grissell has been training me this past year," she continued. "My mother learned cures and midwifery skills from her and taught them to me. When I returned, Mistress Grissell thought I *was* my mother. I look a lot like her but have my father's dark hair." She shook her head, glancing into the forest even though she knew the elderly woman didn't eavesdrop. She somehow knew every secret on the isle without having to resort to listening to spoken words.

"She wants ye to stay," Eagan said.

Tessa exhaled in a rush. "I think she worries about the children she'll leave behind when she dies, those in her care."

"Ye...ye could do it," he said. "The way ye are with children. Wee Elizabeth can't stop talking about ye and is making everyone call her Princess Elizabeth."

Tessa thought of the pretty little girl with blue eyes. "Perhaps...if my father never returns." The notion twisted her heart. He was all she had left.

"Life on Wolf Isle would be better for ye than a life at sea."

She frowned. "You don't know me, Eagan Macquarie. I might be part mermaiden." She looked back at the choppy waves. "And my father may decide to leave the sea, and we could live in Paris or even on his family estate somewhere in the countryside." Her mother said he had one, but they never went to it.

"Did he say that?"

He'd said little except he wouldn't see his daughter selling herself in the gutters of Paris. She'd explained she was managing to live by singing at court, but she wasn't naive and realized the men had been circling her for some time. It had been an exhausting dance of keeping safe while trying to earn money to eat without accepting their distastefully lurid proposals.

"If he didn't say he'd—"

"'Tis complicated," Tessa said, her temper licking higher. When Captain Lemaire found her in the apartment she and her mother shared, she'd been overjoyed, even if she barely remembered the last time he'd visited. He looked like an older version of the sketch in her mother's locket.

Like her mother had said, her father was a natural protector with his tall, broad form and intense look. People scurried out of Captain Lemaire's way when he stalked through the streets in his captain's uniform to escort her to boutiques for new frocks. He'd sent two men to pack her belongings. He was moving her to his ship with him, having been assigned another mission starting the following week. He'd even given her a small cabin, locking her in to protect her from his men, who looked half frightened of him and half ready to slit his throat. But when he'd rowed her over to Grissell's shoreline under a full moon, he'd promised her he'd return.

I promise to wait for you, mon père, she'd answered earnestly. He'd rowed back to his ship, setting sail immediately in the glow of the moon. When she'd turned away from the sea, tears in her eyes, Grissell had nearly struck her dead with surprise, standing there amongst the trees, her two white cats sliding along her legs.

The first heavy drops of rain sounded like acorns hitting the few leaves left above, pulling Tessa back to the present. One landed on her nose, making her blink. "You can come see my cottage," she said, grabbing his hand. It was warm and wrapped instantly around hers as she maneuvered through the trees.

The clearing between the cottages was vacant, the stone well standing alone with its bucket ready to fill with rainwater. Tessa led Eagan up the steps onto her porch made of hewn planks that Grissell had unburied from a stockpile she hid. "I built the porch myself with the help of the children," Tessa said. "Bann and Charlotte helped me, but little Grace just played with Orphy and made flower wreaths."

"It looks sound."

"I'd like a roof over it, an overhang so we can sit out here in the rain." She plucked a purple flower from the box and stuck it in her hair, then pointed at the garland over the door. "Grace made that with scraps of fabric Grissell had."

She pulled him through into the clean room. When she'd arrived, the cottage had been empty and full of cobwebs. Tessa had poured her worry over her father and her future into reviving it with a thorough cleaning, glossy wax, and paint. She'd even added her own designs in the corners, painting swirls and birds.

Rain began to pour down, but the earthen roof softened the violent thrashing. The cottage was cozy and warm, and opposite the cold, bare apartment she'd shared with her mother with its few pieces of gilt furniture.

"Where is yer fawn, Orpheline?"

She smiled. "You remember her name." *A man who pays*

attention to more than a woman's curves. Unusual.

"Names are important," he said and reached up to touch some of her dried herbs. "They tell a lot about the giver of the name and the person named." He was careful when he touched the dried chamomile heads so as not to knock them to the floor. He lowered his strong arm and grinned at her. "Like Tempest. I think there's a whirlwind perhaps hiding within ye."

Warmth slid through Tessa, a different kind of warmth from the heat that their kiss had ignited last evening. It was gentle and infused her, warming her to her toes, whereas the passion that had hit her before was like lightning. Both drew her to this large, chiseled man.

She glanced toward the door. "Orpheline has a nice paddock in the barn with my little goat, Grissell's milk cow, and the chickens. The cats walk out there, too, giving the rooster a purpose to protect his lady hens even though Saint Joan, Saint Margaret, and Sia wouldn't touch them."

"Such odd names for cats," Eagan said, running his finger along the snugly fit panes of glass. She watched the trail of his finger across the chilled surface and wondered what it would feel like across her skin.

"Saint Margaret is the patron saint of childbirth and women with child. Joan of Arc is strong and brave, helping to defend our bit of land. She *should* be a saint. And Sia has six toes on each paw. The names fit."

He walked to the hearth and added a square of dry peat before crouching to blow under it. He must think they were remaining there. Was he presumptuous or merely seeking her comfort?

Tessa watched the play of muscles under the white tunic that was stretched across his back from broad shoulder to broad shoulder. Was Eagan Macquarie a good lover? He looked fit, confident, and every inch a man.

Her mother had endured sloppy and selfish attentions in the bedchamber, first with the king and then some of his courtiers, but Rebecca had wanted her daughter to understand how pleasurable physical love could be with an expert lover. She'd explained much with words and sketches and then hired a tutor for her daughter once she reached the age of twenty. Tessa knew the difference between an attentive lover and a selfish, hasty-witted coxcomb. And from the kiss and how Eagan touched various things in her cottage, she guessed he was of the attentive variety.

"You should stay," Tessa said. Eagan looked at her over his shoulder. She indicated the windows where rain beat a rapid pulse. "Unless you wish to return to the castle soaked through."

He stood slowly, glancing at the door like a maiden realizing she was locked in with a wily fox of a man. "I won't attack you," she added. "And you can leave. I'm merely saying that 'tis—"

"Do ye attack men?" The edge of his mouth rose, and she remembered how those lips felt against hers. Warm, soft, but powerful, too.

She returned his half grin with her own. "Not frequently enough to answer oui and not never to say non."

His brow rose, but his mouth dropped to seriousness. "Have ye had to defend yerself then?"

She snorted softly. "In this world, everyone must defend themselves, from the smallest kitten to the surliest butcher."

He walked over, gently resting his hands on her shoulders. "I have no right to pry, Tessa, but my sisters-by-marriage have had to defend themselves from villainous men before they came here and married my brothers. Ye can find comfort talking with them."

She met his gaze with steely determination. "I've met many villainous men, but I thwarted them." She'd learned to get out of every situation, even crawling out a window to slide along a ledge to safety. Staying physically fit, agile, and silent had saved her emotional stability and even her life several times. One didn't circulate in the viper's nest of court without becoming slippery as a serpent, too.

Tessa raised her hand to Eagan's cheek, feeling the soft bristle of his closely trimmed beard. "You, Eagan Macquarie, are not a villainous man. I believe you to be a good man." He was also tall, so she slipped her hand up to his neck and around the back. Eagan lowered his face without resistance, claiming her lips.

Despite the confidence she displayed in her movements, her heart slammed hard. Eagan's arms came around her like the granite walls encircling a castle, and she felt protected within them. And that feeling of trust and protection was intoxicating. Perhaps that was why the heat had risen from a wisp of smoke to an inferno in moments.

She trusted Eagan Macquarie.

To enjoy the passions of the flesh in full, one must have absolute trust in their partner.

She hadn't been attracted to the sophisticated instructor her mother had hired to teach Tessa about feeling satisfied in passion, but she'd trusted him enough because her mother did.

Tessa slanted her lips against Eagan's, pressing against the taut muscles of his frame. His erection pressed against her, feeling long and hard and very capable. *Mon Dieu.* A rush of heat slid down through her abdomen to dampen the crux between her legs, and thoughts of what she should do and what Eagan should do faded from her mind as instincts took over.

Sliding one leg behind his, she rubbed her crux against his thick thigh and let the moan that had built at the base of her throat breeze out with her exhale. One of his large hands cupped her backside, helping her lift and rub.

He kissed a path along her jawline to her ear as Tessa tipped her face to the slanted ceiling so he'd have complete access to her throat. Perhaps it was the throbbing in her that made the skimming of his lips not tickle.

"Tessa," he whispered at her ear. "I want ye, lass, but I won't dishonor ye." His hands rose to her upper arms. She felt him step back and heard his groan of frustration as if his body warred with his honor.

Her eyes opened, catching his intense stare. It mirrored her own low-lidded desire. "I am no maid, Eagan, and I do want to dishonor you, garçon." Her accent was thicker with the passion, the flow of the French language being made for love. "And you're full of muscle and passion and honor."

She could see desire flare up in his gaze, and his hands fisted at his side like a starving man resisting a sweet tart. His ready verge pushed outward against his plaid.

"I wouldn't take advantage of yer trust, Tessa. Ye don't know me."

Sliding one of her palms up his tunic while the other slid down, she rose on her tiptoes to reach his ear. "All I know is that I want to feel you moving within me." Her lower hand slid over him, and she heard him exhale.

He was larger than her tutor, and the thickness of his stiff verge sent another wave of heat through her. She moved her hand down to the edge and pulled the wool up enough to reach him underneath. Her breath was ragged as she slid her hand along the hard length.

"Bloody hell, Tessa."

She met his fevered gaze. "I ache, Eagan, and so do you. I can feel your ache." She stroked up and down the smooth skin. "Touch me where I ache."

Eagan's hands grabbed her to him with one arm around her back. She continued to work him as his free hand rucked up her simple green petticoat. His fingers climbed the flesh between her thighs, and she opened her legs more.

Relax and feel.

The words burned away as her body wound tighter. She certainly could feel, but there was no relaxing, not when she wanted Eagan's length inside her, parting her flesh and stroking her until she reached her pleasure. Her world tipped as he touched the joining of her legs.

"Mon Dieu," she moaned, pressing her pelvis against his firm hand. He rubbed and stroked, building her to a frenzy. When he sunk his fingers inside, she climaxed right on his hand, her eyes and mouth flying open.

She released him and grabbed his shoulders to keep herself from falling as waves of pleasure crashed through her. "Mon Dieu. Mon Dieu." She kept murmuring as he held her up, his hand still stroking her but slower, gentler, letting her float back down to the ground. She'd never peaked so quickly nor so intensely.

Before she could form coherent thoughts, Eagan lifted her off the floor and carried her to her bed. Breathing heavily, he released her amongst the pillows, staring down at her. His hand slipped under his wrap as if he were in pain.

"I can… I won't if ye…"

His words trailed off as she plucked the laces of her bodice and moved her shoulders back and forth until the edge dropped. Her full breasts swelled out the top, perching on her chest like pale puffs of flesh with hard, dark pearls in their centers. A thin gold chain held her locket shaped like a birdcage. It lay against her skin close to her heart.

"Mo dhia," he murmured, and she could see him stroking his length. The sight of him pleasuring himself sent a new wave of heat surging through her.

Pinching her nipple with one set of fingers, she raised her petticoat until her still throbbing crux was exposed. "Let me see you."

He lifted his wrap so she could watch him stroke his length. She touched herself, and he groaned as he watched her rub and touch. She knew he'd like that as much as she liked watching him. "Come to me," she whispered and spread herself wide.

Eagan yanked his belt open, letting his woolen wrap fall with it. In a swift arch of his arm, he yanked his tunic off over his head while kicking off his boots. He was naked in seconds, and her breath caught at the beauty of him. She licked her lips as her gaze followed his chiseled muscles from his shoulders and powerful arms down his chest, over the ridges of his stomach muscles where she stopped on his thick verge straight and long against his abdomen.

Spreading her legs more, she beckoned, and Eagan fell upon her with a growl from deep within his chest. "Oh yes," she exhaled as he braced himself over her, his biceps mounded on either side of her head.

"Ye're...sure?"

"Oui, yes!"

Her breath caught as Eagan thrust into her, his groan rising to the rafters of the cottage, mixing with her answering moan. He pulled out and thrust again, so deep, so completely deep. She felt his strokes along all her sensitive spots all at once. *Mon Dieu!* They fit together perfectly, him filling her entirely. She lifted her feet, wrapping them to ride across his lower back and contracting derriere. She kissed him with fierce, wild abandon. They moved together as if they'd truly become one writhing, hot beast.

The wave of sensation built slower this time. She felt him shift higher on her so that he also rubbed her exposed bud, teasing her pleasure. Her fingers curled into his shoulders. When they broke to breathe, she stared into the taut lines of his face. A mix of pain and ultimate pleasure reflected her feelings.

"My God, aye," he said as he stroked full and fast.

Tessa's eyes flickered shut, and she crested. "Mon Dieu, mon cœur!" she yelled, imagining her cry cracking the glass panes in her windows.

With a growl, Eagan rolled off her, catching his release in a rag she hadn't seen him place on the bed. Her hand went to her crux, pressing against the waves there, enjoying the continued sensations. She turned her face to the side to watch Eagan stroke himself, the two of them panting next to each other on their backs. He didn't release inside her because he didn't want to get her pregnant.

As much as she agreed getting with a child outside of marriage would be life-shattering, she felt cold as she thought of her father's words: *If you get pregnant out of wedlock, Claudette, make sure 'tis with a Macquarie.*

Chapter Eight

Eagan held Tessa against his body, her face curled into his side as she slept. 'Twas dark now, and no one had come to her cottage. Did Grissell know he was inside with her? Had their roars and moans of climax been heard? He ran his free hand down his face.

"You wish you hadn't visited?" Her whisper stilled him. She looked up to meet his eyes without moving her head. The firelight reflected in their depths. They were piercing as if looking deep within his soul. 'Twas a bit unnerving.

He dropped his hand from his face and rolled toward her, pulling her closer into his arms. "Just thinking about the repercussions."

Her head slid onto her pillow so she could reconnect with his gaze. "You withdrew so I shouldn't become with child."

He nodded, his head brushing against a pillow. "Not a guarantee but that's not what I was thinking."

"What then?"

He slid one rough finger along her chin. "How ye would think of me, lusting for ye so quickly," he said. "We met two days ago."

Her expression was a mix of shadow and flamelight. "How do you think of *me*?" she asked, repeating his question. "Lusting for you so quickly?"

He stroked her cheek. "I think ye are…adventurous and passionate and the loveliest woman I've ever met."

She smiled from her position. "Those are good thoughts. I'm not too…forward, too lustful for you, Highlander?"

"Nay." His brows rose slightly. Even though they hadn't engaged in other positions or pleasured each other in different ways, her confidence exposed her experience. Although she'd never tried to hide it. "Ye weren't a maiden."

She shook her head, her smile tighter. "I have only been with one other man."

Eagan instantly hated the other man but knew his thought was unfounded. How many women had he bedded before? Quite a number yet he doubted Tessa would have such a reaction at the thought of him with another.

"A husband?" He caught the gold birdcage in his fingers. "Someone who gave ye this?"

She shook her head, catching the delicate locket. "This was my mother's, and I've had no husband."

"A lover then?"

She shook her head again, and a cold blade of fury slid through him, almost cleaving him in two. Perhaps he would kill the man. Unclenching his fist, he concentrated on keeping his hand gentle as he laid his palm against her cheek. "Did a man assault ye, Tessa?"

She shook her head, and he released a breath, his eyes shutting for a moment. "Taing Dhia," he murmured.

Tessa took his hand from her face, holding it. "He was hired by my mother to teach me."

"Teach ye?" His brows lowered. He'd heard of fathers taking their sons to brothels to gain experience but never a mother.

She nodded. "Everything a knowledgeable man should do to give pleasure to a woman, and then what I can do to bring pleasure in my partner. 'Tis best if both end the session satisfied."

Eagan stared at her perfectly aligned features. A straight nose sloped gently to a generous bow of a mouth. Thin, dark brows arched over her large eyes, and the shadows accented her high cheekbones. She watched him, and he kept his expression neutral despite swirls of scenarios playing through his flying thoughts.

Was her mother preparing her to be a mistress? A whore? A wife? Had the man been a tutor in educational subjects and convinced her that she should also learn how to give a man pleasure? *I will kill him.*

"Yer mother wanted ye to learn pleasure from a man?"

Tessa snaked her hand under the blanket covering their naked bodies. Eagan's cock jumped back to life as soon as she found him, sliding from his base to the tip and back again. "And how to give pleasure," she said.

"Why?" The word came out on a growl as his hand curved behind her hip to palm her sweet arse.

Tipping her head back, he saw blooming passion in her eyes. "Pleasure is a gift," she said, her lips remaining parted. One of her hands gripped him while the other moved under the covers. Was she touching herself? The thought spiraled more heat within Eagan.

He pulled the blanket downward and saw that she was indeed rubbing her mound. Reaching forward, he replaced her hand with his. "'Tis a gift," he said. "I like that." So many lasses were taught to feel shame in the light of their own pleasure.

She worked him faster, teasing his aching stiffness. "She wanted to make sure that if I was to devote myself to a man,

I should either make sure he was knowledgeable about giving and taking pleasure or be prepared to teach him."

With the blankets pulled back, Tessa slid her body down farther into the bed. With a small smile, she hovered her mouth over his straining jack. "Let me wash first, Tessa." With the agility honed by battle training and quickened by his lust, Eagan rolled from the bed. Tessa rose up on an elbow to watch him as he dipped a rag he found by the hearth into the pitcher for washing and quickly washed his growing erection.

"Now," he said, capturing her hand to kiss her palm as he slid back into bed. "What was that ye were saying?"

She chuckled and slid down his body. His eyes rolled back into his head as her warm mouth descended over him.

She knew exactly what to do with her tongue and lips, and the bloody suction nearly drove him mad. His body tightened as she sucked for several minutes, but before he released, she pulled her lips away and straddled him. Hands braced on his shoulders, she sat slowly down upon him, impaling herself with a long, low moan.

Looking up at her wavy dark hair cascaded over her straight shoulders, her full, pale breasts peaked and begging to be sucked, Eagan knew he'd never seen a more beautiful sight. She moved slowly, stretching out the pleasure that threatened to spill into completion. Eagan groaned, his face taut with restraint.

She leaned down, their lips meeting, their breaths mixing as their bodies moved as one. In that moment, Eagan felt he'd never been close to anyone in the world until then. And he didn't want to let go.

His hands moved to her churning hips, helping her move faster as he released her mouth to reach his lips to her nipple. He sucked, tugging on it, reveling in the sound of her soft mews as she rubbed herself against him, and he imagined creating friction against her sensitive nub. Faster they moved toward a common goal of searing pleasure. And then...Eagan groaned, the wave of pure pleasure rolling through him. He exploded inside her quickly shifting body, flooding her.

He heard her higher-pitched moan over him as she rode her own wave before collapsing across his chest.

...

Morning began as usual with the cat, Sia, touching her nose to Tessa's. Without opening her eyes, her hand slid up to stroke the soft fur of the six-toed cat who had come to Wolf Isle with Lia, the wife of the fourth Macquarie brother. Since Lia was deathly allergic to the cat, Grissell had taken her in like she took in every other creature without a home.

As Tessa shifted in the bed, she felt the warmth and heavy form of Eagan beside her. Thoughts of their afternoon and night together spiraled through her, and her eyes flashed open. How had Sia gotten inside her cottage?

The answers stood inside the doorway in the form of two children, Bann and Grace. They smiled. Orphy, her fawn, nudged her way between them to skip on spindly legs, the small, pointed hooves tapping on the floorboards.

"Bann? Grace? Is something wrong?" Tessa asked, sitting up in the bed, remembering to yank the blanket up high over her breasts.

They shook their heads, Grace smiling and Bann frowning. "You had a sleepover party and didn't invite us?" Bann asked.

Tessa glanced over at Eagan, whose eyes were open, wide awake. Although he remained flat on the bed as if not sure if he should act like he was actually another quilt.

"Orphy stayed with us last night," Grace said. "Grissell said we weren't to let her in or knock on your door until this morn and only if we didn't hear any noises from inside."

Eagan's large hand slid down his face. "Bloody hell," he murmured.

"Thank you," Tessa said to the little girl, who stared curiously at the pile of clothes dropped in heaps on the floor. "I'll come by once we're ready for the day."

Bann, who was a year older than the five-year-old girl, tugged her arm. "They need to be alone to get dressed. Come along."

Grace waved. "We'll be breaking our fast out in the clearing where Charlotte said she found a fairy ring, and the golden leaves have blanketed the ground."

When the door clicked shut, Eagan released a small groan. Tessa rolled away from Sia and across Eagan's broad chest. Ignored, Sia jumped down to follow Orphy to the bowl of water in the corner.

"You're embarrassed," she whispered and gasped with a laugh as Eagan rolled her over, bracing himself above her. She could feel his arousal against her, and it sent another wave of heat through her.

He looked down into her eyes, and she reached up to catch a lock of blond hair that fell over his eye and brushed it back. His eyes were a clear blue like the water of a lake she saw in the Alps once. "I don't want ye to think I only came here to… I don't want people to talk about ye." He looked sincere.

"You're a man who doesn't brag about his conquests," she said with a little nod of approval.

The space between his brows cleaved downward. "No honorable man does."

"Ah," she said with knowing inflection. "I suppose kings aren't honorable then, or do they fall into another category?"

He rolled off her. "I know little of kings, but I assume they do whatever the hell they want without fear of condemnation."

She followed him and rubbed her finger across the lines

of his forehead. "The children won't speak of this, nor will Grissell. She might narrow her eyes at us but won't interfere."

"I have experience with quiet condemnation. My Aunt Ida judges as fiercely as the pope."

Tessa rolled from the bed and felt his gaze on her as she walked naked over to a trunk to pull out a clean smock and stockings. She turned toward him, bending forward to slide each stocking on up over her knee and securing each with a ribbon. Her breasts hung before her, nipples peaked from the cold and his gaze. She gave him a wicked smile and then threw the smock over herself.

He sighed, and she felt her own smile fade. With the morning light, reality pressed in on them. They were not two lovers without responsibilities. She was waiting for her father to take her back to France, and Eagan was planning to leave for mainland Scotland and far-off adventures. Whatever had sprouted between them was temporary. She'd have to lap up all the deliciousness that could be had with Eagan before they parted.

...

Eagan squeezed Tessa's hand. "Someone will ask me where I was all night," he said as they walked through the portcullis of Gylin Castle. "Probably Lark."

"Shall I tell them you spent the night loving me well?" she whispered.

He laughed. Tessa was like no lass he'd ever met. Confident in herself, whether it was birthing a bairn or teasing pleasure out of him without remorse. "They will call the priest to wed us before the moon rises."

"We could run away to France together."

Was she serious? He turned to study her face in profile, the slender nose and smooth skin. Would living a life with her be terrible? Would she demand he marry her?

"Eagan!" Drostan called, jogging out of the castle.

Mo chreach!

His brothers and their wives hurried out after him. "We're headed to Mull," Adam said, his hand on the handle of his sheathed sword. He looked ready to charge to war.

"What's going on?" Eagan asked, his gaze falling on Tor Maclean's war coordinator, Keir Mackinnon, who walked with Tor's brother-in-law, Alec MacNeil from Barra Isle. Both fierce men looked ready to lop heads off.

They turned to stride toward the ferry. "Do we need our mounts?" Eagan asked.

"Nay," Keir said, "she hasn't been taken off Mull."

"She?" Tessa asked, breaking into a jog to keep up.

Lark looked from her to Eagan. Any suspicion about their whereabouts and activities last night was squashed by true concern. "Walter Gleeb, the witch hunter, has arrested Aunt Ida, accusing her of witchcraft. He wants her tried and hanged as soon as possible."

Chapter Nine

"Ida Gunn Macquarie, ye are charged with consorting with Satan to bring curses down upon these good people of God." Walter Gleeb's inflated voice swept over the center square, where the elderly woman sat on a stump as if her legs couldn't hold her.

Tessa's heart squeezed as she watched Eagan and his brothers surround the man and woman before the gates of Aros Castle. Eagan's aunt's hair was down and wild in dark gray and silver around her head, and she squeezed her eyes shut as if to block out the horror around her. Tessa had seen condemned people shut out the world when she was at the French court, as if they wished to lose themselves into the darkness behind their eyelids and block out the scornful looks from witnesses.

"My aunt is no witch," Eagan said, his voice as powerful as his arm holding his sword.

The woman lifted her head, and the fear Tessa saw in the old woman's face tore through her. Her mother had been afraid in the last days before her murder when she'd sought a way out of her courtly tangle. A jealous, powerful woman wanted Rebecca gone, but the king had decided she should remain. Fear had struck her mother with weakness. The paralyzing emotion was an internal enemy. Tessa hated to see it in any woman.

Walter Gleeb, the pompous bastard, had been eager to identify a witch in the town. If Tessa hadn't been able to return to Wolf Isle, she had little doubt that she'd be the woman bound and teetering on the edge of condemnation and torturous death.

Gleeb's voice rose. "Ida Macquarie is known throughout Aros and the surrounding countryside of the Isle of Mull to create cures from unusual ways, cast curses and lethal glances, and—"

"My aunt never killed anyone with a glance or curse," Adam said. The five Macquarie brothers had formed a circle around Gleeb and their aunt, each of them holding a thick, no doubt razor-sharp sword.

"She's sickened people," Gleeb said, his jaw firm in obstinate conviction.

"People become sick," Tor Maclean, the chief of Aros, said. "And I won't stand for your villainy on my isle."

"Even if our royal regent commands that I dig out all those who are corrupt?" Gleeb asked. "Would you bring down the might of the crown upon your isle?"

The warriors who'd come to Wolf Isle stood beside Tor, along with another man, each with their arms crossed and frowns on their faces.

"I am Cullen Duffie," a dark-haired man with a pointed beard said, "chief of the Macdonalds of Islay Isle, and I support the Macleans and Macquaries."

Keir Mackinnon nearly growled his words. "Even if troops from Edinburgh show their faces here."

The fourth man stared at Gleeb with intense, narrowed

eyes. "I am Alec MacNeil, the Wolf of Barra Isle, and I support the Macleans and Macquaries. We don't fear ye or yer absent men." He waved an arm out, indicating that Gleeb was all alone.

Father Timothy jogged up, his thin face pale with ruddy cheeks from exertion. "Master Gleeb…I've…been told…" He rested his hands on his knees and then straightened. "Mistress Ida Macquarie is not a witch. She has lived amongst us for decades as a God-fearing citizen of Clan Maclean."

Ava Maclean stood with several other women. "Mistress Macquarie has participated in all the church holidays." None of the women wept or hid their faces. They all held themselves in determined stances as if ready for war along with their husbands.

"We rely on collected herbs and cures from the wise women of the village, like Ida Macquarie," a lady with light hair said, her frown fierce. "I am Lady Mari MacNeil and have come here with my husband, Chief MacNeil, to bring some back to Barra."

"Would you condemn us all?" Lady Grace said next to her, her English accent even stronger than the night of Cecilia's birthing. Her hands sat on her hips, and then she let them slide off as if it were a habit she wished to break.

Gleeb ignored the women as if they hadn't spoken, as if their words were merely the brittle fall leaves sweeping through the streets on the autumn wind, useless and forgotten. Gleeb raised his arms in the air, looking up at the gray sky. "Thou shalt not suffer a witch to live, so says the Lord."

Tessa stood back from them, unnoticed, but she couldn't keep silent. Her voice rose up higher than his as she cast her gaze across the men and women of Aros Village, who frowned silently at Ida Macquarie. "You shall not spread a false report. You shall not join hands with a wicked man to be a malicious witness. Exodus 23:1." She repeated it for them in

Latin and then in French. Her gaze held as much judgment as the witch hunter, but her judgment was on Ida's neighbors for not defending her.

"How dare you speak as if you are God," Gleeb said, spittle jumping from his sharp little teeth.

"I merely quote the same good book you do, Master Gleeb," she said. "And I'm certain the good people of Aros don't wish to offend God by providing false witness on this fragile woman."

Gleeb's face turned a ruddy shade of purple and red in his fury. He pointed at Tessa. "A witch protecting her own."

"A witch?" Lark said, coming up to stand next to Tessa. "Who can speak the Lord's words without stumbling over them and in three languages." She shook her head. "There are no witches here, Master Gleeb. Report that to your patron back in Edinburgh."

Eagan re-sheathed his sword and walked past Gleeb to his aunt, helping her stand. As far as Tessa could see, she hadn't been abused. From the look on Eagan's face, the witch hunter's blood would have been spilled if she had.

"Ye will come back with us to Wolf Isle," Eagan said, and his four brothers encircled her, the oldest, Adam, taking her other arm. Ida said nothing and allowed them to lead her away while Gleeb fumed and threatened.

"I will bring soldiers back with me," Gleeb called. "The Macquaries will all be condemned."

"That's never stopped us before," Eagan said.

...

"I will request a bath to be sent up," Lark said as she slid out of the bedchamber that had been made ready for Ida Macquarie. Lark's sister, Anna, followed her out. Tessa stood near the window and realized she was the only one left with the matriarch of the small Macquarie Clan. Ida sat on the edge of the neatly made bed, still not talking.

Tessa nodded to her, her smile pleasant but shallow, and walked across the room to leave.

"Are you going to marry Eagan?" Ida's voice was soft but clear.

Tessa froze as if she were caught by a net. She met her sharp eyes. "We are courting," Tessa said. "But we only just met."

"You could keep him here, ask him to stay here with you."

The woman knew Eagan planned to leave. As far as Tessa could tell, the rest of his family didn't.

"He hardly knows me," Tessa said. "None of you do. You may not want me to stay."

Ida weighed her words. "You know the ways of herbs and have the skills of an experienced midwife. You speak French and have a French accent, but you live with Grissell. You know Latin and English, too, and quotes from the Bible. And you are brave enough to speak against a witch hunter who might likely go after you next. Who are you, Claudette Tempest Ainsworth?" Her eyes slowly turned to Tessa.

Rap. Rap. "I have the chamomile." Lia pushed inside the room, bringing the brew to a table before a mirror. She looked between them. "Supper will be served when the sun drops below the horizon." She indicated the window where a sliver of the sea could be seen. "Perhaps you'll be recovered enough to come down to eat with your family," Lia said.

Ida's gaze released Tessa from its strong grip. "I have no clean clothes, and I would not be seen in dirty rags."

"I'll ask Lark if she has any of your sister's old clothes here at Gylin. She lived here for some time," Lia said. From the peeved look on Ida's face, it was obvious that she knew her sister had lived there.

The door clicked shut behind Lia, and Ida's gaze was back on Tessa. *The best defense is often a good offense.* Ida Macquarie was intelligent, observant, and hid behind her gloomy temper. "Who broke your heart, Ida Gunn Macquarie?" Tessa said, her voice even and steadfast.

Silence hung in the air for long seconds.

"Tell me, child," Ida said, "why are ye here and what do ye want?" Ida stood, walked over to the steaming brew, and sat in the chair to sip it.

Better to calm the beast rather than run from it. Tessa picked up a brush made of thick bristles. Gently, she lifted one tangled strand of Ida's gray hair and slid the bristles down it until it was smooth. She met the woman's eyes in the mirror. "My father brought me here after he rescued me from France. My mother died, and I was cast into penury. My father knew of this isle, because my mother, Rebecca Ainsworth, lived with Grissell for a year or two before going to France. I await his return so we can return to France together."

"You have no intention of staying with my nephew," Ida said.

The woman had the sharpness of a cut diamond. She'd spot a lie before it left Tessa's tongue. Tessa shook her head.

"At least she tells the truth," Ida murmured and took another sip of the steaming brew.

Tessa continued to brush the woman's hair, carefully removing the angry tangles.

"Why are you a Macquarie and not a Gunn?" Tessa asked. She'd wanted to take her father's last name, Lemaire, but her mother wouldn't allow it. Sometimes Tessa wondered if they'd actually been married.

Time passed, and with each second Tessa knew more and more that Ida wasn't going to tell her anything. Well, not without a little nudge and some relaxation. Tessa drew in breath and began to sing one of the mesmerizing lullabies. It felt good to let the ribbon of sound flow from her.

Ida said nothing, but Tessa continued to work through the tangles of her hair like she used to do with her mother when she came back from the king's bedchamber. Slow and soothing, the notes matched the gentle strokes of the brush. The song ended, and the old woman exhaled long.

"Why are you a Macquarie?" Tessa whispered the question.

Ida sniffed, pulling a bedraggled handkerchief from her sleeve to dab at her nose. "I think you are a witch with that voice."

"Non," Tessa said, setting the brush down to gingerly pull the long silver waves together. "I have a talent for singing. It relaxes people."

"Into talking?" Ida asked.

"Sometimes."

Ida snorted softly. "Why would I tell you anything?"

Tessa reached around her to pluck some hairpins off the table. "Because I'm not a Macquarie. I'm from France, far away from here. Because I have a heart that could be bruised by silent neighbors and those who whisper about me being a witch." Tessa stuck a few pins into the curls she made around the crown of Ida's head. "I think talking will lift some burden off you."

Ida met her gaze in the mirror. The only change to her face was moisture gathering in her eyes. "I am bitter because the man I loved died," Ida said. She paused and drew in a long breath through her thin nose. "But first he married my sister."

Chapter Ten

Eagan paced before the hearth, stopping to blow under the peat and logs now and then. Lia had told them that Tessa was helping bathe and dress Aunt Ida. Why? Lark had a lady's maid that could attend her, but Ida had sent the maid away when she'd come up with the bath. Instead, Tessa had remained with his aunt.

Daylight was fading, and it was almost time for the last meal. Eagan hadn't seen Tessa since they'd returned from Mull that morning. Was Ida interrogating her? Would she find out that their courtship was a farce? Was it? They'd lain together. *I'm still leaving.* Would she go with him if her father didn't return? How long would they have to wait until she consented to go?

He closed his eyes and faced the fire. The heat of it was nothing compared to the internal heat they'd created in Tessa's bed. She said she'd had some type of sexual tutor. Bloody hell, she knew how to bring pleasure to herself and her partner.

Callum came to stand next to him. "Can Tessa hold her

ground with Ida?"

Eagan looked at him. It didn't look like Callum was teasing. "How am I supposed to know? We just met at Samhain."

"And yet," Callum said, "ye're courting and remained at her cottage all last eve."

Because of the danger to Aunt Ida, no one had yet questioned Eagan about his whereabouts last night. "'Tis none of yer affair, Cal."

"It is if ye get her with child," Callum said. "Even if ye pull out there's a chance. Was she a virgin?"

Eagan crossed his arms over his chest, feeling the muscles flexing over his fists. "She was not a virgin, and she did not seem concerned."

"No one is concerned in the heat of it," Callum murmured, running a hand down his beard.

"Are ye asking me because ye want to break the curse? Not because ye're worried over Tessa's honor?"

Callum placed his hand on Eagan's shoulder. "I want the curse broken as much as the rest of us. Don't fok it up."

Eagan used to literally look up to his older brothers. Now he was taller than all of them and equally broad. He also didn't take everything they said as gospel. They all worried about the curse that their ancestor, Wilyam Macquarie, had brought over their clan a century ago. Grissell was the last descendent of the witch who cast it in her fury and grief. Would the curse be broken upon Grissell's death? Or would it continue until the last Macquarie brother married and truly loved another?

Callum traipsed away toward his wife, Anna, scooping up their two-year-old daughter, Elizabeth, from off the back of the large wolfhound she rode like a horse. The girl giggled as her father tumbled her in his arms, cradling her against his chest. Callum was devoted to his wife and child, like each of

Eagan's brothers. The weight of their worry over the curse and their younger brother's part in helping break it lay like sopping bags of oats upon Eagan's shoulders. That was a big part of why he must leave.

Beck strode in, heading to Adam, although he looked at Eagan, one eyebrow raised as if to add to Callum's prying questions. Beck stopped before their oldest brother, turning to him as he spoke. "There's a ship off the west coast, close to Gometra Isle."

"One of Cullen Duffie's ships?" Adam asked.

Beck shook his head. "It flies no flag. Perhaps 'tis a Mackinnon ship. Brode Mackinnon is still looking for a wife. Tor and Keir said he was returning to hunt."

Anna's gaze was on the archway behind them. "Aunt Ida?"

Eagan's breath caught as he looked toward the archway. What sorcery was this?

Aunt Ida wore a blue gown, simple but well preserved. Her gray hair was lifted and woven into an elegant crown of curls circling the top of her head. Her face was cleaned of the grime from her ordeal and shone with a suppleness that resembled youth. There was a faint tint to her cheeks and lips, which looked natural although he'd never seen it on his aunt's face before. The effect made her look young and almost sweet.

She stepped into the great hall, and Eagan spotted Tessa behind her. She smiled gently at Ida as his aunt walked across the room. Had Tessa wrought the changes? Gone was Ida's hesitant walk that bordered on stomping. Now she moved with limbered grace, not as smoothly as Tessa who seemed to float, but Eagan couldn't remember a time when Ida had looked so…unburdened, so pleasant.

Perhaps Tessa was a witch and had worked her magic. Whatever she'd done, magic or not, had been powerful.

"Aunt," Adam said, standing from the table as Ida approached. "Ye are welcome to our table."

The room was silent, everyone waiting to see what words would come from the woman who'd continually harangued them as children and young men. Eagan was probably the only brother who felt a tug of love and respect for her since she'd raised him from birth when their mother died.

She nodded, and her hair remained secure, so the curls didn't flop. "'Tis been too long since I've broken bread with my nephews." She sat in a chair at the table, and those brothers who had been sitting took their places again. "Too long," she continued, "since I came to Gylin Castle."

Lark glanced first at Tessa and then took a seat next to Ida. Adam's wife rested her hand over Ida's on the table. "We are glad to have you."

Eagan walked around so he could meet his aunt's eyes. He smiled. "I've never seen ye so bonny, Aunt Ida."

She frowned at him, and he saw the familiar glint in her eyes, which made him smile broader. "Running after you lads and then living alone gave me no time and no reason to do my hair." She nodded to Tessa as she patted at the curls on her head. "The lass has talent."

Lord, did she have talent, more than he would ever tell anyone, especially not his elderly aunt. But Aunt Ida's look was more than a clean gown and smoothed curls. The stiffness that had seemed to haunt her brittle spine had been gentled.

Tessa sat on the other side of Ida. "I think it would be best if Ida stayed here on Wolf Isle until Walter Gleeb leaves Mull."

"Of course," Lark said, and all the brothers murmured their "ayes."

But it would be up to his aunt to decide. Unmarried and vastly independent, they'd never gotten her to bend from her course. Adam had told Eagan that their mother, Ida's sister, had tried continually to get her to move with her and their father onto Wolf Isle, but she'd refused. Then when Hilda had died, leaving their father, John, a widow, Ida had implored them all to return to Mull, saying that the curse had killed Hilda and Eagan's twin sister. Without a mother for his five sons, John had finally relented, bringing them back to Mull to share the cottage with Ida.

"I think it would be prudent to stay for a while," Ida said, and Eagan watched the shoulders of his brothers lower in unison as if her words had released their clutched breaths.

"The Macquaries are all together again," Eliza, Beck's wife, said as she held her toddling son's hands as he practiced leaping in the air with all the energy of a two-year-old who'd been cooped up inside all day.

"You have a natural dancer," Tessa said, looking across at Richard.

Eliza nodded. "He never sits still."

Tessa stood, going to the little boy. "Would you like me to teach you a dance from the French court?"

The boy nodded vigorously and lunged for her without looking at his mother. Richard had Eliza's brave but rash personality, which Eagan knew made his brother both beam with pride and frown with worry.

Tessa laughed softly, the tinkling of her voice like a song. Richard tilted his head as if caught in its notes. "After we eat our meal," she said and handed the boy back off to Eliza and took her seat.

Questions filled Eagan's mind as he watched Tessa take small bites at the last meal of the day. She seemed relaxed, but he wondered how she could be in a new home where people might be judging her, and yet she smiled and spoke with man, woman, and children alike.

"I used to teach the children at King Louis's court how to dance the branle," she said. "It was perfect for those wanting to get their fidgets out." She nodded toward Richard.

"Ye were a dance instructor at the French court?" Callum asked.

She nodded and took a silent spoonful of venison stew that their cook had seasoned perfectly. She set her spoon down, touched the napkin to her lips, and set it back with such grace it was like a dance in itself.

"I'm a fair dancer," Callum said, glancing at Anna with a grin. "Especially when I have a couple swords to jump over." Anna leaned against his arm and got a kiss when she agreed.

Eagan watched Tessa as she chewed and smiled and spoke in melodic tones. The lass was always performing. The thought soured his stomach. Eagan had felt like he must perform at times, being who his family wanted him to be, but did Tessa ever get to be lazy or disordered?

"I spent time at the court with my mother," she said. "I sang, and danced, and taught lessons to the aristocrats and their children."

"That must have been exciting," Lark's younger sister, Kat, said, her eyes wide with a desire for adventure.

Tessa smiled at her. "At times. At first."

Anna's brows furrowed. "I've been around courtly people in England. 'Tis a dangerous line one walks with them. They can take advantage of those under their control."

Tessa looked down to her platter and worked at spreading butter on a fresh bun. "One must always stay a step ahead of the dangers at court."

"Is that why you left?" Lia asked.

Eagan looked up and down the long table. Everyone stared at Tessa, nearly salivating with questions. "Why don't we let her eat in peace," he said.

"Of course," Lark said and waved her hands, reminding them of their manners. It was the role she'd taken on years ago when marrying Adam, back when he and his brothers had been near-savages when it came to eating.

Tessa finished chewing her roll. "I withdrew from court when...my mother died, and then I left France when my father returned from his post at sea. He brought me here because my mother had lived for a while with Grissell, and he knew about her sanctuary."

Everyone around the table froze, their spoons and napkins stopping in the air. Ida and Tessa kept eating, along with the toddlers taking cut apples from their parents' plates.

"Yer mother lived with Grissell?" Drostan asked, from next to Lia.

"Oui, yes," Tessa said. "Otherwise, I doubt my father would have known about her or your isle."

"Captain Lemaire?" Adam asked as if trying to place the name.

"I'm sure you haven't met him," Tessa said. "'Twas my mother who knew of Wolf Isle."

"What an interesting story," Lark said.

"Does Grissell know?" Lia asked.

Tessa smiled, her lips quirked slightly. "I think she knew before I finished wading to shore from my father's rowboat."

"If anyone is a witch," Ida said, "'tis she."

Eagan felt a line of loyalty twang through him like a bowstring being plucked. "She belongs to Wolf Isle, and even if she won't admit it, she's descended from the Macquarie Clan."

"Aye," Adam said. "Gleeb will not get near her."

Ida sniffed softly. "Then she is exceedingly fortunate."

Chapter Eleven

Laughter bubbled into the rafters of the great hall as two-year-old Richard turned in a circle with Callum's daughter, Elizabeth. The two children were adorable. They didn't need the velvets and silks of court dress to be beautiful, only the whimsy of youth. Tessa clapped her encouragement, because there was nothing else one could do to train two-year-olds who couldn't yet follow directions.

She turned to the older girls, some of Beck and Eliza's wards and Anna's sisters. "We will start with couples standing together in a line." She took Eagan's hand. It was warm and dry and strong. The pressure of it against her palm made heat kindle within her. "Each couple should hold hands, facing one another."

Eagan tried to catch her gaze, but Tessa couldn't lose her concentration with everyone gathering and watching her. They hadn't talked since they'd left Grissell's that morning. She knew he had questions, could almost feel them leaking from him every time he looked at her. But they would have to wait.

Tessa released Eagan's hands and crouched before the youngest children. "On the morrow, I will teach you a game called bilboquet. I'll need to fashion a cup with a small ball attached by a string."

"I can help you make it," Dora said, her dramatic freckles giving her a beautifully natural look. She'd paired up with her sister, Aggie.

"I used to play bilboquet for hours when I was a child," Tessa said, remembering how she'd walk the grounds of Versailles, waiting for her mother to emerge, swinging the ball at the end of the thick string.

The two musicians, called in by Eagan's oldest brother, played a light tune. Tessa spoke with them about the cadence for the first dance she would teach. She hurried to stand opposite the line of adult and older children dancers and waved Eagan to join her. "Two steps left," she called, taking Eagan's hands so they could follow her instructions as an example. The line of dancers moved. "Two steps right. Now forward three, release hands, and circle around to a count of six."

Varying degrees of grace brought laughter and good-natured teasing. Beck knocked Drostan almost off his feet when he spun without care. Anna was quite the dancer and kept close to Callum, who swung her around. They whispered together as if sharing sweet memories of another dance they might have shared.

"Often the steps are similar to the Galliard," Tessa said and released Eagan's hand to demonstrate. Pointing her toes, she gave little hops, fluttering her feet back and forth. It reminded her of a fledgling bird trying to get off the ground. When her mother first taught her the steps, Tessa flapped her arms, too, trying to gain height, making her mother burst into fits of laughter. Tessa had joined her with giggles. Everything about her mother had been joyful and fun. Until she'd been killed, her swanlike white neck stained red with blood.

Tessa pushed the nightmare from her mind, her practiced smile unwavering. She startled slightly as Eagan took her elbow.

"Are ye well?" he asked, his mouth dipped toward her ear.

Her face turned to him, her smile in place. "Do I look unwell?"

"Not to the room," he said, nodding to the laughing dancers, all trying to flick their feet with steps in time with the musical beat.

"But to you I look unwell?" she asked. Only her mother had ever cared enough to read behind her mask.

He raised his hand toward a curl that she'd left down to lie tantalizingly against the creaminess of her skin above the edge of her bodice. But then he lowered it before he touched her. Her skin still tingled as if he'd stroked the sensitive area, and she almost reached for his hand, forgetting the watchful room.

"For a moment, yer eyes looked…haunted," he said.

The word was accurate. Her smile softened into a true one. "My mother loved to dance and laughed when doing so."

"And she has died," he said, nodding.

Rebecca Ainsworth hadn't just died. Rebecca Ainsworth had been murdered, her laughter and joy stolen away from Tessa.

"Was she ill?" Eagan asked.

"Pardon," Lark said, coming closer with several of the sisters. "I've heard there's a new dance sweeping Europe."

"Something rather scandalous," Eliza said. "'Tis called La Volta."

"Do you know it?" Dora asked.

Tessa's full smile returned. It was practiced but had bits of authenticity to it. At least she thought it did. She'd played the part of entertainer for the court her entire life, making it impossible at times to know where the fun-loving woman ended and the real Tessa began, if there even was a real Tessa.

"Oui," she said with a nod. "Yes, 'tis a dance where the man lifts and turns the woman, his hands on her waist and his knee riding up under her backside to help lift her."

None of them seemed shocked. Some rose upon their toes as if ready to leap all on their own. Lark clasped her hands and looked about for her stoic husband, Adam. Eliza traipsed off to snag Beck, dragging him over, her petticoats kicking out with her steps as if she hated the cumbersome ensemble. Anna and Lia found their husbands, and Tessa looked at Eagan. "We can show them and then you can dance with your nieces."

"I don't know the dance," he said but let her lead him out into the circle of onlookers.

"Trust me," she said and laughed when he looked doubtful. "Go on, take my arm and listen to my instructions."

The couples waited, watching closely. Even the two-year-olds looked on, holding hands as if not to be left out of the fun.

"The dance starts with a Galliard led in a circle." Tessa tugged on Eagan's arm, and the musicians provided a jaunty tune to match the step, accenting the three counts. "One, two, three," she called as Eagan led her around. She had danced with many men at King Francis's court, some clumsy, some stiff, some taking the lead role with dictatorial vengeance.

Tessa was delightedly surprised. "You dance lightly despite your broad frame," she said as they turned.

"We train for war, and war is just a dance with weapons."

The thought percolated through Tessa. She tipped her head slightly and smiled. "That is true. I fought a war at court, and often dancing saved me." She thought of the roguish looks from the men who watched her from the shadows of the grand ballrooms. How she would smile and glide, and then when the moment was right, disappear to hide away for the night when those with muscle or power stalked the halls?

Eagan's hand gripped her a little tighter, his jawline tense. "I've heard court is a dangerous place for a lass."

She turned her face, meeting his gaze. "The world is a dangerous place for a lass."

After a beat, she turned back to the dancers. "Now watch. Eagan, place your hand behind my back and as we turn, lift me using your knee..." She lifted her knee to show it bent. "Lift under my backside to help. Ladies, throw your legs out slightly, or wide if you wish it, then slide the feet together as you touch down again."

Eagan's arm went around her back, holding her parallel to him. "There should be a space between the dancers," she said. "Now turn and lift."

Eagan turned her, lifting her easily. "Good," she said, "but use your knee to lift under me."

"I don't need to."

"We have more muscle than French courtiers," Callum said and swooped Anna up into his arms, tossing her as she let out an unladylike curse.

"'Tis part of the dance," Lark said, looking at Adam. "Lift with your knee, too."

"Try again," Tessa said to Eagan.

He turned her in a circle, and she felt his knee rise under her. The power in the lift boosted her so high she felt like she might fly. She yelped. "Too high," she yelled when she felt herself lift from his arms into the air. He caught her easily and twirled her around. Tessa couldn't help but laugh. "Not so high!"

But it was too late. All the Macquarie brothers were tossing their wives high in the air and catching them as they turned, ending with the Galliard point and hop in their boots.

Laughter was punctuated with squeals and gasps as they did it again on another turn.

"Me! Me!" Richard and Elizabeth ran up to their fathers for their turns to be tossed.

"How did we do?" Eagan asked, grinning broadly.

She turned to him. "Perfect."

Tessa glanced at the far corner where Ida sat next to the older of the two wolfhounds that roamed about the castle. Her toe tapped even though her face sat in a frown. Perhaps it was how her face rested. The woman had been heartbroken decades ago and had never healed.

Tessa squeezed Eagan's hand. "Ask your aunt to dance."

"La Volta?"

"Or the Galliard or just turn her in a circle."

"She will say nay."

"Ask anyway."

He bowed politely to Tessa and walked over to Ida. Tessa's heart thumped faster when the woman stood. The boy she'd raised for her dear sister wanted to dance with her. It was good.

I loved once, and he married my sister.

Ida had confided in Tessa that she'd loved John Macquarie. She and Hilda had come over to Wolf Isle for Ida, the older of the two sisters, to marry him. But one look at Hilda, and John had asked Ida to break the betrothal so he could marry her sister.

At first, she'd refused, but watching the two of them together became torture. Ida thought of sending Hilda back to Clan Gunn, but their parents had died and no one was left to take her in. It was an impossible situation.

Tessa had watched women at court falling, day by day, further into bitterness like a bird caught in a bog. 'Twas like a cold grip on their happiness, leading to a slow decline toward misery and death. And the same had happened to Ida. Even after her sister died in childbirth, John could not bring himself to marry her, rejecting her all over again.

The woman walked on Eagan's arm across the hall. "Don't throw me about," Ida said. "I'll have none of that foolishness."

"I promise not to toss ye," Eagan said.

Ida nodded to Tessa as she walked past. Tessa followed and called out, "Everyone, choose a partner and stand next to them around me, in a circle."

"Don't delay," Ida said, her words coming out strong as she eyed the Macquarie brothers. 'Twas obvious she still saw them as rambunctious lads.

"Despite the strength you all have," Tessa said to the once again quieter room, "do *not* toss the ladies in the air when dancing in public. Just a gentle carry across the floor for the leap, please. Let's try again." She looked at Ida but spoke loudly as if to the room. "If you don't wish to leave the ground at all, tell your partner, and he will continue to turn you with the Galliard flutter step."

Ida said something to Eagan, and he grinned, nodding. As they turned with the others, he lifted her gently, setting her back on the ground like a bag of delicate cups. "Beautiful," Tessa called. "Everyone, watch how Eagan raises and lowers his graceful aunt." They turned again, and Eagan gently lifted and set Ida down. The woman had grace when she relaxed the stiffness in her shoulders.

Hands clapped, and color came to Ida's cheeks. She laughed, a little breathless. "'Tis like dancing in my youth, although we never danced anything so scandalous."

The elderly man named Rabbie stood apart drinking a tankard of ale. "Times have changed." His gaze remained on the older woman, and he shook his head once, turning to pick up a tart that had been left on a platter. But Tessa noticed him watching Ida as Adam took her hand to partner him in a line dance where men and women stood opposite each other, weaving in and out.

"Will ye dance with me again?" Eagan asked, coming up to Tessa.

"She has been lonely," she whispered. "Ask her again to remain here, either in Gylin or the village close by."

He followed her gaze to his aunt. "I'll talk to Adam. We've asked her before, but this is the first time she's visited since she came to whisk us all back to Mull."

"Times have changed," she said, repeating Rabbie's sage words. "Maybe with the threat of Walter Gleeb's witch hunt, she'll let her family protect her."

Eagan led Tessa over to join the dance, which the family seemed to know, adding their own flourishes as each couple turned and strutted down the center. Even Ida made a simple turn in the middle, and a smile softened the tightness of her lips.

When the dance ended, Richard toddled up to Ida and took her hand, leading her over to the wolfhound by the fire as if introducing her to the beast.

"We've had no chance to be alone today," Eagan said. He stood next to her, away from his brothers still dancing with their wives and children. He stared out with her. There was an undercurrent of want in his words. It called to her desire she'd set aside through the ups and downs of rescuing Ida and helping her clean up and deftly pulling out her poisonous secrets over an hour.

"'Tis been a long day," she said, glancing at him. Eagan stood strong, his muscles full beneath the cloth of his tunic. She wanted to clutch those hard biceps again, not as a partner in dance but as his lover thrashing with pleasure. He must feel the same.

"Aye," he murmured. "Ye must want to find sleep." He tried to hide the note of disappointment in his tone but failed.

A mischievous smile curled her lips as she looked out at the firelit hall where his family created an intimate tableau of humble celebration. She didn't bother to lower her voice since the music lifted into the rafters and the dancers' feet tapped while they laughed.

"I doubt I'd be able to sleep right now," she said. "Not with this ache in the crux of my legs and the heat coursing in my blood."

Out of the corner of her eye, she saw him swallow, the masculine knot in his throat rising and falling, and he breathed in fully through his nose. It brought to mind a bull smelling the air for a mate. Could he smell her desire? She shifted, her legs squeezing together, but she knew the throbbing would not dissipate easily.

"If you can't get away from your family to walk me back to my cottage," she said, "I will pleasure myself."

Eagan's gaze dropped to her. "Pleasure yerself?"

She cocked her head. "Have you never brought yourself to pleasure on your own?"

"I..." His lips remained parted for a moment. "I have... done...that."

"Bien," she said and looked directly into his eyes. Flames of desire raged in Eagan's intense stare. "I could touch myself until I rid myself of this hot ache, but I'd prefer your company."

His lips opened on an exhale, and his mouth quirked up at the corner. "Ye want me to get rid of yer hot ache?" The rumble of words in his deep voice teased the line within her that was already taut, plucking it to send vibrations up through her pelvis.

"Oui," she said, and her voice softened so he must lean in to hear her. "I want your hot mouth on me. And..." She clamped her legs together as if to keep the lid on Pandora's box. "I want to hold you in my mouth."

His teeth clenched for a moment. "I would taste ye, too, Tessa." He leaned into her ear so that she could feel the heat of his breath. "Until ye flood with yer own honey, and I ram my cock up into yer thrashing body, impaling ye to me while ye explode, milking me until I join ye."

Her eyes widened at the scandalous words. *Mon Dieu*, the man had talent. Tessa had been taught by her dry tutor how to say things that tantalized men, but Eagan's words shot through her with much more intensity, opening all her floodgates. Her mouth went slack, loose as if already salivating for him. "I think I'm already flooding," she said, his face close enough to hers that she could lean forward into his lips.

Her logical mind wondered how things had turned so quickly out of her control. But the rest of her didn't give a whit about the play of power she'd been taught to parry. Before her mind could swim its way out of the fever Eagan had lit in her, he was leading her toward the door.

"Are you leaving already?" Lark asked as he passed.

"Don't follow," he managed to say, and Tessa hurried along next to him.

The cool evening air brushed Tessa's cheeks, but it did nothing to cool the lava invading every inch of her body.

"I'll take ye back to yer cottage," Eagan said, his words almost angry, but Tessa knew it was the rumbling of need.

"Eventually," she said, tugging his hand toward the side of the castle within the wall, back where even the moon couldn't follow them.

Chapter Twelve

Tessa led Eagan past the willow tree she'd studied earlier from the window in Ida's room. Its leaves were unfurled but an unnatural green for this late time of year. In the darkness, the shadow of the dagger stuck into the trunk elongated. But she paid it no attention as she pulled him along, her gaze scanning the darkness broken only by glimpses of moonlight.

There toward the back was the kitchen garden, most of the herbs already harvested. But she'd seen the maid hang blankets out on thick ropes to dry and several remained, having been forgotten in all the drama of the day.

She ducked behind one, yanking it from the line in the darkness. Before she could decide where to put it, Tessa was pulled into the vault of Eagan's arms. Steel wrapped around her, and his mouth descended onto hers. Her hands scratched the muscles in his back through his tunic, and her body melted against his. His dominant, hard verge rose between them, pressing against the wrap around his powerful hips.

Reaching around to tug on her laces, Tessa nearly ripped her bodice down from her breasts. Her nipples pearled with the coolness of the breeze, and the moonlight glinted on the gilded birdcage that rested against her collarbone. She hitched one leg up to his hip.

Eagan's hot mouth lowered onto her nipple, sucking and bringing a soft moan from her. She desperately batted her petticoat upward, as well as his wrap until she felt his hot skin. Sliding her leg higher, she brought her naked crux against his thigh. The contact, along with the hot suction on her breast, sent a spiral of intense desire through her. She thrust her pelvis along his leg, reveling in the brush of his skin across her sensitive nub. Her breaths came in pants, and she almost cried out when his strong, deft fingers found her.

Eagan groaned and nudged his verge against her.

"Oh God, yes," she said, abandoning thoughts about keeping the upper hand in the tryst. He lifted under her arse, and Tessa's feet left the ground. She wrapped her other leg around him until she straddled him, her petticoat bunched around her.

"Do ye want me?"

She looked down in his eyes as he brought the head to her heat. "Yes."

"Do ye want me inside ye?"

"Right now," she said, pressing herself against him.

His gaze was so intense, she couldn't have looked away if she'd wanted to. He thrust into her as he brought her down. Passion pinched his face, hardening his jaw. Tessa's gasp turned into a deep moan as he completely filled her body. She tightened her legs around him, squeezing as he moved. The stone wall behind her gave her more leverage, her raised petticoats cushioning her back as Eagan began to pull out and thrust back in hard, pushing her breath out of her with each stroke of his body against hers.

Her breasts bobbed, perched along the edge of her bodice as they met each other over and over. His mouth found hers again, and their kiss was as wild as their straining bodies. His mouth kissed a trail from her lips, along her jaw and to her ear where his indecent whispers tickled.

"Can I fok ye from behind?"

"You can fok me however you want."

She heard his deep chuckle, and he withdrew, setting her feet on the ground. Cool grass told her she'd lost her slippers somewhere along the way, but she didn't care as he spun her to face the wall.

He pulled her body into him, covering her with the heat from his large form, and raised her skirts. The mere tickling of the fabric against her thighs made her pulse race with want, and she spread her legs, arching her back. She felt him seeking her and then he thrust back inside.

"Mon Dieu, Eagan." It felt so glorious to be full of this man.

Her breath caught as he moved within her and rubbed against her on the outside, his other hand releasing her to palm a breast, pinching her nipple until the pleasure shot down from it to meet up with the other taut lines in her pelvis. Her breasts jiggled as he thrust into her, her locket thudding against her upper chest. The rubbing, the pinching, the thrusting: they all worked together to build her higher and higher.

And then his tongue tip slid along her ear, the heat of his breath an added pleasure. "Yer body is like a vessel of hot honey, Tessa, lass. And I'm going to sample all of it. I'm going to feast on it."

His words pushed her over the edge into hot, pulsing oblivion. Eagan followed, pumping into her, curling his arm around her to secure her as he lifted her off her feet with each thrust. Then he joined her, his yell of satisfaction muted in her thick, soft hair. They breathed hard together while the rhythm of their bodies slowed. As he slipped from her body, turning her in his arms to hold her, Tessa realized he'd released within her once again.

...

Eagan rolled over, his arm dragging across his face to block the early morning sun coming in the cottage window. Memories of his wild night with Tessa sent heat to his already-hard jack since it was morning. He should piss before touching her or he wouldn't be able to go.

Instead, without opening his eyes, he rolled toward Tessa, inhaling their joint essence in the rumpled sheets. She was a sweet dessert he could not ignore, a roasted cut of beef to a starving man, a tankard of ice-cooled ale to one dying of thirst. There was no choice but to roll toward her.

A niggling thought tried to sour his mood. He'd released his seed in her several times last night, unable to pull out at the critical moment. So much for his brothers, Rabbie, and Aunt Ida hammering into him he should never release inside a woman other than his wife. He would need to wait until her monthly courses came before he left the isle. The thought made his tight chest open back up. That meant he could spend more time with her.

Eagan's arm slid across her side of the bed unimpeded, and his eyes opened. She was gone, and his stomach gripped into a fist. "Tessa," he murmured and sat up, the sheet falling to his lap. The room was empty.

Eagan rolled out of the bed and grabbed up his white tunic, throwing it over his head. He shook out the long woolen wrap and folded it quickly around his waist to support it with his wide leather belt, throwing the end over one shoulder to secure it. His feet slammed into his leather boots, and he grabbed his sword, heading out the door.

The clearing was empty except for a red squirrel that ran

across, stopped to chitter at him with a nut in his little hands, and then hurried on. He would yell her name but didn't want to alert everyone to the fact he'd once again spent the night with Tessa.

Grissell walked around the corner, her two white cats and the multicolored cat, Sia, trotting in a weaving pattern around her, somehow avoiding being stepped on or tripping the old woman. Without a word, she pointed toward the water behind her.

"Is Tessa there?" he asked and cleared his throat. "I came out here to see her this morn."

The unspoken word "liar" passed over Grissell's face, before she poked her finger toward the trees bordering the rocky shore. She continued to the children's cottage.

Tessa was easy to spot standing at the tip of a stone jetty where a rowboat was tied. She wore a thick wool robe of pale blue, but he could see the lace edge of her long white smock blowing about her ankles in the breezes off the sea. She stared at the horizon to the west, her hair dancing like dark ribbons.

As he walked closer, he heard the notes of her song flow upon the breeze. There were no words, only notes, rising and falling in clear perfection. He could imagine the song as a rope pulling him to her. He stopped next to her, feeling the spray of the sea when a wave crashed hard against the rocks as if the Greek god of the sea were trying to abduct her. It made Eagan's arms itch to wrap around Tessa and drag her back to the forest. But he didn't want to disturb her, so he stood guard against Poseidon.

Her lashes fluttered, and she let the song fade. A single tear dried in a path down her cheek before he could pull her to him and wipe it away. "What's wrong?"

"He said he'd return for me." She looked at him. "My father. And yet he does not come." Her face turned back to the sea. "I thought I saw a ship far off this morn, but it was a mere speck that disappeared around the isles to the west."

Eagan found her hand in the folds of her cape and clasped it. Her fingers were cold. He cupped them in his two hands, blowing a warm exhale onto them. The frivolous joy from the day before, the laughter and mischievous light to her large green eyes, had been squelched with worry.

"He's in the French Navy?"

She nodded. "A captain of his own ship. He's been gone too long. A year now."

"I could ask Beck and Adam if we can sail to the major ports along Scotland and France to see if ye can spot his ship." After the pirate Jandeau had attacked and Beck set his own ship ablaze to ram into Jandeau's ship, he'd rebuilt a new *Calypso*, and Adam was working to build a second carrack under Cullen Duffie's guidance.

"I don't know," she said. "I think he was headed south, perhaps around to the African coast."

"For the French Navy?" Was King Henri involved in the African slave trade?

She stared out at the sea. "I worry a storm has taken him. I may truly be an orphan."

He squeezed her hand. "Ye can have a family here."

She turned to him with a look that flexed between hope and dismay. "Here? On Wolf Isle? With you?"

Eagan's throat constricted, and he cleared it. "Grissell won't live forever, despite her prayers or spells or whatever she uses to cling to life. Ye could continue her work. Live here and help lasses and bairns. Ye're a midwife."

She nodded, looking back out. "She has asked me to do so."

"Stay on Wolf Isle to take over her orphanage?"

Tessa nodded.

Eagan's whole body tensed. If she stayed, would he want to stay? Would he abandon all his plans to explore the world or at least the far reaches of Scotland?

"I've told her no," Tessa said, and like a honed blade, her words cut the idea of abandoning his plan.

"Why?" he asked with more force than he wanted as relief surged through him. She didn't want to stay on Wolf Isle. Would she consider going with him?

She turned her face to study him as if she'd heard the emotion behind his question. "Because I must leave if my father comes. My mother always said he'd come for us when the king did not need him. Now that she's gone, I'm meant to be with my father."

"Then why didn't ye stay with him on ship?" Eagan asked. *Mo chreach! I don't want to go to France.* The words were soft in his head under the thrumming of his quickened blood, but they were insistent. At least if she remained on Wolf Isle, he'd know where to find her.

"He had king's business to do, and his men didn't like the idea of a woman on the ship. They thought it was bad luck. So he rowed me over to Grissell where I would be safe until he returned. That was a year ago."

Eagan had heard the sailing superstitions from some of the sailors who'd left the sea to live in Ormaig Village when Beck's wife, Eliza, settled on Wolf Isle. She had been raised by them on the ship, so they considered her more mermaiden than woman.

"Ye should speak with Eliza about life onboard a sea vessel. 'Tis not easy. She grew up on a ship constantly under threat by pirates, storms, and persecution. She had to learn to be as tough as the sailors and ready to kill."

Tessa stood straight, her face turning slowly to his. Her expression was set firm as if suddenly chiseled in granite. "I can and will kill if threatened. I know the danger of men, devious louses who prey on women. Men who think we are weak, but I'm not weak."

"That is fortunate," he said, not wanting to annoy her further even though the thought of her going up against a man like the pirate Jandeau curdled his stomach. "Still," he continued, "ye should speak with Eliza about life onboard ship. Saltwater baths that leave ye sticky, tainted food when supplies run low, no privacy with two dozen stinking men. The list of unpleasantries goes on and on."

Her lips quirked in a dry smile. "It sounds like you're trying to convince me not to sail."

Eagan couldn't stop himself this time. He reached for her, his hands curving around her upper arms to pull her into him. She came willingly but still looked up into his face. "Ye could stay here on Wolf Isle; whether ye settle at Grissell's or in Ormaig, it doesn't matter."

"You don't want me to sail away."

"Nay."

"And yet you plan to sail away to mainland Scotland and beyond. In fact, you should already be gone." Her brows pinched. "You would have me watch another man sail away from me. Have me always watch the horizon for a ship." She tipped her head, peering at him. "How is that fair?"

Eagan rubbed his mouth. It wasn't fair. Daingead. "Ye could come with me." The words came out before he thought better of it.

She pursed her lips tight and pushed her finger into his chest, the end hard. "Then you wouldn't be lonely. Isn't that what you said you wanted? To be all alone on your journey?" With each word, she tapped his chest and then left her fingertip against him, pinning him there as if the little appendage was a dagger.

"I'm not sure now. I've always wanted to leave, have a chance to make my own way without a cluster of brothers and kin telling me what I must or mustn't do." He grabbed her finger to pull her closer until his arm could snake around to her back. "The only thing I am sure about is that we fit well together, Tessa." He lowered his face to her neck, kissing a trail along it. "Very well together."

When he raised his head, she took his hand and silently led him back to her cottage so he could show her just how well they fit.

...

Two weeks passed with simple entertainment.

Grissell no longer discouraged Tessa from going up to Gylin Castle, and the Macquarie Clan was respectful and accepting. Even though Eagan had been staying with her at her cottage at night, the ladies of the castle still spoke with her. None of the men leered or tried to catch her alone. They seemed enamored of their wives, which was so different from court life where dalliances occurred nightly.

A few times, Tessa had nearly forgotten to study the horizon off the shore, searching for her father's ship. The gripping thought that she might be abandoned was lessening its painful hold. And Eagan hadn't said anything to his family about leaving.

The breeze blew Tessa's hair around her shoulders as she sat with the ladies on a blanket in a spot of sunshine in a pretty glen north of Ormaig Village. The woven colors of gold and brown in the blanket matched the falling leaves that the children built into a mountain for jumping. The crunch and crackle excited them even more, but their squeals weren't too sharp with the fresh air carrying the high-pitched notes away. Orphy, Tessa's fawn, leaped around with them, staying out of reach of the two-year-olds' clenching fingers.

Even Ida had accompanied them. She sat on a stump watching the children and stroked the large heads of the Macquarie wolfhounds. She'd frown at their antics occasionally, but she seemed softer than before coming to Wolf Isle. Lark's lady's maid had been trying different coiled and woven styles on her gray hair, and color was once again in Ida's cheeks.

Whether the woman wanted it or not, she'd captured the attention of the old man, Rabbie, who'd begun to wash more frequently. He carried a basket over to Ida, offering her a tart that Anna had baked that morning. Ida took one, thanking him, and turned back to the children rolling in the leaves.

"They will all need baths," Anna said.

"We'll send them to bathe with their fathers in the loch," Eliza said. "Cold water will do them good."

"As long as they don't catch a fever," Lark said.

Lia lowered her voice. "Rabbie is sweet on Aunt Ida."

All the ladies turned to see the man trying to talk with her, the basket hanging from the tips of his fingers.

"He must be," Lark said, "even though Adam says it can't be. The two have always disliked one another."

"That was before Ida had a smile," Dora said.

"She's always had a smile," Tessa said, her words soft. "Bitterness was weighing it down."

The ladies looked at her. They didn't ask, but their gazes were curious. Tessa stood, brushing her skirts. She'd never betray Ida's confidence about her love for John Macquarie and the pain his rejection caused. A woman's heart was a private landscape.

Tessa walked toward the trees. The brothers and a few men from neighboring Mull readied a thick rope, stretching it out over a five-foot-high pile of leaves to play tug-o-war. She wove through the trees, first finding a place to relieve her bladder, and then walked the short distance to the rocky coast. The glen was inside the north shoreline of Wolf Isle where an inlet stretched west out to the open ocean.

As she emerged from the trees, Tessa's breath caught

at the sight of a ship. It had four masts and collapsed sails. *A galleon.* Men moved along the deck, and a rowboat sat against the hull in the water. Her heart hammered, her gaze scanning the deck where men moved about calmly.

The ship flew no flag so there was no way to identify it. Her father had said he rarely flew a flag, because it would draw pirates who wanted to steal the riches of France. Could it be her father who was finally coming to retrieve her?

Tessa's stomach dropped, bringing an emptiness with it. Was she ready to leave Wolf Isle? Perhaps that's why Grissell hadn't wanted her meeting the Macquaries, because she knew the pain of leaving them would be terrible. Leaving Eagan now after the weeks they'd spent in each other's arms would feel like something ripping away from her.

Maybe her father wouldn't want her to travel with him. Then she could stay and take care of the orphanage. Tessa should alert the Macquaries about the ship. She turned and gasped at the large figure standing before her. She blinked, her mind spinning away from thoughts of her father. "Master Gleeb?"

The witch hunter wasn't alone. He had a group of men with him, all of them armed with swords. One held a rifle. Gleeb's watery blue eyes gleamed with feverish zeal. "Thou shall not suffer a witch to live."

Chapter Thirteen

"I've come to take ye to Edinburgh to be tried as a witch," Walter Gleeb said, "since I cannot do my duty to God and the crown here in this heathen land."

His sharp gaze pierced Tessa as if she were a butterfly being pinned on a naturalist's board. He stepped toward her with hands outstretched. She turned to run but found her way barred by the sea. She looked left and right, spotting two other rowboats moored farther down the rocky coast. Should she flee to one of them? Would Gleeb and his brutes follow?

Gleeb lunged, catching Tessa around the waist. "Let me go!" she yelled, striking out with her elbows.

Gleeb grunted but yanked her off the ground and hoisted her from the rocks back to the dirt. She pried at his solid hold, her nails digging into the fleshy bulk of his arm. He hissed in pain but didn't release.

"Let the lass go," Eagan said, his voice deadly calm. A growl came from the trees as the dogs emerged. Adam followed and yelled a command to stop the dogs from attacking, and Eagan's other three brothers moved forward between them.

Tessa stopped twisting, her gaze fastening onto Eagan as if he were a floating barrel in the open ocean. His brothers faced off with Gleeb's men. The wives must be back in the woods with the children, but Tessa saw Lia holding her bow and arrow, nocked and ready.

Tessa's breath stopped as she felt the sharp edge of Gleeb's knife graze her throat.

"One step and I'll send this witch to Hell right now."

She'd protest she wasn't a witch, but, like so many women before, Tessa knew she wouldn't be believed by the likes of Gleeb. She barely swallowed against the cool blade. Her pulse beat with such fury she imagined her blood pressing against the knife.

"I am Chief Macquarie," Adam said. "And ye and yer men will leave right now."

"Without Tessa," Eagan added.

"By royal writ, I am invited anywhere belonging to the country of Scotland if I believe there is a credible suspicion of witchcraft."

"The lass isn't a witch," Callum said, his gaze on the brute directly across from him. They were of similar build and would cause each other much loss of blood if they clashed.

"I will examine her to see," Gleeb said.

"Examine her?" Eagan yelled. "Ye mean torture her with pins pricked into her skin."

"Demons and witches are clever," Gleeb answered with the self-assurance of a priest discussing original sin. "They appear innocent and weak when they can rise up with spells and witchcraft to attack at any time. The testing keeps the accused under control during the inquiry."

"'Tis foking wrong," Rabbie called from his place next to Drostan. Now they were only outnumbered by one. Except that one of Gleeb's henchmen was leveling a firearm and pointing it at anyone who spoke. That single weapon multiplied the deadliness of Gleeb's side fivefold.

"Unless ye want this woman's blood on your conscience," Gleeb said, "I suggest ye back up and let us leave without harassment. As it is, I'll report how the Macquarie Clan interfered with an official edict about—" His words cut off in a gasp, and Tessa felt his whole body stiffen.

Then Gleeb's hand was ripped away from her throat. Her hands replaced the blade on her neck, and she felt the sting of the shallow cut. A bit of blood smeared on her fingers.

Eagan lunged forward, catching Tessa before she hit the ground. He hauled her up against him, using his arms and body to shield her as Gleeb's men began to slash.

Blast! The gun fired, making Tessa lurch against Eagan.

Loud yells and the cracking metallic sound of blade hitting blade filled the small shoreline, and Tessa turned wide eyes to the scene. Gleeb's men fought, but it looked like they fought each other. The dogs barked but remained by Adam's side, under his control. The Macquarie brothers and Eliza stood back, their faces slack as Tessa watched the battle from the safety of Eagan's arms.

Callum wrestled up from the ground, triumphantly holding the matchlock pistol. Gleeb lay face down across the rocks where he'd fallen, blood pouring from a stab wound in the back of his white tunic.

"Bloody foking hell," Eagan yelled behind her. "Run, Tessa." But when he let go to draw his sword against one of Gleeb's men, Tessa stayed rooted to the ground as she looked at the man dressed in a sea captain's long coat, holding his sword, red with Walter Gleeb's blood.

"Father?"

He wore his ice-hard frown, his dark eyes glittering like a clear, star-filled night sky. "Ma fille," he said. "I've come for you." Chill bumps swept across her skin from head to toe.

Without any other words, her father strode to her, yanking her away from Eagan's side to stand before him. Her father had just saved her again, this time from the witch hunter.

She twisted toward the Macquaries, her arms out. "Don't shoot. He's not with Gleeb. He's my father."

"Father," she said, glancing up into Captain Lemaire's stern, focused face, "these are friends I've made on the isle. They aren't with the witch hunter."

Her father murmured in rough French behind her; the vehemence more than the curses made it sound like he hated Eagan's family. It sent a nauseating chill through her.

Her father's black eyes turned down toward her. He smelled of the open sea and tar and some spice. "We are leaving now."

"Nay!" Eagan yelled, stepping forward.

She'd been waiting for her father for over a year, every day watching the horizon for the sign he'd not abandoned her again. But now… Leaving like this wasn't right.

Boulders weighed down her stomach so much that if she were to find herself suddenly in the sea, she would certainly sink to the cold, dark bottom.

Her father's voice boomed out. "Claudette Tempest Ainsworth is my daughter and lawfully under my protection. She's coming with me now."

"Non, mon père. I must say farewell," she said in rapid French.

All traces of the earlier laughter from the glen and the warmth of the sun had transformed into an eerie, stilted silence as the Macquaries stared with widened eyes.

"Get into the rowboat. We leave now," her father ordered.

"Now?" Tessa's heart squeezed. She thought of her sweet fawn and the six-toed cat that she cuddled with. And then there was Eagan, the honorable, pleasure-giving, adventurous lover and kind man.

"Immédiatement."

His men lined up on either side of him. Two of them held muskets ready against their shoulders. They had killed all of Gleeb's men with little blood loss and looked to be ready to end the lives of all the Macquaries.

"The Macquaries are our friends, mon père."

"Nay, Tessa," Eagan called across to her. She turned, her breath catching. Eagan's teeth showed as he spoke, his lips slightly rolled back. His nose wrinkled as he held his sword before him, staring over her head at her father as he spoke. "Captain Claude Jandeau is no friend of ours."

...

Blood pounded in Eagan's ears as if the sea raged inside him. He kept his gaze on Jandeau, the French pirate loyal to no one but himself and his greed. The madman who'd tried four other times to steal away the wives of his brothers along with children and defenseless women who would be raped and sold to brothels if they survived.

Furious bewilderment shot pain through Eagan's head as the blood thumped in his ears. Captain Claude Jandeau was Tessa's father?

Impotent rage swirled like a wicked storm in his gut. Of all the lasses he could become entangled with, he'd spent the last amazing weeks with Jandeau's daughter. Had the pirate left Tessa on Wolf Isle to ensnare Eagan?

"A father who uses his daughter as a shield," Eagan said, trying to keep his voice even. "Ye bloody foking coward."

Tessa stared at him with wide eyes. She shook her head. "Captain Claude Lemaire is my father, Eagan. Everyone put their weapons down." But no one relaxed.

Eagan's blood thrummed with violence and dread. "Tessa, I don't know if Jandeau is your father or not, but the man behind ye is not a naval captain for King Henri of France. At least not an honorable captain. He's a pirate who sells women and children as slaves, or worse."

Eagan remembered her tale of salvation, of how Jandeau rescued her when she was nearly starving after her mother died. Then he'd brought her to Grissell for safekeeping. Jandeau was the man that Tessa had watched for every day upon the rocks, her eyes scanning the horizon for his ship, her sorrowful song lamenting his absence.

Questions bombarded him, but they fell away in light of his need to stop Jandeau from taking Tessa away. The infamous pirate had a new crew after they'd set his second ship on fire when he'd abducted Drostan's wife, Lia. But like a plague, the man kept rearing back up to threaten the Macquarie Clan. And now he was taking away the woman that Eagan… What? Found immense pleasure with? Laughed with? Considered taking with him? *Bloody hell.* She could be with child!

A bastard born will doom Clan Macquarie.

"Ye're outnumbered, Jandeau," Adam called out, and Eagan noticed the wives and the unmarried women had come from the forest, too, some holding daggers and some holding large throwing rocks that Anna had them practice with daily.

"I will put this blade through your skull," Eliza said, aiming to throw her sgian dubh. "You know I can."

Lia didn't bother to say anything but loosed her arrow at one of the two crewmen holding muskets. A strangled sound came from him, the heavy weapon dropping as his hands rose to the arrow's fletching feathers, the shaft embedded through his throat. He dropped to his knees on the rocky shore and fell over.

"I said I'd kill you if I ever saw you again," Lia called unrepentant.

Before the second gunman could discharge his musket, Beck shot his own musket, hitting the other man's weapon and making a small explosion that knocked the man backward and destroyed his firearm.

"Throw!" yelled Anna, and fist-sized rocks shot through the air, hitting several of the men. One hit a pirate's nose, and blood gushed from it. Another rock bludgeoned a pirate's jack, making him double over and fall on the ground. Adam released the wolfhounds, who leaped at two men running forward with curved swords slicing the air. The men stopped in their tracks as the dogs' front paws slammed into their shoulders, toppling them.

Jandeau dragged Tessa backward toward the two waiting rowboats. Eagan re-sheathed his sword, drawing his sgian dubh from his boot. With a lunge and flick of his wrist, he threw the blade, and it stuck into Jandeau's forearm. If he grunted, Eagan couldn't hear it over the yells from the battle.

One pirate was dead, and the other six had scurried about, ducking from Lia's quickly releasing arrows and the rocks that whizzed through the sea breeze. Two of the fiends were now under the two-hundred-pound dogs. Eagan dodged another man battling Callum with a sword in one hand and a dagger in the other. At the last second, Eagan threw his leg out, tripping the pirate, and kept running. Jandeau dropped his arm, the blade protruding. It was all Eagan needed.

Eagan reached Tessa, grabbing her to him.

"No," she yelled, the words cutting through him as if she'd wielded a knife. Tessa's face snapped back and forth between Jandeau and Eagan.

"He's not what ye think," Eagan yelled over the chaos. This was no time to talk about all the sins the infamous, foking-lucky-to-be-alive pirate had committed against men, women, children, and probably animals.

Her face was tight with indecision when it turned to

him. "He's my father. I know it to be true." Her hand went to her locket. The small birdcage shape was a lump under her smock. He'd never looked inside it. Was there a picture of Jandeau there? Daingead, he should have looked inside!

Jandeau wiped his blood off the sgian dubh, seething rage darkening his tanned face. There was no time to convince her. Eagan lifted Tessa off the ground, setting her over one of his broad shoulders, and turned.

"Put...me...Putain, Eagan...put...me...down!" she yelled as he ran toward the forest, his shoulder probably ramming into her middle, making it hard for her to talk. The rest of her furious words came out in French. But he didn't stop, not even when she kicked her legs.

One watching without knowing who the players were in this horrid act might think him the villain, stealing the daughter away from the father who'd come to retrieve her. *I'm not the villain.* He'd seen what Jandeau did, how he stole innocents, using them for grotesque pleasure and profit. Tessa needed to hear the truth before she chose to go with him. Would Eagan let her walk away with Jandeau if she chose to? He couldn't even think about that without wanting to roar.

Eagan ran through the woods, the well-hewn muscles in his legs churning to push them as far from Jandeau and his men as he could get Tessa. Before he reached the meadow, Eagan heard Jandeau's chilling words behind him.

"I will return for my daughter, and she will come with me, or all of your Macquarie sons and daughters will be slaughtered."

Chapter Fourteen

"The loutish beast," Tessa said over the sound of her boots cracking on the wooden floor as she paced.

She'd been led to Eagan's bedchamber of all places. Despite being inside the hulking stone fortification of Gylin Castle, the room was full of light from two large windows paned with glass. A fire had been started in the stone hearth, and rugs lay about the wooden floors, keeping the room warm. Gylin wasn't Versailles with its gilt trim and priceless furnishings, but it was strong and solid like the Highlanders who inhabited it.

She stopped at the large bed, which had obviously been built to accommodate the dratted man's large form. All that muscle made it easy for him to pluck her off the ground and throw her over his shoulder, running her away from the shoreline while his brothers battled her father.

Mon Dieu! She picked up one of the plump pillows and yelled foul curses into the feathers under the linen casing. A feather poked her in retaliation, making her inhale briskly. *Putain!* She could smell Eagan on it. He smelled of a certain garden spice, mixed with leather and fresh air. It was damnably alluring.

She huffed, narrowing her eyes at the offending pillow in her hands, and threw it hard at the bed. It rolled off the soft plaid blanket onto the floor on the opposite side. She paced back to the fire, then the window, then the bed, making a triangular path. Her boots clacked on the hard wood and then became muffled as she traversed the scattered floor rugs.

Eagan had grabbed her away from her father without hearing what she wanted to do. Her mother had loved the French naval captain, had wed him, and waited in France for his return like Tessa had been waiting for him to return to Wolf Isle. He'd saved her from the gutters, clothed her, and left her safely with Grissell.

No one had been willing to talk. Lia, Drostan's cheerful wife who'd saved Sia as a kitten, had started the battle by shooting one of her father's men. She'd killed the man without a single sword strike or gunshot as if she sought revenge. And after Tessa's father had just stabbed Gleeb through the heart and then signaled his crewmen to attack the royal soldiers.

She frowned, her hand sliding along the line of dried blood across her throat. "He'd been saving me," she whispered in the room. But then... *He held me before him like a shield.*

She shook her head and strode to the window, pushing it open to breathe in the crisp air coming from inland. Had her father been protecting himself, using her as cover? His men had two firearms to the Macquaries' one. Although, her father had apparently known that he was the Macquaries' target.

Tessa continued to pace a triangle across the room over a thick rug. *Crack, crack, crack, muffle, muffle, crack, crack.* She flopped unceremoniously onto the bed. All she wanted was to bury her face and forget that day. She inhaled and drew in Eagan's essence. Her body responded immediately with an ache through her abdomen to the crux of her legs.

"Bloody hell." She used his favorite curse and rolled onto her back, pressing the ache through her petticoat to push it away.

She turned her mind to her father. What had he said exactly when he'd rowed her over to Wolf Isle in the middle of the night over a year ago? "I haven't the permission to dock," she murmured, repeating his words when she'd asked why her landing was so clandestine.

Remain with Grissell, the old woman who lives in one of those huts. Be a good girl, but if you get pregnant, make sure 'tis by a Macquarie. He'd spoken in soft French. Before she could assure him she wouldn't get pregnant, he'd touched her cheek and continued.

Await my return, and I will take you to France. And then he turned and pushed the small craft off the shore, rowing quickly back to his ship in the darkness.

"Pregnant by a Macquarie?" she murmured, staring up at the canopy over the bed. Did her father believe the curse Grissell told her had been placed on Eagan's clan a century ago by her ancestor? Did her father hate the Macquaries as much as it seemed Eagan's family hated Captain Claude Lemaire, whom they called Jandeau?

Tessa fingered the golden birdcage locket that was warm from sitting against her skin. If only her mother were still alive, because Rebecca Ainsworth, despite her flirtations and rash behavior, always answered Tessa truthfully. At least that's what Tessa had always thought.

Rebecca hadn't mentioned anything about what her father did on the sea for the king, but Tessa had never asked. And now she didn't have anyone to ask who she knew would tell the truth.

In the silence, Tessa heard light footsteps in the hallway. One set and then another, firmer set. She stood, not wanting to be caught in such an undignified sprawl on the bed. But no one knocked on the door.

She moved closer to it and heard low voices, so she laid her ear against the wood.

"I was Jandeau's prisoner," the woman whispered. "He raped and killed my mother and killed my father and gave my baby brother to a brothel."

Tessa stopped breathing, her stomach turning sour. He'd raped and killed? It couldn't be the same man.

"If ye tell her all his sins right away like that…'tis too much, Eliza." Eagan's voice was low as he spoke rapidly with concern.

"She deserves to know the truth."

"She doesn't deserve to be hit over the head with it."

"There's no easy way to tell someone that their father is a beast," Eliza said, "but it must be done."

"Maybe he's not even her father," Eagan said. "Either way, I'm not letting him take her on his ship."

Indignation over Eagan's authoritative tone blew on the sparks alit inside Tessa. A fiery anger grew within, and she laid her fist against the solid wood door.

The words, which were coming faster and faster between them, slid around in Tessa's belly, making it boil. "I can hear everything you're whispering out there," Tessa said, her voice at a normal volume but her tone terse.

Silence. Then, *rap, rap*. "May we come in?" 'Twas Eagan.

Tessa pressed the latch and swung the door inward to find both Eagan and Eliza standing there. Eliza held a tray with some biscuits and a decanter of what looked like whisky.

Worry pinched Eagan's ruggedly handsome face. She pivoted and strode to the hearth. If she was going to be hit over the head with her father's alleged sins, she wanted to be warm. It was also better to put some distance between herself and her lover, for that's what Eagan Macquarie was, merely her lover, a very masterful lover, but nothing more than that.

Her mother had taken lovers but had never loved them. She used them for pleasure and prestige. It had upset Tessa that she could be intimate with another man while she was waiting for her husband to return from sea, but with each letter Rebecca received from Captain Lemaire she became rasher, her smile and laughter more brittle. 'Twas as if she knew he would never return.

Eliza walked into the room wearing trousers. She looked much more in command with her legs free to run and kick than in the tiresome layers of petticoats. If Tessa was going to sail with her father, she'd need to acquire a few pairs. The thought of sailing away with him didn't feel as comforting now.

Setting the tray down, Eliza poured a cup of amber liquid.

Eagan closed the door behind him. "I was helping bury Walter Gleeb and his men. No one will reveal that they were here in case anyone from Edinburgh comes asking questions."

"Do the Macquaries have enemies in Edinburgh, too?" Tessa asked, her eyebrow arching as she frowned. A look of disdain was stronger than glaring.

"We get some interference from the crown, and sometimes English soldiers come north to cause trouble," Eagan said. "They harass the Scots mainly on the border."

"I mean the Macquaries, not other Scotsmen."

"Nay." He frowned. "We don't have enemies. Except for Jandeau."

"Drink this," Eliza said, handing her a cup. "You'll be better with a sip of whisky."

"Better?" Tessa said, taking the cup. "Better from having my father, whom I've been waiting to see again for over a year, attacked by the people I thought were my friends?" She stared at Eagan. "By the man who *was* my lover." She emphasized the past tense.

Eliza tipped her head left to right. "Perhaps you should do more than sip. Drink the whole cup down."

Tessa swallowed a mouthful of the smooth, fiery liquid and breathed out the sharp essence on a long exhale. Her gaze slid across both of them and landed on Eagan. "You call my father Jandeau," Tessa said. "His name is Claude Lemaire, and he works for the French Navy under King Henri."

The whisky had wound down to Tessa's stomach, and she felt a flush suffuse her, rising to her neck. She placed her cool hand across it.

"Did Lark give ye ointment for the cut across yer throat?" Eagan asked, fury edging his words.

"Oui," Tessa answered in French but kept going in sharp English. "Claude Lemaire is my father. He was married to my mother. She was English." She waved a hand. "And somehow came to this isle to live with Grissell. But then my father rescued her, taking her to France when she became pregnant with me. He sailed throughout my life, only stopping in to visit us once a year. When my mother was…murdered at court, he rescued me from the life of a beggar in Paris."

"Yer mother was murdered?" Eagan asked.

Tessa stared at him. "Because she trusted when she shouldn't have."

"Why did he leave you on Wolf Isle?" Eliza asked.

"His men are rough, and mon père didn't want me to sail with him until he could find sailors with more integrity for his ship. Then he would return."

Eliza passed a glance to Eagan and then back to Tessa. "His men still seem pretty rough."

"Did you kill them all?" Tessa asked Eliza. Eagan had run Tessa back to Gylin Castle without pausing to rest, explain, or respond to the curses she hurled at him in French, English, and even Latin.

"A few were dispatched," Eliza said cooly. "Jandeau and

the rest got away into their rowboats."

"Jandeau!" Tessa threw up her one hand that wasn't holding the whisky. "That's not his name."

Eliza met her glare, her own eyes narrowing. "If you could hear me through the door then you already know that he has raped and killed innocent women and sold children into slavery."

Tessa shook her head. "Perhaps that is your Jandeau, but Claude Lemaire is an honorable captain in the French Navy."

Eagan's hands fisted and slid over the top of his head to the back of his neck as if it ached. "If ye say that man standing on our shore today, the man who without any conversation killed Walter Gleeb, the man who used ye as a human shield… If ye say that is yer father, Tessa, then they are one and the same. He calls himself Captain Claude Jandeau when he's sailing the seas, destroying, torturing, and cruelly using people."

"Now who's hitting her over the head," Eliza murmured. She looked between them. "I think I'll leave you two alone to discuss…" She moved her hand in a circle like she were stirring a tempest. "Discuss this bloody mess."

She turned and traipsed out of the room while Eagan and Tessa stared at one another. The door closed.

Eagan exhaled. "I'm sorry I picked ye up like a sack of barley, but I've seen Jandeau take women right off our shores. Lark, for one. I didn't want ye within his reach, and there wasn't time to convince ye that he was dangerous."

"If they are the same person…" She couldn't meet his gaze. "Then he is dangerous to you perhaps, but not to me, his daughter." Her cheeks burned at how that sounded. She couldn't imagine her father doing such terrible things. There must be a mistake.

Eagan shook his head, his open hands landing on her shoulders as if to hold her there so he could hammer his version of the truth into her. "That man today, standing on our shore, holding ye before him…he's a bad man, Tessa."

Her brow rose. "So am I a bad woman for having his blood in me?"

"Of course not," he said, letting his hands slide off her shoulders and down her arms. "But ye can't go with him. He will… Well, I don't know what he has planned for ye. Maybe he'd be kinder to a daughter. But ye'd be exposed to his men, to his slavery business and murder."

She'd planned to petition her father to remain with Grissell for a time, but she hadn't been given the opportunity with daggers, arrows, and gunshot flying around. But she wasn't going to tell Eagan that. He'd assume it was because she wanted to stay with him. *I do. Merde.* She couldn't say that. Not when she was spitting furious.

"Has he left Wolf Isle?" she asked. "Abandoned me here again?"

The word "abandon" sunk into her gut like a rock tossed off a dock into the sea.

"His ship has sailed away from the isle, but we're watching for it."

"So you can fire upon it and scare him away if he tries to return to see me?"

"Jandeau cannot be scared away," Eagan said, his face grim.

Her eyes narrowed. "Then you watch for him so you can kill him."

Eagan didn't answer, which was answer enough. The Macquaries would kill her father the moment they had the chance, the man she'd prayed for all her life.

Eagan tried to take her hand, but she snatched it behind her so he couldn't. "I've been abandoned my whole life," she said quietly and tried to strengthen her voice. She leveled her gaze with his. "I was raised by my mother, knowing I had a father who would always sail away. And even though Mama did not say it, the money he'd sent at first dwindled away. She'd been a guest to the French court, and I would sing. But once we had no funds..." Her words trailed off. "Mama would leave me for a time, going to the court. I never knew when she'd return, and then one day she didn't." Tessa was certain that Rebecca had resorted to taking lovers who could pay her for her talent in bed.

"Do ye know what happened to her?" Eagan asked.

Tessa crossed her arms. "I went to Fontainebleau, which was where she'd said she would be. A servant led me down into the cellar where..." Tessa's body stiffened at the memory. The dank cold penetrated her cloak and wet seeped up through her slippers. It smelled of dirt and decay, and the sound of dripping water in the dark would forever haunt her nightmares. "Where her body was wrapped for burial. She lay on the cold stone floor." She swallowed against the constriction in her throat.

"I'm sorry, Tessa."

"She'd had her throat slashed." She said the words quickly as if that would make the memory less horrifying, as if speaking briskly would give her only a peek at what she remembered.

He tried to pull her into his chest, but she turned away. "Do they know who...?" he asked.

She gave a brief shake of her head and walked to the window, looking out at the trees beyond. "I was told she was found in the gardens that way. Her petticoats torn. They hadn't even washed the blood from her skin." It had dried down her throat and chest like dark crimson paint, staining her lily-white skin. "I think the king's powerful mistress hired an assassin because King Henri still called my mother to his bed."

"What did ye do?" Eagan's voice was close behind her,

but he didn't touch her.

Tessa could lean back and knew his strong, warm arms would go around her. How she'd longed for someone to comfort her back then when she had little money, a mother to bury, and no way to avenge her.

"I...I sent word through the court to my father telling him his wife, my mother, was killed by an unknown assailant. I left directions to my apartment even though I wasn't sure how long I would be able to live there without income. I used the coins I had left to bury her."

Eagan stepped to the side of the window so he could see her face. "No one helped ye?"

She shook her head, the anger licking up inside her. "They said she was..." Her gaze flicked to him. "A whore." The slurs had come from members of the court, jealous wives and their daughters who used to be Tessa's friends and students when she taught dance there. And each word had cut Tessa a little more until she felt weak with blood loss.

To Eagan's credit, he didn't ask if the slurs were true.

"I sold off the few pieces of furniture we had and my mother's clothes, keeping only this." She clasped the golden birdcage and slid her finger between the layers of the locket. Inside were miniatures of her parents.

With an exhale, she held it open so Eagan could see them. "Mama in this one, and my father is the other. Mama had left it home when she went to court as if she worried someone would take it."

Eagan bent to study the portraits. Tessa knew that he'd come to the same conclusion. The man was a younger version of his pirate, Jandeau.

"Yer mother was lovely."

"And funny and graceful and full of joy and love." Tessa felt her tears gather. "She didn't deserve to be abandoned in France by my father, then the court. Even justice deserted her."

Tessa lifted her gaze to his. "I prayed for my father to come, and he did. It took a year, but he found me selling flowers and surviving on the pittance I earned away from court. I managed…" She swallowed hard, hoping he would believe this truth. "I managed to earn enough to live without selling my body."

Eagan bent so his eyes were level with hers. "Honor in the face of starvation and extreme neglect is as useless as gold when there's no food to buy." He set his hand on her shoulder, and she remained still. "Whatever ye did or didn't do doesn't matter, Tessa. All that matters is that ye survived."

She wiped at a stray tear. "Father returned and saved me. Bought me new clothes and boots and food. He said he wouldn't have a gutter rat for a daughter." His tone had been brisk, but Tessa was so relieved that there was someone else she could trust that she didn't mind. "He took me away from France on his ship after visiting Mama's grave."

"They were married."

She nodded. "When they were young, and she became pregnant with me. Her family disowned her, and Claude Lemaire brought her here to Grissell's. He returned to take us to France."

Eagan rubbed a hand over his mouth. "'Tis a lot," he said. "What ye've been through."

"And my father finally returns to rescue me for good, and you chase him away." Tessa's words grew in strength as the return of her anger buoyed her. "He is all I have left!"

Eagan shook his head. "Nay. Tessa, ye have me and my clan. Ye have Grissell and Orphy and Sia and all the children."

She snorted. "After they hear my father is your infamous pirate, and my mother was a murdered whore?" She shook her head. "My blood is tainted."

Eagan grabbed her shoulders. "Nay, Tessa. Ye belong…

with me."

Was he asking her to wed? Tessa wasn't certain, and the disappointment if he wasn't proposing marriage was too painful right then. Tessa's heart thrummed in her chest, making her breaths come too shallow. "I want to return to Grissell's. She must worry over where I am, and I need to feed Sia."

"I'll send someone to tell her and feed yer cat," Eagan said, "but I don't want ye left alone there where Jand—yer father could return and take ye."

"Take me? Steal me away? He may have a reasonable explanation for what you say he's done. He may promise to take me to his family estate in France." Her hand wrapped again around her birdcage locket, remembering the assurances of her mother. "You don't even want me talking to him? My father? Someone who may be able to take me to the only family I have?"

Eagan released a long breath but didn't answer.

"I'm going back to Grissell's. Now," she said and met his gaze. "Unless I'm your prisoner, Eagan Macquarie."

Chapter Fifteen

Adam stood before Eagan and Tessa in the great hall. "'Tis not safe for her, for ye," Adam said, his gaze moving between them, "to go back to Grissell's until we know for certain that Jandeau has left the area."

"He's my father, the man who rescued me twice now. There must be a mistake about his identity, about what you feel he's done. I need to talk with him," Tessa said. "He's my only connection to my family."

The words make Eagan's stomach clench again. There was no mistake. The most dastardly, brutal person he knew was Tessa's father. How could an honest, kind person come from such vile seed?

Her mother must have been a saint, he thought. Would a saint solicit income with her body at the French court? No. But to keep her daughter fed when her husband abandoned them? Bloody hell, he didn't know. And it didn't matter. Tessa was her own person, and her heart was the opposite of the black, charred remains of Jandeau's heart, if the man had ever possessed one.

"There's no guarantee your kinship will keep ye safe," Adam continued. "The man is a devil, I'm sorry to say. Even if he is your father, it may not be enough. You must heed our warnings."

"I need to return to Grissell to ensure the children and my animals are well."

"You've taken Sia as your own?" Lia asked from beside the table.

Tessa nodded. "She's the sweetest creature."

Lia's face relaxed into a wistful smile. "She is, but I can't touch her, or I swell terribly."

"And we'd all rather have ye alive and breathing," Drostan said, pulling her against his side.

Adam cleared his throat. "Jandeau will likely come back and abduct ye if ye're at Grissell's. We should put all the children and the old woman up here at Gylin. If Grissell will come."

"She won't," Tessa said.

Eagan agreed. The old woman would remain at her cottage until she died. She might go for a walk now and then with her two white cats named after saints, but she'd never sleep somewhere else.

"The children then," Lark said, holding her son on one hip. "Jandeau will take them to sell."

Tessa's face tightened, her gaze hardening. "I'll protect them if that's what he's done in the past. He saved me from the Paris gutters." She shook her head, glancing downward at the wooden floors. "If what you say is true about him, perhaps I can change his ways by talking to him daughter to father."

Lia stood beside Lark. "Or he will realize you don't have his black heart and add you to his list of assets to sell."

Tessa's face grew red, her lips pinching tight. *Daingead.*

The front doors in the entryway opened, and one of

the older children from Grissell's hurried in behind Beck. "Tessa," the girl called. "We need you."

Tessa hurried toward her. "What's happened, Charlotte?"

Eagan's hand went to the hilt of his sword.

"Mistress has become ill, so ill she doesn't move from her bed."

Eagan followed Tessa and Charlotte toward the doorway.

"I'll fetch my bag of supplies," Lark called behind them, but they were already heading out into the cool autumn air. Adam would have to bring Lark because Tessa wasn't waiting for her, so Eagan wasn't, either.

They hurried out past the willow tree with its unseasonably green leaves swaying in the breeze. It was quite bonny now, lush and full. But the dagger hilt still protruded with dark sap that looked like blood dripping from it, which turned the scene into something macabre.

Eagan had fought fierce pirates before, battled them until blood soaked the ground. He'd been shot and left to drown and survived fiery ships. But it was the willow tree that spun through his darkest nightmares.

Tessa and Charlotte led the way with Eagan following them past the turnoff toward Ormaig Village and into the woods toward the south shore where Grissell's cottages sat. Only the brush and crunch of fallen leaves heralded their passing as they ran and dodged bramble and trees over the mile.

The clearing in the middle of the five cottages was empty, and they continued to the oldest cottage, the one that had survived through Grissell's ancestors, each of them adding onto the original building.

"Let me," Eagan said, surging up before Charlotte and Tessa. Before they could refuse his protection further, he opened Grissell's door. The old woman lay in her bed, eyes closed while the two smaller children sat upright with wide eyes turned to Eagan. The white cats walked sentry before the bed, and Sia meowed loudly from the rafters as if threatening to cough up a furball on him.

"Are ye alone?" Eagan asked the children, his gaze sliding to the corners of the main room and the dark doorway beyond.

They nodded in unison.

Tessa and Charlotte surged past him. The little girl rolled off the bed to run into Tessa's arms. "Mother Grissell is ill."

"Lady Lark is on her way with medicines," Tessa said, hugging the child close while also pulling a chair up to the bed.

"Mistress?" Tessa asked.

From the doorway, Eagan could see the old woman's eyes flicker open. "Ye're still here," Grissell said, her voice weak. Her hand looked bonier than usual as she slid it out of the covers to clasp Tessa's. "Stay here. Watch my bairns, the animals, and children with nowhere else to go."

If Eagan had questioned allowing Tessa to return to Grissell's before, he completely reversed his thinking. Grissell could convince her to stay on Wolf Isle far better than he, especially after the throwing her over his shoulder disaster.

Footsteps on the porch heralded Lark. "Eagan, why don't you keep Adam company outside." She walked briskly past him to the bed. "Good day, Mistress Grissell."

Charlotte couldn't have been more than twelve years old, but she shooed him out, shutting the door firmly in his face.

"Let's check the perimeter," Adam said, pulling Eagan away.

"Aye, but I'm keeping the cottage in sight."

"Drostan is rounding up Callum and Beck, and I've sent Rabbie to Aros Castle to alert Tor and Cullen Duffie that

Jandeau is in the vicinity. Cullen will no doubt hurry back to Islay Isle to mobilize his ships to patrol the waters."

Eagan nodded silently but kept his gaze on the cottage. How badly did Jandeau want Tessa? And how badly did Tessa want to believe her only remaining family cared about her?

...

"I want you, Tempest Ainsworth, to succeed me as keeper of this refuge." Grissell lay in her bed, her face lined but still warm with life. They were alone, Lark having left.

Tessa squeezed her skeletal hand. "Lady Lark says she thinks you're exhausted and underfed. With sleep and nutritious food, you'll be full of life."

Grissell's straight lips thinned even more into a tight slash above her chin. "I am in my nineties, child. Even if I do remain on this earth, I can never be full of life again."

Tessa gave her a wry smile. "Full of temper and dictatorial force then."

The thin lips relaxed, and Grissell snorted. Her sharp eyes shut. "No matter. I will not remain long on this earth."

"Even so," Tessa said, "I can't take over your sanctuary, since I'm to travel back to France." Despite her anger with Eagan, saying the words wound tightly around her stomach, cinching it until it ached.

The slash of lips curved downward in Grissell's wrinkled face, and her eyes opened. "Captain Jandeau will not keep his promises."

Tessa sighed. Even Grissell knew her father as Jandeau. "I owe my life to him. He's my father."

"One does not owe fealty to blood ties when family has proven themselves unworthy."

"But I'm his daughter," Tessa murmured. Didn't that

matter? Otherwise, she truly was an orphan.

The old woman stared with her pale blue eyes that almost looked white below tiny lashes. "I doubt you're his *only* child, and I don't think that matters to the devil. Jandeau only acts if it will bring him profit." She tipped her head slightly on the pillow. "What profit will you bring him?"

Tessa shook her head. "He saved me from starvation in Paris." Her words were soft but bolstered with stubborn hope that the woman was wrong. "He bought me clothes and food. He said he wouldn't let his daughter end up…" She paused as the memory came back, memory of that hollow-bellied time when she merely survived. Her father had found her, lifting her up, giving her bread and wine.

Claudette Tempest Ainsworth, ma fille. I won't let you end up on your back, selling yourself, like your mother and my own mother.

The words had been cruel, but Tessa was so desperate for a chance to live that she'd obediently followed behind him, leaving the home she'd shared with her mother. Tessa had sold everything to remain there, so it was merely an empty shell anyway.

Grissell continued to stare at her as if reading the memories in Tessa's eyes. It was a wonder that she never seemed to blink. "So, he's put money into you," Grissell said. "You will need to make him a profit. The man works in no other way."

The cottage suddenly felt too warm with its pungent herbs and dancing fire. "He cares for me because I am his legal blood daughter. He married my mother— how could he not?"

"He took her from here with a promise of marriage," Grissell said. "I don't know if they married."

"Why would he have saved me then if I was just one of his many bastards?"

"He may have cared for Rebecca before greed tainted his soul. And he always has a plan and you no doubt are one of them. Tread carefully."

"Then perhaps I can…heal his soul." Tessa realized she'd stood from the chair and now paced. Snatching Sia off the bed, she took full breaths that didn't feel full enough. Dizziness propelled her toward the door.

"When dealing with the devil," Grissell said, "one always must pay a price. It sounds like your mother paid a harsh price for trusting him."

Tessa yanked hard on the latch, making the door fly open. Murmuring an apology, she closed it behind her. Tessa descended the step and rubbed her cheek on Sia's fur until the animal squirmed and jumped down to trot across the middle clearing.

Tessa's heart was already thudding hard like a drum, and then Eagan strode around the corner of the cottage, making her pulse pound faster. Tall and broad through the chest and shoulders, Eagan's body slimmed through the waist and hips, leading to sleekly muscled legs. He was the perfect example of strength in a man. She should know since she'd kissed and nibbled along it during their nights together. And during that time her worries had evaporated under the temptation of bliss.

Eagan stopped when he saw her. "How fares Grissell?"

Tessa walked toward her cottage, feeling the brush of his deep voice and tumbling northern accent through her. "She is weak but as nosy and opinionated as ever."

The pebbles crunched behind her as Eagan followed. The sound was a balm to her anger. She remembered the heat of his naked skin on hers, the play of his muscles as he moved with her. *Mon Dieu!* Everything about the Highlander was mind-numbing like whisky. And right then, she wanted to feel, not think.

Tessa turned at the top, her hand on the latch. Eagan looked up, his blue eyes connecting with hers, and they stared for a moment. His jaw looked clenched as if he were waiting for a pardon or writ of execution. The breeze moved the longer layers of his hair. If she buried her nose in the mane, it would smell of Eagan, a mix of wood smoke, spice, fresh Highland wind, and something all his own that drew her. It would overpower her memories of the rank Parisian sewers, the smell of desperation and scorn and loss. She could lose herself in Eagan's smell and forget about the crack in her heart that threatened to widen, pulled between her father and a possible future on Wolf Isle.

But would Eagan remain on Wolf Isle? He'd never once said he'd stay. But right that moment he was there.

"Are you coming in?" she asked, watching Sia weave between the trees chasing a squirrel.

"I didn't know if I was invited," he said, the lowness of his voice a potent spark. He placed his large paw on the wooden rail leading up the steps, squeezing it slightly so that the muscles clenched up his arm. He wore a short-sleeved tunic, apparently not bothered by the crisp air. He took a step up.

She held out a hand to stop him. "One condition."

His brow rose. "Speak it." The words were simple, but the underlying heat told Tessa that he'd been thinking about their nights together, too. That under his plaid wrap, his hard verge was probably already seeking her.

"No talking," she said. "No asking me questions I can't answer. No words." If she was going to leave Wolf Isle, she wanted to be with Eagan once more. The pain of the thought made her push it away. *No thinking. Just feeling.*

Heat flared in his gaze as he gave a slow nod, his nostrils widening as if he were a stallion sniffing after a mare in season. The man was full of seductive power, and she wanted to feel it.

She lowered her hand and pressed inside the room. 'Twas cold without a fire in the hearth. She walked to it, crouching to place squares of dry peat and kindling on the grate. Did Eagan follow her inside? She didn't want to look. Her ears strained to hear his footsteps.

The gentle sound of the door shutting relaxed her enough to inhale, and she struck the flint in the wool balled in her palm, watching the spark flare. She blew a gentle stream of air into the smoldering fluff until it caught and lowered it slowly to the peat and twigs, setting it where it was likely to catch.

There was no sound behind her, but the spell of desire swelled within the cottage. Tessa could feel Eagan's hungry gaze, and it added to the prickle of sensual awareness. She added more twigs and leaned down to blow on the growing flame, the heat of it sliding across her face. Once it was stable, licking up the two dry logs she'd added to the peat, Tessa stood.

Before she could turn, she heard the step, and then two arms came around her from behind. She leaned back into the heat, inhaling the familiar scent that shot quicksilver through her blood. Lips touched the skin at the juncture of her neck and shoulder. Light and warm. The sensation split off from it, shooting through her like an exploding star. Her lips parted as she leaned her head back, and Eagan kissed along her neck up to her ear. Instead of saying anything, a low growl resonated from him, as if he were a beast. She shivered as lust flowed down through her, and he turned her in his arms.

Tessa set her hand along his bristled cheek, meeting his gaze. They were locked there. Together, as if they were already joined as one. Her eyes shut as lips met lips in a frenzied kiss. Untamed and raw, full of longing and wishes and…farewell? Tessa reached behind Eagan's neck, holding him there so he couldn't leave, so she couldn't leave.

Everyone left her, but, at that moment, Tessa knew Eagan was hers. He lifted her in his arms, moving without breaking the kiss. Her fingers tangled in his hair, reveling in the softness of it. She breathed through her nose, smelling his familiar essence, tasting him. All of her senses came to life.

Without words, they took cues from each other. She slid his hand to her breast where he squeezed gently. Working together, they fully undressed until she lay naked on her bed. The crackle of the fire punctuated the thump of her heart. His body was exquisite, so much power contained in one man. His erection stood proud, and her core clenched with desirous heat.

Tessa slid her arms up above her head, stretching like a feline. Her breasts perched high, nipples hard, and when she reached down to the triangular patch between her legs, Eagan's hand slid along his length. The sight made her moan softly and spread her legs.

As if he could no longer stand the torture of separation, he moved over her in such a fluid movement that she could imagine he flew. But then she was awash once more in his kiss and the touch of his fingers as they licked a path of pure delight down her body.

Eagan pulled back from the kiss so that they stared into each other's eyes, and then he thrust deep. Tessa's lips opened on a gasp, and he groaned. Pulling out, he thrust again and then again. She answered each and lifted her legs to wrap them around his powerful hips.

In the wordless room, the only sounds made were sighs and moans and the brush of skin upon skin with the fire crackling, adding to the heat. As Tessa neared her climax, breathing in all of Eagan, she bent her attention to memorizing every little detail. 'Twas as if she already felt herself sailing away.

Her breath caught as the wave of ecstasy broke, and pleasure washed through her straining body. A single tear leaked from her eye. For the first time, Tessa hoped her father would not return for her.

Chapter Sixteen

"She's staying?" Adam asked Eagan as he turned, jumping back. They were training in the bailey before Gylin Castle. "On Wolf Isle?" Adam surged forward, but Eagan anticipated and sidestepped the assault. "Taking Grissell's place with the children and lasses?" Adam asked, his breath coming in gusts.

The crunch of their boots showed the tempo of their dance as they fought with wooden swords, turning, thrusting, and stepping backward in an effort to throw off the other's balance.

"Grissell asked her," Eagan said. *And then we fell into bed and nearly incinerated the sheets.*

It was a wonder he'd disentangled himself from Tessa that morning with her scent and warmth ensnaring him. Only the direct orders from his brother, the chief, to come back to Gylin pulled him from her arms. It was midmorning by the time he'd emerged and Sia had run inside Tessa's cottage, ready to take his place in the warm bed.

"And how did she answer?" Adam asked, his gaze sliding

to where Drostan and Callum battled against Beck.

Eagan took the momentary distraction to knock against Adam's unguarded hand, making his sword drop as he grunted. Adam grabbed his sword from the dirt but nodded to Eagan, giving him the point. With real swords and real foes, Adam would likely be dead.

Eagan caught his breath as Adam worked his fingers, making sure nothing was broken. "She didn't answer," Eagan said, making Adam's gaze snap back up to him.

"She's still considering going with her father if he returns," Adam said.

The other three had paused, breathing hard.

"*When* he returns," Beck said. "The devil will harass us until he draws his last fetid breath."

Callum nodded, his face grim. Drostan stared, but they all knew Beck's words to be true. With each failure to win what he considered his prize, Jandeau's obsession with the Macquarie Clan had increased.

"Bloody foking hell, I should have killed him when he was unconscious," Callum grumbled, not for the first time. He was the only brother to have actually caught the infamous pirate when he'd gone to retrieve Anna and her sister, Dora, from England.

Drostan's hand came down on his shoulder, but he didn't say anything. They'd each gone round and round with Callum since that time, telling him that an honorable man didn't kill an unconscious, unarmed man, but Callum continued to berate his honorable actions.

"Then we'll take turns guarding Tessa until he returns," Beck said.

"And do what?" Eagan asked. "Kill Jandeau in front of her?" For that was the only outcome that rid the Macquaries of their tormenting adversary. "Her father."

"If she happens to be looking," Callum said, and Eagan

threw a glare his way. "What?" Callum said. "They're not going to have a good father-daughter conversation over tarts and ale." He threw his sword on the ground. "Do ye imagine them having a picnic where he tells her how he's always loved her and will quit selling children and women into slavery to become a loving father, supporting her in France?"

"Hold yer tongue," Eagan said. "'Tis just…for Tessa to witness us killing her father might turn her away from us, make her…" He trailed off. *Make her hate me.* He looked at his brothers. "I think I want to marry her." Was that true? Would he stay for her, abandon his plans to leave? *She'll go with me.*

They all stared at him. "Ye want to marry Jandeau's daughter?" Drostan asked.

Eagan felt his blood begin to boil. "'Tis not like she has tainted blood. The sins of the father don't transfer to the daughter. She barely knows him."

"Ye love her?" Adam asked. He'd set his wooden sword aside and crossed his arms over his chest, studying Eagan.

Eagan scratched at a prickle of drying sweat on his forehead. "We get on well together."

Callum snorted. "Having a good fok doesn't mean ye get on well—"

Eagan charged his brother, his fist cocked back. Fool Callum wasn't expecting his youngest brother to attack and didn't even get his hands up to defend himself before Eagan delivered a punch to his jaw.

The momentum threw Callum backward so that he landed on his arse, his head thrown back to hit the ground.

"Daingead!" Adam yelled, running to Callum while Drostan grabbed Eagan's arms.

"Well, hell," Beck said casually, his elbows out on either side of his head as he cupped the back.

"Ye don't talk about her or any woman like that," Eagan

yelled at Callum. "Ye foking arse."

Adam leaned over Callum. Eagan shook off Drostan's hold, so Beck came over to stand with Drostan. "Ye need to calm yerself."

"How calm would ye be if foking Callum said that about Eliza or Lia?" Eagan looked at his two brothers.

Behind them, Adam had clasped Callum's hand and was giving him a lift off the hard ground.

Callum rubbed his chin, wincing. "Ye've got a hell of a hook, brother," he said, though the words were slurred from the injury to his mouth. Blood flowed from a cut on his lip, and Adam handed him a rag from his belt.

As if reveling in the turmoil between brothers, the willow tree danced in a sudden gust of wind. The spindly branches snapped toward them like whips.

"And ye've got a hell of a foul mouth," Eagan said, and spit on the ground as if bitterness coated his tongue.

Callum turned and strode toward the well on the other side of the bailey.

"Ye need to talk to Tessa," Adam said. "See what she's planning."

"If ye ask her to marry ye," Beck said, "she'd have a reason to stay."

Eagan scratched his fingers through his sweaty hair. Would she go with him if they married first? He met Adam's eyes. "I plan to leave Wolf Isle. I meant to weeks ago, but Tessa showed up."

"Leave the clan, yer family?" Drostan asked.

Eagan didn't break his gaze with Adam. "I plan to go north to Orkney and decide from there if I will sail to Norway and Denmark or travel the east coast of Scotland."

"Ye're serious?" Beck asked, coming to stand next to Adam so that he could stare in Eagan's face, as if weighing his commitment to his plan.

"He's had a satchel packed," Adam said, still staring at Eagan. So Adam already knew.

"If ye've gotten Tessa with child, then ye must ask her to marry," Drostan said. "Or do ye plan to doom our clan?"

Eagan felt a flush prickle along his skin. He hadn't pulled out every time Tessa and he had come together. He glanced at the willow tree, but no leaves had turned brown, not that they would right away. He released a breath. Fok, he'd been so stupid. What if she were pregnant and Jandeau took her like he'd tried to take Lia, dooming the Macquarie Clan when they didn't marry?

"I'll wait until her monthly courses come," Eagan said, his stomach growing sour. It had been his plan before, but then they'd fallen into bed again.

"And we have to make sure Jandeau doesn't take her before then," Adam said, his brows pinched. He exhaled. "And I would like to talk more about ye leaving before ye do. Don't run off in the night."

He looked worried, his stoic, always-in-command eldest brother. As if he might miss him and not just because he wouldn't be able to order him around. Either that or he was worried about the curse not being broken.

"I'll give ye notice."

"Stay away from Callum right now," Drostan said.

Eagan glanced down at his knuckles where the skin had broken open on impact. The blood had already dried. "Tell him to keep his filthy mouth away from me." Eagan grabbed up his sparring sword to set it against the barn before he strode out the gate. Some laps across the small loch north of Ormaig would help him think and cool his blood.

Despite the calm breeze, Eagan felt a storm gathering, and changes were already in motion.

. . .

It had been late afternoon when Tessa watched Eagan ride up, dismount, and stride toward her, standing on the cottage porch.

One kiss had swept them both away in the familiar storm of their passion. 'Twas as if they both hid away in the sweep, not wanting to talk about hard things—things like her father, Grissell's request to stay, his plans to leave Wolf Isle, and whether he truly wanted to marry her. The topics seemed too weighty to voice. So, instead, they'd blocked out the world with passion.

Eagan had left as the sun began to descend. *I'll return tonight*, he'd said.

Perhaps I wish to sleep tonight, she'd answered.

Then I will stalk around your cottage, protecting ye.

From my own father? Her smile had left.

He'd looked her directly in her eyes. *Aye.*

Darkness had descended, but Eagan hadn't yet returned. Tessa looked around the cottage that she'd grown to adore with its exposed rafters and chipped hearth. She'd hung herbs from the rafters, much like Grissell, the old woman teaching her even more than her mother had about the combinations of plants, animals, and elements in the world.

Tessa had learned midwifery from her mother, but Grissell had taught her so much more. Everything from how to calm a rolling stomach to powerful sleep tinctures to even poisons that would stop a heart. It should have been obvious that Grissell was preparing her to take over once she died.

Did she want to leave this place? Leave her pets and the friends she'd made? Leave Eagan? No, but she'd also prayed her whole life for her father to return, for him to love her as his daughter and tell her stories of her mother when they were young and newly in love.

Your father, Tempest, was so riveting, her mother had

said. *A beautiful man, dark and mysterious. His mother had abandoned him, yet he kept his heart open to love. He loves me, loves you, ma chérie.*

Rebecca had told Tessa that they'd met when they were young, when he'd attended the English court with the French ambassador as his page. How their passion had exploded into an inferno. Her parents didn't approve, but she wouldn't give up her Claude for their strict English ways. She'd run away with him, but due to his unexpected appointment to the navy, she'd been left on a small isle off the coast of Scotland where the French ambassador had known of a place for women with nowhere else to go.

But Claude had returned for her, and when she'd told him she was with his child, he'd taken her to France, and they wed. It was the most romantic story Tessa had ever heard. Her mother had told her it repeatedly, like history, like she must convince herself it was true. As a child, Tessa hadn't recognized that, but now she wondered.

Tessa helped bring in money by singing and teaching the royal children how to dance, but it was never enough to create the lifestyle her mother sought. Rebecca also sought protection, and she gained it from the powerful players at the French court—that was until the king's powerful mistress had her throat slit.

Tessa moved to the window, peering out. Two rough-looking men turned to her, and she stepped back, her heart pounding. But then she remembered them from Ormaig Village. They were patrolling the grounds until Eagan returned. Peeking back outside, she could see the outline of swords strapped to their sides.

Tessa's brain was so tired from churning through possible decisions that when she lay down on the quilts, she quickly drifted into sleep. The sound of the door opening startled her, and her eyes flew open. Still groggy, she pushed up from the bed where Sia sat beside her at attention like a lioness. The cat hissed.

"Mon père?" she whispered. Was this a dream? She'd had them before. Her father coming to find her, hugging her and telling her that he loved her. But this man didn't smile.

Claude Lemaire stepped inside the cottage, shutting the door behind him. He wore a soft-soled boot that made no noise when he walked toward her. "Ma fille," he said. "I've come for you." They were words she'd prayed for, but they were said in a cold voice. He'd come back for her. She was worth sneaking into enemy territory to retrieve.

"I…" Her mouth remained open for a moment, and she wondered what would come out. She rubbed her hands down her face and slid her feet to the floor. Would she tell him she didn't want to go? The thought was ridiculous after a lifetime of praying for his return. But Eagan…

"Mon père," she said, "I've been making my home here. May I… I mean…" She took a full breath. "I must remain here on Wolf Isle. The old woman who cares for the children—"

"There's no time for talk, Claudette. We must be away now. Take what you'd like or leave it all. I will purchase new clothing for you once we make port among the Caribbean Islands."

"Caribbean?" she whispered and frowned. "You're not taking me back to France, to your family's chateau in the countryside?"

"Chateau in the countryside?" He narrowed his eyes.

"Alsace. You said we would live on your estate there. Mama said you had family in the French countryside."

Jandeau rubbed his chin. "Your mother spouted fairy tales."

The belittling grin growing on his mouth made tears gather in Tessa's eyes. He thought her mother was a fool and Tessa for believing her..

"Why did you leave her in France then? Leave us both?"

Her father looked over his shoulder. "My men are waiting on the shore. We go now."

"But—"

His face hardened. "I don't care if you wish to stay with the Macquaries. They are my enemy and as my daughter, your enemy, too. I could squash them with one attack this very night. My men are vicious and will rape and plunder and kill. But I've reined them with loyalty to me."

Tessa stared at him, trying to take in this information while her brain fought with the discrepancies between a loving father and this man staring at her in the dark.

He huffed. "Come now, Claudette, and I will leave this isle unharmed." The deadly threat was evident in his even tone.

Tessa swallowed hard and felt herself nod. "I'll gather a bag."

"Rapidement."

Tessa threw her jars and pouches of herbs, two flasks of weak ale, and several clean smocks into a satchel. She made sure her necklace was in place, the birdcage locket nestled between her breasts, and threw on her heavy woolen cape.

Meow. Sia rubbed against her legs, and Tessa scooped her up with her free arm. She couldn't let her go. Eagan had said that Sia had been on a ship before when she voyaged with Lia.

Tessa threw her satchel over one shoulder and nestled Sia under her cloak against her chest. "I am bringing my cat," she said to her father's back, but he continued to stride away, expecting her to follow.

In the darkness, she saw men running about the other cottages. "What are they doing?"

"Patrolling against the Macquaries." He glanced at her. "Especially the one you've been foking."

The crude word pierced, lodging in her chest. Of course her father would be angry about her indiscretion, and there wasn't time to defend her actions. What would she say if she did have time? *I love him like Rebecca loved you.* The words jumped through her mind, but she brushed them away. Even if they were true, they'd only bring more cursing from her father.

And what did she know of romantic love anyway? Her mother had sworn that her father loved them both, yet he never came to visit and let them fall into penury. And Eagan still planned to travel across Scotland.

Tessa clutched Sia, and the cat squirmed. She loosened her hold but wouldn't let go as she followed her father through the quiet woods to the shore where three rowboats waited with a man at each.

She swallowed hard when she saw two men tied to a tree, their mouths gagged. The men who'd been guarding her. One was unconscious while the other glared at her father as he strode by. The captain clasped his hands behind his back as if he stood on his ship's deck. He ignored them and Tessa, as if he didn't expect anything less than complete cooperation.

Tessa looked back at her cottage and the clearing in the small compound. "Wait," she said and stopped on the rocky shore. Dawn was creeping upward. She hadn't even gotten to say farewell to the three children and Grissell. "I must—"

"There's no time. A storm is moving in." Her father turned to stare at her. "You will come with me." He spoke as if she were his property. Tessa had been independent her whole life, and his tone grated on her.

"I have no choice in staying on Wolf Isle?" she asked even with a lanky sailor gesturing for her to climb into the small boat.

Her father dropped his hands, and they formed fists at

his sides. He walked back over to stand before her, and she looked up into his black eyes. A chill slid down her. "I will take you, ma fille, or I will take Wolf Isle and every breathing soul on it," he said, his words as cold as the dark sea at his back.

Chapter Seventeen

Tessa's lips parted at the threat. Either she went with him, or he would take the lives of the people sleeping peacefully on the isle. Could her father be so ruthless?

"Oui," he said as if answering her silent question. "And if you decide to stay, ma fille, England's boy king will hear that the Macleans on the Isle of Mull are aiding the French…" He shrugged. "'Twill be your stubbornness to blame for their annihilation, too."

Tessa's heart beat hard against the tightness in her chest. Sia began to squirm, so Tessa stroked her, trying to loosen her tight hold without letting her go. "But if I go with you now, you will leave the Macquaries alone, and the Macleans?"

His mouth turned up at the corners. "Oui."

Tessa nodded the briefest amount and released her breath. "I would bring my cat," she said, forcing her voice to sound steady.

"It will piss all over the ship."

"I'll clean up after her." She took a step back.

He cursed under his breath, glancing behind her at the

quiet cottages, and then brushed a hand through the air.

"Amenez le chat," he said, and she exhaled with relief. "Now get in the boat, ma fille."

Tessa lifted her skirt and cloak with one hand while holding Sia and let the sailor steady her as she stepped in. She wobbled on the uneven bottom and plopped down onto the seat to steady herself. Sia pushed against her chest, and Tessa closed the cloak around her so the cat could hide from the cold, damp air. Rain had already begun.

The small boat bobbed on the waves as the sailors rowed back toward the ship anchored around the curve of the isle. The last rowboat remained as if waiting for more of her father's men. Were they setting traps for Eagan and his family? She turned to ask, but when she glimpsed the hard face of her father, the question died on her tongue. Instead, she looked back and watched Wolf Isle grow smaller as she was carried out to sea.

...

Eagan stepped out into the muted moonlight and tipped his face up to the first heavy drops of rain. He'd been unable to sleep apart from Tessa. Lark and Anna said she needed time alone to think, to take in all she'd learned about the man she knew as her father. Adam had agreed and said he should let her sleep, that he could convince her in the morn to stay when they were both well rested.

Eagan snorted. He'd certainly not be well rested, and he wasn't sure he could convince Tessa of anything.

Beck and Eliza had asked some of her old crew to guard Grissell's area. They took turns through the night like they used to when on Eliza's ship. In the morning, Eagan would return to Tessa and crawl into her warm sheets, asking her to marry him. The thought made his chest tighten. What if she said no? What if she said yes? What if she were with child?

He glanced at the willow tree's thrashing branches as he walked past it toward the closed portcullis. The growing wind caught his breath, and he broke into a jog. Grissell clung to the bars, her long silver-white hair loose down to her waist. She wore a night smock and robe with unlaced boots on her feet, a mile from her cottage. Her two white cats trotted through the bars, meowing at Eagan as he ran forward.

"Grissell?" Eagan looked up at the tower where the night guardsman's head appeared.

"What is it?"

"Open the gate."

"Bloody hell," the guard called. "I never saw her walk up."

The iron clink of the chains heralded the toothy maw rising. Grissell held on, moving her hands until it was too high, and then Eagan caught her.

The old woman was fragile. He lifted her easily, carrying her swiftly across the bailey through the rising wind, but his mind was flying out the gate.

"Tessa?"

"He's come for her," she whispered, and he surged forward into a run.

Eagan pushed through the doors, running with Grissell into the great hall where one of the kitchen maids yelped with surprise. "Wake Adam and Lark," he ordered.

Eagan lowered Grissell gently into a seat by the hearth and crouched before the old woman. The two cats had followed them in and leaped up onto her lap. Their ears were flattened. Eagan ignored their hissing. "Who?" But he knew.

Grissell's gaze lifted, and he saw the exhaustion war with stubbornness in her eyes. "Jandeau came with his men."

"What's happening?" Adam asked as he ran into the room, his tunic untucked and his kilt barely pleated. Lark followed, running straight to Grissell.

"Jandeau is taking Tessa right now!" Eagan's voice rose through the hall like thunder.

Lark took his place before the woman. "Mistress Grissell, you've walked all this way?" She touched her wrist to feel the strength of her pulse.

"Ye said she would be safe with guards from the village," Eagan yelled. "Let her sleep, ye said!"

Adam's hard features didn't change.

"Did he take her?" Adam asked, looking at Grissell, "or did she go with him willingly?"

Eagan grimaced. "It doesn't matter. She could be with child." He must see Tessa again. Talk with her. Hold her. Foking ask her to be with him, permanently.

Lark looked to Adam. "Isn't Cullen Duffie patrolling the waters?"

"What's going on?" Callum asked as he and Anna descended the steps, Anna holding their two-year-old Elizabeth against one hip.

"I believe he is," Adam said.

"Jandeau's taken Tessa," Lark answered Callum.

"And my bairns," Grissell said. They all looked at her. She lifted her head, her gaze going to Eagan. "Jandeau lured Tessa away, and then his men dragged Bann, Grace, and Charlotte out of my cottage. Gagged them and rowed them out to his ship."

"Oh, dear mother of God," Anna whispered.

"We'll go after them in the ship," Adam said.

"There's a storm coming," Callum said.

Grissell looked at Eagan. "Jandeau might sail anyway."

"I have a rowboat on Grissell's shore," Eagan said, running toward the doors. "I'm going after her now."

• • •

Tessa paced in the small cabin below deck she'd been led to as soon as she boarded her father's hulking ship. Dawn was hours away, but she couldn't sleep.

She listened to the men above through a small ceiling hatch as they tied sails because a storm approached. She'd been taken to the ship's rear, the wood around her creaking with the turning tide. Fresh water was in a basin, and two small apples sat in a basket. She ate one, barely tasting the sweetness while she watched Sia explore the room with its small bolted-down bed, privacy screen, chairs, and empty bookshelf.

Thump, thump.

Tessa jumped, propping one knee on the bed to stare at the wall separating her from the sea. Something had bumped against the hull. She held her breath as she heard what sounded like scratching. Sea animals couldn't break through a hull, could they?

The sound of a key in the lock made Tessa pivot. The cat shot off the bed to hide on the bookshelf. The door swung inward, and her father's large form filled the opening.

"Dine with me in my cabin." He nodded toward a chest that she'd already opened to find gowns of many colors and fabrics. "Choose a dinner ensemble, and I will have you brought up in an hour's time."

"'Tis still dark."

"The storm will grow fiercer. We eat now or possibly not for another day." His gaze caught the cat's flicking tail. "Leave your feline friend here. I wouldn't want it to leap into the sea."

The thought of sweet Sia falling into the black deep sent tingles up Tessa's arms. "I will keep her locked in here. Could I have a key to do so?"

Captain Lemaire stared at her, assessing. "The person leading you to my cabin will relock your door so no one will open it." He met her gaze. "One hour. Punctuality is a sign of good breeding."

"I will be ready."

He turned, striding out. Tessa listened to the scrape of the tumbler turning in the lock. Was he keeping his men out or was he keeping Tessa in? The cold in the room seemed worse, and she wrapped her arms around herself. Hopefully she'd find a warm ensemble in the wooden chest. Although the ice that covered her bones wouldn't thaw with woolen clothes. That chill came from the stark command in her father's voice.

Tessa felt the ache of tears behind her eyes and a hollow sickness in her middle. *Eagan.* "I would have said farewell," she whispered and sat on the bed. Sia leapt onto her lap, and Tessa rubbed her face in the cat's soft fur. "And I think…I would have stayed."

...

"Eat," Captain Lemaire said, indicating Tessa's full plate. "Once we're farther out at sea, the food is harder to come by and can be tainted. 'Tis part of this seafaring life."

Tessa took a bite of the tender lamb, wondering if it had been stolen from the herds that roamed Wolf Isle. She chewed. "Your cook knows seasoning. The sage and thyme blend well together."

Her father tilted his head as he studied her. "You also have a talent for knowing which spices pair and enhance one another. Perhaps you, darling Claudette, will become the ship's cook."

Tessa managed to swallow the chewed meat and blinked at her father. "I am to stay on the *Bourreau*?"

"For the time being. I must stop in Portugal and have no plans to head back to France until I find some treasure for

King Henri in the Caribbean."

The growing waves under the boat tilted the room, but all the large pieces of furniture remained bolted in place. Tessa held her plate with one hand and her wine goblet with the other. It reflected her tilting world.

"Is that how you earn coin?" She took a sip of the red wine as if everything wasn't literally swaying beneath her. It tasted smooth with an earthy undertone that reminded her of France. "You capture enemy ships for the king of France?"

Lemaire's dark eyes locked with hers. "Oui, but I have many ways to acquire gold."

Tessa swallowed as the prickles rose along her nape. *How will you profit him?* Grissell's question niggled through her like a burrowing parasite. "Grissell said something about the slave trade, that you might be…bringing in profit through selling people."

Lemaire flipped his hand, his polished gold rings catching the lamplight. "On occasion when the opportunity presents itself. 'Tis quite a lucrative business."

Tessa felt her worry inside harden into temper. But her father didn't seem the type to respond well to outbursts. "'Tis a horrid business," she said, her voice as even as she could manage. She remembered whispers at court about various people disappearing. Rumors circulated that enemies of the king and his mistress were sold to slavers, never to be seen again. If Tessa hadn't seen Rebecca's cold body, she would think her mother had been shipped away. Tessa wondered which her mother would have preferred: her throat slashed or being owned and mistreated for the rest of her life?

"Of course you would feel that way, child," Lemaire said, stabbing a piece of the lamb with the tip of his knife. "You were gently born and are not made for such business."

The knot in Tessa's stomach remained, but it didn't sound like he planned to sell her. He was her father, the father whom her mother had loved and the man who'd saved Tessa from the gutters. Once she knew him better, she'd ask him never to involve himself with such despicable practices again.

They continued to eat and sip the excellent wine in silence while the ship swayed and pitched with the swells of the waves. Tessa's legs tightened, trying to keep her level in her seat, her forearm bracing her periodically on the table. Rain hit the glassed portholes, and she was thankful the motion didn't make her nauseous. Her father said they'd ride it out overnight anchored closer to an isle before continuing out into the open ocean.

When she finished her meal, Tessa set her knife and napkin down beside her plate. "Will I live in France after this voyage?"

Her father stared down into his wine, swirling it. "I'm still considering what to do with you, Claudette." He glanced up. "You're beautiful and graceful like your mother. Do you possess any talents?"

"I…I sing and dance. I've taught lessons at the royal court while Mama lived." Her hand rose to the birdcage necklace.

The thoughtfulness on her father's face hardened like a bolt of lightning turning a clear sky into storm. "Rebecca took you to the French court?"

She felt her cheeks heat in embarrassment. "Only to teach lessons and sing for the children." She left off the part about singing to the king and his subjects.

He took a gulp of wine and set the goblet down on the table with a *crack* that made her jump. "And where was your mother while you entertained and taught? On her back with her legs spread, I'm sure."

Tessa's heart thumped hard. Did he expect her to answer?

"Tell me, Claudette," he said, picking up his wine, "do you have bastard brothers and sisters about France from Rebecca's infidelity?"

She held her own wine so it wouldn't fall over and shook her head. "No, Father. Mother was careful and only…she only took lovers to keep us fed and clothed. She also taught English to the children at court. But we didn't earn enough to keep our positions there, and when your funds stopped coming…"

"My funds stopped coming because she'd become a whore." His tone had such a cutting edge that Tessa felt blood loss.

She drank the rest of the wine in her glass and set it on the table. Her fingers found the birdcage locket and held it up with shaking fingers. She pried it open to show him the two tiny portraits, faded with age. One was her mother when she was young, her face full of joy. The other was a version of her father that Tessa barely recognized. The cutting lines and thick skin from living at sea weren't on his face yet, and he grinned in the picture like a man in love.

"She wore this always when at home," Tessa said. Telling him that Rebecca loved him seemed dangerous, as if he'd strike her for lying, so she kept her mother's declarations inside.

"I would see that," the captain said, and she slid it off over her head. She waited in silence as he held it, staring at the pictures as rain pelted the porthole windows like pebbles.

Her father spoke softly as if to the picture of her mother, his thumb brushing over it. The emotion Tessa could see in his tortured face showed that he'd loved Rebecca.

He glanced up at Tessa. "You have my coloring but her eyes."

She nodded. "She would stroke my hair and say that it was like running her fingers through your hair."

Pain sliced across his face. His brows furrowed and his white teeth clenched down behind parted lips. His narrowed eyes rose to Tessa's. "Did she think of my hair when she thrashed with pleasure under some rutting aristocrat?" He snapped the locket shut, dropping it to the tabletop. "Non, la fille. Your mother was like every other woman, a whore to her pleasures."

Her father's fist slammed down on the locket, making Tessa jump. Her empty goblet tipped over, rolling off the table to continue across the floor. He rose abruptly. "I will take you back to your cabin. The storm is making dessert impossible."

Tessa's constricted heart twisted when she picked up the crushed locket, an indent in the gold top. Would it even open again?

"We will have to stay here near Tiree until the storm passes," her father said, beckoning her impatiently.

Rain slanted across the deck as Captain Lemaire held her arm firmly so she wouldn't fall. The crewmen they walked by skittered out of her father's way. Was he also cruel to his men? They all looked like criminals with their dark glances, as if they weighed their chances of survival with Captain Lemaire if they risked touching her. Tessa pulled her cloak tighter closed.

"Bampot is retching down in the hold," one of the men was saying to another. "He hurled his last meal out on me shoes." The man used a ladle to pour water over his leather boots, his feet bare.

The other man laughed. "Did ye tell him that the ship was like an isle like the one he'd lived on, so he should just ignore the swaying?"

"Aye, but then he puked again."

The other man laughed and, catching sight of Captain Lemaire, cut off the chuckle and nodded as they passed.

"I have ginger from the Far East," Tessa said to her father once they'd reached her cabin door. "For the poor soul who is sick. It can calm a stomach."

"Save it for the truly ill," he said, his tone uncaring. Had he never been tortured by nausea before?

Lemaire unlocked her cabin and ushered her inside. Before she could turn and argue for the poor soul, he pulled her door shut and locked it, leaving her alone. Once again, he didn't leave her the key. "Good eve, Father," she whispered, her hand clutching around the crushed locket.

She turned around in the dim room but didn't see her cat. "Sia?" Tessa walked toward the darkness. "I've brought you some lamb." She put her hand in her pocket for the small pieces of meat she'd hidden there when suddenly a hand clamped down over her mouth, trapping her scream inside.

Chapter Eighteen

The hand smelled dank like sea and tar, and Tessa clamped her teeth down into the palm.

"Bloody hell," the voice hissed, and Tessa's pounding heart lurched, her rigid body going slack.

"Eagan?" she said, but the sound that came through the bloody hand against her mouth was muffled. She turned out of his arms, staring with wide eyes at the only person she wanted to see.

He held the finger of his unbitten hand to his lips. Grabbing a rag from the washbasin, Tessa grabbed his hand, pressing it against the bite. Her other hand went to his cheek, her face full of unsaid apologies. For leaving without saying goodbye. For having a father who might be a terrible person. For biting him like a trapped wildcat.

Eagan was damp and windblown, the hair around his face curling in wild disarray. He brushed her hair back from her face. "Are ye well?" he whispered.

She nodded and leaned into his ear. "How are you here?"

He did the same, his breath tickling. "Grissell came to us,

said Jandeau was taking ye and her three children."

Tessa's breath caught. "Children?"

"Bann, Grace, and Charlotte."

Tessa's fingers clenched into his damp tunic, and she shook her head. "No. He said he'd leave them if I went with him quickly."

Eagan's eyes closed for a moment, and he exhaled. "He lies, Tessa. Grissell watched the children taken from their beds after ye'd been rowed across."

Her legs felt weak, and she pressed a hand against her lips. Would her meal come up? She turned and lowered onto the edge of the bed, trying to breathe through the nausea. Sia came up to sniff at her pocket, and she mindlessly drew out the bits of meat for her.

Eagan crouched before Tessa, whispering. "I ran to a rowboat I had set behind Grissell's cottage. I knew he'd come back. I should have been with ye."

She met his gaze, her voice certain. "If you had, you'd be dead, Eagan. He had two rowboats of men."

His eyes were dark in the lamplight. "I should have convinced ye to stay at Gylin."

She shook her head. "I still…" She wanted to say that she still had hope that he was wrong about her father, but her conviction was crushed. Her hand went to her locket, holding its jagged form. He'd taken Grace, Bann, and Charlotte. *Mon Dieu.*

"The others are following in Beck's Carrack ship. I didn't wait for them to board and push off. As it was, the *Borreau*'s sails were being raised when I tied to a line off the stern. I then had to figure out where he was keeping ye. I heard a meow." He glanced at Sia, who sat on the bed. "I was hoping the children would be with ye."

"I didn't even know they were on board."

The waves under the ship rose and fell, and the wind

raged against the portholes of the small cabin. Where were the children being kept? They must be terrified.

Footsteps passed overhead, and Eagan pulled a long dagger from a sheath tied to his chest. The ship tossed, jarring her and making her stomach twist with nausea. The wind blew across the small hatch in her ceiling that allowed in fresh air. It also let in voices.

"The little girl is too young even for my tastes," said one of the crewmen as he walked by the porthole.

"How about the older one? She's got paps you can bury your face in."

Tessa's breath caught, her fingers curling into the quilt.

"Aye, but she's covered with the lad's puke."

"Pull her out in this rain. It'll wash her clean enough to fuck."

The first man laughed over the wind. "And have the captain slice my throat for lowering her value at auction."

Whatever else they said was lost under the lashing rain, and they stomped away. Cold slid along Tessa's skin like the hand of death stroking her. They must be talking about Bann, Grace, and Charlotte. Not that Grissell or Eagan would lie, but here was proof. Bann couldn't even swing on a rope without feeling ill from the back-and-forth motion. "Mon Dieu," she whispered and let Eagan gather her in his arms.

On occasion when the opportunity presents itself. 'Tis quite a lucrative business.

Meow. Sia slid against her back as if to give comfort. Grissell was right. Eagan was right. Tessa ran her thumb over her smashed locket. Her mother had been deceived.

Captain Claude Lemaire was indeed a monster.

• • •

Eagan wanted to grab Tessa, toss her overboard, and row her

as far away as he could from Jandeau and the vicious pirates who made up his crew. But not without the children and not in the storm.

His hand ached from her bite, but he couldn't blame her. He'd have struck out with whatever weapons he had if he'd been grabbed. Eagan went to the washstand to clean the wound better and then he'd think of a way to get everyone off this ship from Hell.

Tessa came closer, helping him tie a clean strip of linen around his palm. "I'm so sorry, Eagan. I'd been raised to believe my father was a good man. I didn't want to believe you." The shock of what she'd learned about Jandeau was still obvious in her tone.

Eagan slid his palm along her cheek. "We all want to believe our families are good. My father struggled with what his grandfather did. All the Macquaries have."

Swinging lamplight flashed along her pinched face. "My mother had hope that he had goodness within him, but whatever was there is lost."

Light and shadows swayed with the small room. Eagan pulled Tessa to him, hugging her close, wishing he could pull her into the protection of his body. As if they could become one. He'd never felt the need to protect so strongly before. He was the lone wolf, protesting whenever his family said he must always be connected to people, saying that since losing his twin in the womb, he must always want companionship. He'd fought his whole life to prove them wrong. But now... Right there, he'd throw all of that away if he could just be with Tessa. If he could pull her inside and keep her safe.

His lips opened. *Will you marry me? Stay with me?* sat on his tongue. But the ship dipped in the trough of a wave, and he swallowed the words down.

"Bann must be so sick," Tessa said, pulling away. "He gets motion sick just swinging on rope."

Eagan released her, his hand running up his forehead to scratch his damp hair. "We need to break out of here and find them."

Tessa tested the latch on the door without making a sound. She shook her head when she turned to meet his gaze.

Bloody hell. The door had been unlocked when he'd followed the sound of Sia. But now he'd have to use force to open it, which might be noticed even with the storm raging around them.

He walked back to her. "Let's make our plans through the night and act when someone comes to open the door in the morn."

"We can work together," Tessa said, a question in her tone.

Eagan looked deeply into her eyes and allowed the corner of his lips to pinch upward. "Someone once told me doing things alone can be satisfying but doing things with another pulls on two sets of strengths."

Tessa's mouth relaxed. "That together we can do more than apart."

"Wise words."

She smiled, and he began to scan the contents of the room. "Let's construct our plan of attack."

Tessa nodded, her smile sharpening into determination. "I have poison."

...

Rap. Rap. Rap.

Tessa shot up out of sleep, and Sia leaped silently to the top of an empty bookcase. For a moment, Tessa didn't know where she was, even though she felt the heavy oppression of fear and fury like a crushing blanket.

Eagan? Her gaze snapped around the room until it

landed on him standing just inside the privacy screen in the corner. He nodded to her, and Tessa pushed out of the bed. With the storm still blowing, 'twas impossible to know the time, but it was past dawn.

"Mademoiselle Claudette," a voice called through the door. "I'm coming in if you're decent."

Did the crew think she slept naked? She'd only changed out of the rich gown that she'd worn for dinner into her regular woolen ensemble.

She said nothing and listened as the key turned in the lock. A medium-sized man stood in the door holding a tray with what looked like bread, cheese, and fruit compote. He had close-cut brown hair and a beard that looked recently trimmed. He was wiry and moved from foot to foot as if he were ready to bolt or had to piss.

His eyes were lowered. "Are you dressed, Mademoiselle?"

"Oui."

He looked up timidly as if she were tricking him and a breast might be sticking out of her bodice. He exhaled when he saw her completely and modestly dressed. "If I was to see you naked," he said, "the captain would probably carve my eyes out."

She walked closer to him, which made him push the door shut behind him just like she'd wanted. "Does my father do that often? Cut people's eyes out?"

"Oh…I…umm… I'm fairly new to the crew, but I've heard stories."

"And you are?"

"Hubert Lautrec." He nodded in greeting and strode to the small table bolted to the floor, setting the tray there. A clamp was on the tray, and he screwed it in place to keep the tray from sliding off with the rocking ship. Eagan remained behind the screen, giving her time to dig some information out of the man.

Tessa eyed the unlocked door. "Hubert?"

"Oui?"

"Where are the three children imprisoned on this ship?"

His gaze snapped up to hers and then he looked back down. "We don't discuss our cargo on the *Bourreau*, Mademoiselle. The captain would cut out my tongue."

"Mon Dieu! Does the captain take enjoyment from cutting things off people? Tongues? Eyes?" Thank God he hadn't visited often when she was a child.

Hubert's wide eyes stared at her for a moment. "Captain Jandeau is most efficient at dealing with misdeeds on his ship."

So the crew knew her father as Jandeau, not Captain Lemaire of the French Navy. He truly had become a pirate.

Tessa whirled around and grabbed her thick woolen cloak, throwing it over her shoulders as she strode to the door. "You will give me a tour of this ship, Hubert Lautrec."

"I cannot let you leave this cabin." He ran to intercept her at the door, barring it with his scrawny body.

Tessa stood tall, looking down her nose in the offended way her mother had perfected when dealing with those who tried to walk over her. And the presence of Eagan just feet away bolstered her rashness.

"Will you wrestle me to the bed, Hubert? Strike me to stop me from leaving this cabin?"

He blanched, blinking rapidly. "God help me, no! The captain would cut off my hands and then my arms and then throw me overboard tied to a cannonball."

Tessa wondered what type of nightmares Hubert had.

"Since you won't tell me where the children are located, I will find them myself," she said, "and if you try to stop me, it will be my word against yours when my father asks what happened." Her stare bored into the man, and his face reddened.

"In the storm? You could be swept overboard."

"I'm assuming they are being held below deck."

When she yanked the door open, Hubert's hands went to grab her arm, but he stopped himself.

If anyone touches ye, I'll kill them. Eagan's words during the night as they made their plans filtered through her mind.

"If you want to live, Hubert, don't touch me," she said, staring him hard in the eyes. Eagan had a sharp blade ready. She could feel his readiness behind her, feel his gaze taking in every movement.

Hubert swore under his breath and followed her into the narrow corridor. The wind whistled, and Tessa's heart thumped hard. Moisture hung heavy in the air and dripped between the floorboards overhead.

"Mademoiselle! Mademoiselle Claudette," Hubert called as he ran after her. "Let me lead you about else you fall into someplace dangerous."

"And my father will cut off some body part of yours."

"Most definitely," he said with exasperation.

"Show me to the galley first," she said, fingering the full linen packet that she'd slipped into her pocket.

She kept her eyes and ears open for any sounds of the children, although the storm howled loudly above. She lifted both hands, palms out flat on either side of her, to keep herself from falling into the corridor walls as the ship tossed.

If she thought about the perils of drowning, trapped inside the small space, she'd either swoon, vomit, or run above deck screaming. She kept her focus firmly on Hubert's bowed shoulders. Behind her somewhere Eagan was sneaking out and down into the bowels of the ship to find Bann, Grace, and Charlotte. She prayed nothing terrible had befallen them yet.

"Where there's life, there's hope." She murmured her mother's favorite saying, her heart clenching.

"Quoi?" Hubert asked.

"Where is the galley?"

"Straight ahead," Hubert said, gesturing to a door at the end of the corridor.

As they entered, warmth hit Tessa's face along with the smell of sage, onion, thyme, and oregano. There was no fire under the small cook stove, and the room had a dank feel to it.

"Pierre," Hubert called, and a large man emerged from another doorway. His stomach hung over his tied trews, and many stains dotted his tunic. His face had a greenish tinge, and his brows were furrowed.

"No hot food on a day like this. Too dangerous for a fire."

"Uhhh…" Hubert stammered.

Tessa ploughed ahead. "I am Captain Jandeau's daughter, Mademoiselle Claudette. I asked Hubert to show me the galley."

The man's small eyes narrowed until they were slits. "Your breakfast not to your liking, Mademoiselle?"

"Oh, 'tis fine, thank you. I needed to get out of my cabin. The rocking of the ship is making me queasy."

"Pierre knows about motion sickness," Hubert said.

Pierre grunted. "Hold your foking tongue."

"I have some ginger that will help your stomach. I can add it to the stew for the crew." She nodded to the pot over the cold hearth.

The cook frowned. "I have no need."

"Have the children been fed this morn?" she asked, and Hubert choked, coughing into his fist.

Pierre looked at him and then back at Tessa. "Everyone on board is given bread and cheese when the weather is foul."

What a frustrating non-answer. Tessa moved over to the unlit hearth and sniffed the open pot that seemed to be waiting for a time when it could be heated. It was some sort of meat stew and there was another pot of grain in water.

"Mmmm…" She filled her inhale and released a mellow song she used to sing in the nursery at court. The notes ebbed and flowed around the brief tale of a boy longing to eat sweets instead of meat. From the silence behind her, the song was having the same effect on the gruff cook as it had on the unruly children. It caught their attention, tangling it in the ribbon of notes.

Using her body as a shield, Tessa leaned over the stew pot, continuing the pleasant notes of the song. She flicked the pouch to dump the contents into the aromatic meal. It wasn't poison to kill, but it would make the crew sleepy or ill after they ate. Hopefully, they'd be too hungry to notice anything different with the bitter flavor of the herb mixture. And any spirits would accentuate the effects. She tucked the pouch through the pocket hole in her skirts and ended the song.

Two heartbeats later, Pierre grabbed her arm, whirling her around. "I don't like people nosing around my galley, even if they do sing like a bloody bird."

Using all her imperial training from her time avoiding grabbing hands at the French court, Tessa looked pointedly down at his hand. "I understand my father cuts off the body part that touches what is his, which includes me, his daughter." She let her gaze slide back up to Pierre's red eyes. "How good a cook will you be without your right hand, Monsieur?"

His fingers snapped open as if she were a blazing hot pot. "The cook is the most important crewmember. If I can't cook, no one eats."

She sniffed disdainfully and walked back to the door, hiding the fact that her heart hammered. "I know the correct way to season a stew, Pierre, and I'll need a task on board. What better place than the galley for me?" She tossed him a knowing smile as she stepped out into the cold, dark corridor. As she shut the door behind her, she let out a long breath, sucking in more quickly to calm her pulse.

With rabbit-like agility, Hubert moved around her in the corridor without touching her. "You sing like a nightingale, Lady Claudette."

"One uses the weapons one has," she murmured more to herself than to Hubert.

Tessa followed slowly, letting the spry man move forward, increasing his distance. She passed one open hatch where the sounds of snoring rose. Tessa slowed as she neared another hatch that sat silent and open a crack, unlike when she'd first passed it. 'Twas Eagan's signal that he'd gone down it.

Without hesitation, she descended, the sound of her petticoat unnoticed with the surging of the wind and sea around the ship. One small lantern hung encased in glass, a bucket of water below it and a crewmember sleeping right beside it, sleeping or unconscious.

Tessa stepped around cannonballs stacked in pyramids about the room.

"Mademoiselle!" Hubert called from above, making her move quickly through an opening into another room full of barrels. The acrid smell of gunpowder tickled her nose, and she held a finger under it to stop the sneeze.

Mon Dieu! How many ways could one be killed on a war ship?

Another hatch was open with a ladder that led down into the dark. Tessa knelt beside it, peering down. A few portholes sat in the walls, but they were at the waterline and showed only gray sea. Tessa took another swaying glass lantern off a hook and swung the lantern down in the hole. A few empty hammocks swung over more barrels. No men.

"Bloody hell," Hubert murmured behind her as she quickly stepped down the ladder, her boots finding the rungs. The ship tipped first one way and then the other, nearly throwing her from the ladder, but she held tight with her one hand, squeezing her eyes shut until she was flung back to the ladder.

When she got to the bottom, Hubert nearly jumped down. "Which way to the children?"

His eyes flitted to a door behind her, but he shook his head, pursing his lips shut as if nothing would pry them open. She didn't need him to speak with words when he gave everything away with his glances. Foolish man. She briefly wondered if her father assigned him to Tessa in order to catch her mutiny.

Tessa strode to the door, pushing it open, and stepped through. The foul odor of human waste and vomit assailed her. Still holding firmly to the door jamb so as not to fall from the pitching floor, she raised the lantern higher until the light penetrated the darkness. Amongst more barrels, a square area was surrounded by iron bars. A dark form moved inside.

"Charlotte?" Tessa asked. She glanced around the dark interior but didn't see Eagan. Inside a barred cell, two people stood covered together with a blanket. A third pushed his head up from a blanket on the floor. Three pale faces looked out with wide dark eyes.

"Tessa." Charlotte's voice was full of hope.

"Mon Dieu," Tessa whispered, rushing toward the bars. She blinked past tears she knew she couldn't stop and grabbed the bars. "Bann and Grace, too?"

Grace's little hand caught hers at the bars. "Eagan was—"

"Shhh," Charlotte said, her gaze going over Tessa's toward the ladder where Hubert stood.

Bann moaned softly from his corner. "The boat won't stop moving," he said and exhaled in a sigh that, considering the circumstances, was not exaggerated in the least.

"Has anyone…hurt you?" Tessa asked.

Charlotte met her eyes, latching onto Tessa's hand, her cold fingers desperate. "Nay, but there were plenty of threats."

"They took us," Grace said, "from the isle." The lantern showed tear streaks down her dirty face.

"I am so sorry, sweet," Tessa whispered. "I'm going to get you out of here."

"Impossible," Hubert said behind her.

Without letting go of the child's clinging hand, Tessa snapped her face to the man who hovered behind her. His eyes were nearly as large as Grace's as he stared into them even though he hopped nervously from side to side as if dodging gunfire.

"And you, Hubert, are going to help us get safely off this ship."

He was already shaking his head. "He'll kill me most foul."

Behind Hubert, out of the shadows, a form rose like a grim reaper, standing a foot taller than the man.

Tessa held up a hand to still Eagan, and she spoke to Hubert. "If you help us, you can come away from the *Bourreau*. Leave this terrible life that torments you with nightmares."

The man rubbed his forehead, probably reliving one of those nighttime episodes. He swallowed hard. "I knew you'd be trouble," he mumbled.

"Much more than trouble if I tell my father you touched me."

He gasped. "He'll cut off my jack."

"Orrrrr," she drew out, "you can come with us if you help us off this ship. You can sail on a ship where they don't sell children or rape, a place you don't need to fear the captain."

Hubert licked his dry lips. "And you can get me on one?"

"Of course. The Macquaries have ships, as do their friends. So, what is it, Hubert? Your jack sliced off and death in the dark, cold sea, or life away from here?"

"I…" He nodded rapidly like a pecking bird. "I will help you and go to another ship."

"What a wise decision," Eagan said, stepping out of the shadows.

Chapter Nineteen

Eagan came up behind Hubert, his blade at his throat. The wiry man seemed to go limp, barely standing with fear buckling his legs. "Yer name is Hubert," Eagan said.

"Aye." The man squeezed his eyes shut.

"How did ye find yerself on the *Bourreau*?"

"I…I followed a line of men signing up at a dock in Dublin. Had no money or food, and both were promised."

Eagan heard the slight lilt of the Irish accent. "Ye've lived elsewhere."

"France, England, Ireland, the northern isle of Scotland, too, wherever I could find work."

Eagan met Tessa's gaze over the man's head. To trust or not to trust. "What say ye, Tessa?"

Tessa scrutinized the frightened man. "I don't think Hubert has any loyalty to Jandeau," she said.

"I don't," Hubert blurted out. "I can be loyal to the lady, though, and to you, milord."

Eagan rolled his eyes. The man would pledge his soul to keep his life. Eagan lowered his mouth to the man's ear. "See that ye do, or I'll be doing more to ye than cutting off yer wee jack."

He waited for Hubert to nod and lowered his mattucashlass, resheathing it along his ribs. "Go stand over there and stay quiet," Eagan said, pointing to the corner where he'd hidden in the shadows. When Hubert scurried off, Eagan met Tessa at the bars. Her breathing seemed ragged like she was enforcing even inhales and exhales.

"I found some more bread above, left in the sleeping quarters," Eagan said. "Brought it down with pouches of weak ale for them."

"We were so relieved when we saw him," Charlotte whispered, her gaze continually going to the hatch entrance as if she imagined a horde of raping pirates barreling down. She returned to Bann, mopping his face with a damp rag to wash some of the vomit off.

"Other than the nausea, they seem to be well enough physically," Eagan said, coming closer to Tessa so he could whisper. "Not sure how long they'll have nightmares, though."

"I thought the worst things that could befall children were in cities. They aren't safe even on a remote isle." Tessa shuddered, his hands on her shoulders. "Because of men like…my father."

"There are people everywhere who take advantage of the weak and young." Eagan pulled her against him and felt her arms wrap under his, holding him to her.

"I should have stopped him somehow," Tessa said, her voice muffled. "I went along with him because he said he'd order his men to leave them alone."

"Ye had no choice." Eagan rested his chin on the top of her soft hair. He could imagine holding her to him in the clearing on Wolf Isle, surrounded by nature and peace. He could imagine staying there with her forever.

"When can we get off?" Bann asked, his little voice weak.

Tessa pulled back, and Eagan turned to make sure Hubert's little mouse eyes were still in the dark corner. The man crouched, his arms wrapped around his knees. "Hubert, come here."

The man stood, coming timidly. "Sneak some more food for the children," Eagan said, "and be prepared to help us leave the ship. I'll leave it up to ye to make it to our rowboat."

"Aye, thank ye, sir. I'll swim to it if I have to." He rubbed his nose aggressively like it itched.

"Don't eat the stew," Tessa said. "'Tis been...adjusted."

Hubert was staring wide-eyed at Bann. "He's sick again."

Charlotte slid her hand up the boy's forehead, her worried glance turning toward Tessa. "He feels hot."

"Oh, mon Dieu," Tessa murmured, rushing to the bars. "A fever."

...

"The storm is calming," Tessa said across the table from her father. After Eagan had thoroughly explained to Hubert what would happen to him if he betrayed them, she'd gone back to her cabin and the crewman went foraging for more bread for the children. Eagan stayed below to guard them. They'd all spent the day waiting for the storm to move on.

Jandeau was more interested in the charts spread across the table than her even though he'd called her to his cabin. Exotic treasures surrounded them in the room twice the size of hers. Carved masks out of wood, golden figures, silken curtains, and velvet throws.

Her gaze fell on the dark portholes. "Will we sail soon?"

"I'm sending some men to the isle to gather more fresh water and game just before dawn," he said. He placed a mark down south on the map. "Then we will sail."

"To Portugal," she said. *To sell Charlotte, Bann, and*

Grace. It took Tessa's training of hiding her true emotions at court to keep her pleasant mask in place. Under it, her stomach roiled in disgust and horror. He nodded, using a straight edge to mark a path through the sea.

How could she have longed for her father's return? Eagan and his brothers, even Grissell, had warned her that the man they called Jandeau was the devil. She hadn't wanted to believe it. Would her mother have confessed his vileness to her eventually or had she not known? Tessa felt the rough edge of the crushed locket scratch against her skin, but refused to take it off.

How will you bring him profit? Grissell's question sent a chill crackling up Tessa's back and over her shoulders until she couldn't push back the shiver.

"You won't feel the cold in the Caribbean," the captain said, the captain named Jandeau. She couldn't think of him as her father without ripples of nausea. He raised his gaze to Tessa, studying her as if he were trying to slice her open to reveal her thoughts and secrets.

"Pardon, Father," she said, realizing she hadn't kept her mask of comfort and hope in place. "The storm has chilled me."

His black eyes narrowed. "Pierre said you were down in the galley this morn."

Merde. Had the cook told Jandeau she'd asked about children on board? If she lied now, the captain would see straight through it into her tormented heart.

Tessa set her napkin on top of her knife beside her plate and sat up even straighter. Meeting her father's gaze, she took a full breath. "I overheard two men outside the hatch in my ceiling talking of children on board the ship. It concerned me. Hubert refused to say anything except that I had heard wrong. I thought I'd trick the cook into speaking about children since he looked as unwell as I felt. He did not, and I left. Hubert took me back to my cabin." Was the explanation too long? Too many details could come across as a lie.

Jandeau's gaze never wavered, his black eyes like bottomless holes. After a long moment, his mouth twitched, and he took a drink of his wine. "Claudette, there are all levels of people. Some aristocrats with fine breeding and gold, and others are boorish and crude. Some are created to be waited upon and others are created to labor." He set his goblet back on the white tablecloth. "You, daughter, were created to survive and deserve to be obeyed by those less able to lead."

She tried to follow his philosophy about a natural hierarchy, but images of people at court kept flashing through her mind. How she and her mother had been treated somewhere between aristocracy and common servants. How undeserving courtiers lounged while others suffered right under their noses.

"I found you," he continued, "in a pest-infested hole, but you deserve to live in finery and comfort." His arm went out to the riches in the room.

He seemed to wait for her to say something, so her mouth opened. "This is a well-appointed room."

"Oui. I thought so when I took it from the Spanish captain. I took possession of everything onboard with it, including his cargo headed for a new life in service. They are no longer aboard."

"Were there children?"

His lips cut into a frown. "Some people are made to labor. I kept them alive and took them to a port to help them find positions."

Was he truly mad or merely trying to convince her that his actions were honorable? Tessa wasn't sure which she preferred. A skewed philosophy or madness? Madness could pass to the child, so she deeply hoped he'd just been tainted by his rearing and life.

She wet her dry lips and tried to keep the horror off her face. Drawing on what she'd learned from her mother while they dodged obstacles and personalities at court, Tessa gave a small nod.

His mouth relaxed. "In the future, remind yourself of this discussion so you don't bother my crew with tiresome questions." His voice had hardened, making Tessa's muscles tighten as if they anticipated an attack. He leaned slightly forward over the table. "Is that clear, Claudette?"

She nodded, but her gaze froze on one of the small portholes opposite her. Eagan's face peered inside, his gaze focusing on her and then on her viperous father. Which did he desire more? Saving her or killing Jandeau?

"I would hear you say it, daughter."

"Pardon?" She blinked, dragging her gaze back to his black eyes shadowed even more by the heavy pinch of his brows.

Jandeau spun in his chair to look at the windows filled only with the vacant dark of night and thick dots of rain.

"Do not talk to any of my crew unless they ask you a question. I would not have them grow fond of you and try to get under your skirts. I'd cut them to pieces, but I don't have time to find new crew. Again."

She could only manage shallow breaths. "I understand not to…bother your crew about any of your passengers in the future."

He picked his quill back up. "Good, because while on board my ship, you're one of my crew, Claudette. If you disobey me…" His gaze grabbed hold of hers until she felt strangled by it. "…I will tie you naked to a mast for a day and night."

Her breath caught. She couldn't move.

"My men know better than to fok you, but they will surely touch and watch and likely pleasure themselves before you, maybe even with one of our impure passengers if we pick one up."

Everything inside Tessa squeezed in terror, her nails digging into the padded arms of the chair.

"You might be my daughter," Jandeau said, "but you are not above *my* law."

...

The storm had abated enough that Tessa could hear the crew clomping around on the deck above. She hadn't heard nor seen Eagan since he'd spied on her with Jandeau. She'd once again opened the small, barred hatch in the center of the room that let in air. She heard a man shouting orders in English, his accent thick.

He must be her father's second in command. Tessa strained her ears for Hubert's voice but hadn't heard nor seen him after he brought her back to her cabin.

Had Hubert gone to her father, betraying them all? Tessa's stomach clenched at the thought of armed men climbing down into the prisoner's hold to slaughter Eagan in that dank, dark hole, the children screaming. Everything inside her constricted, and she clutched the locket.

"Breathe, Tess," she said aloud, and felt Sia push her head against her leg. She bent to pick up the cat, cuddling her and letting her small warm body dissolve the horrid thought. She'd been so relieved, like Charlotte, when she'd realized the man in her room was Eagan. But now it was as if part of her were wandering the ship without protection. Tessa was certain her mind would break if she were forced to watch Eagan's torture.

Tap. Tap.

Tessa jumped, pivoting toward the door while clutching Sia.

Tap. Tap.

Sia wiggled out of her arms, and Tessa went to the door, flattening her palm there. "Yes?"

A key turned in the iron lock, and she stepped to the side as the door swung inward. Hubert hurried inside, closing the door behind him. *Dieu merci.*

He leaned toward her ear, slipping the key he'd just used into her hand. "The dinghy your man brought hasn't been noticed on the port side. 'Tis still there." His brow furrowed. "It doesn't look like 'tis made to hold six people."

"Two are small children," she said. "If you can lower another dinghy or a larger one without getting—"

"Jandeau will notice that for sure. And I'll lose my hands, my tongue, my eyes, my—"

"Then don't." She exhaled a full breath. "We will make do with Eagan's rowboat." She checked the porthole again, and it was still dark. "We must escape when they can't see us."

"Aye." He nodded vigorously.

She pocketed the key. "Did you take bread below?"

Gong!

The bell made Hubert jump, his face losing its color. He closed his eyes for a second. "The men will be eating, so we should go soon while they're busy."

"Busy falling asleep or getting sick."

Hubert blinked, his brow furrowing. "Asleep or sick?"

The clomping of many boots pounded overhead, and the men descended toward the galley at the end of her corridor. Tessa jammed the key in the lock and sent up a prayer of gratitude that the tumblers turned, locking her in. A cacophony of curses and low jests penetrated her door as a line queued up right outside her cabin.

The latch of her door was tried several times as if to see if she were locked up tight. Were they the ones who would touch her if she were tied naked to the mast? A shiver racked her body, and she backed all the way up to the far wall. She had no doubt her father would follow through on his threat if he discovered her disloyalty.

"How will they fall asleep or get sick?" Hubert asked again.

"The stew. If the men eat the stew down quickly and combine it in their guts with spirits, the effects should come on them within the half hour."

Hubert rubbed his chin, a frown taking over his whole face. "The stew."

"Mon Dieu. Hubert." She inhaled, her eyes widening. "Did you eat the stew after I said not to?"

He shook his head as if trying to rid water from his ears. "It tasted fine."

"Merde. I put herbs in Pierre's stew when we visited yesterday."

"I didn't see you do it." His words were slurry. Of course they were. Tessa had added enough sleeping herbs for three caldrons of stew. He stuck a finger in his ear and wiggled it as if he couldn't hear well. "I thought Pierre was too close."

Thump! She jumped at the thud overhead. One of the crewmen falling into a stupor?

"I think...I better lay meself down," Hubert said.

Meow. Hiss! Sia leapt from the bed to the bookshelves as Hubert dropped forward, face down onto her bed.

"Non, non, non, non, nonnnn," Tessa dragged out, hands to her cheeks. She poured water on a rag and tried to wake Hubert by rubbing his face. "Wake up," she whispered. "You'll be found in my bed and then Jandeau will hack you to pieces."

Hubert did not move.

Chapter Twenty

"Who the bloody hell are you?"

Eagan spun on his heel to see a man with a dirty apron striding toward him down the corridor, his width nearly matching that of the narrow space. The man rubbed a fist over his paunch, and a large rumble, sounding like thunder over the sea, tore across his middle.

"New crew," Eagan said.

"Whoever the fok you are, get the hell out of my way." He rushed toward a hatch that led down below, a groan coming from him. Hopefully his roiling bowels would keep him from noticing the three smaller people hiding in the shadows below the ladder.

When a door slammed, Eagan peered down the steps. A little pale hand waved up at him. Grace. The wee lass was brave. He held his palm up, the sign for them to wait silently in a shadowed corner. He'd extinguished the lantern down that hatch, but he'd need to get the children up before the large man returned with less discomfort and more questions.

Eagan hurried toward the cabin Tessa had been locked

in. He'd given Hubert an hour to unlock it and give her the key. Hopefully, he'd been successful, or she'd be locked inside, unable to let them in.

Tap. Tap. Tap. He glanced continuously over his shoulder, but the corridor was empty.

"I don't want any food," Tessa said through the door, their agreed-upon code.

"'Tis good I brought whisky from Mull then."

She yanked the door open, and he took in her wild eyes.

"What's happened?" he asked, and she threw her arm wide to indicate the small bed where Hubert lay half on, half off, snoring. Eagan looked back at her. "He ate the stew."

She nodded, her lips pinched in a look that called the drugged man fool, idiot, and bampot all together without uttering a sound. She glanced past his shoulder into the empty corridor.

"I've got them," he whispered and turned away to the hatch where Grace's eyes already peeked over the edge. He beckoned her and the others followed, walking on tiptoe to slide into Tessa's cabin.

She shut it, turning the key to lock it and opened her arms. All three children gathered into her. Bann wasn't vomiting with the smoother seas, but Charlotte had said his fever had increased. All three were pale with spasms of quaking hitting them every so often. He'd watched over them while they were still in the cell below and knew that at least the two younger ones were tortured by nightmares when they dozed off. No doubt they'd be haunted for years to come even if they did manage to make it safely off the *Bourreau*.

A heavy thump hit the deck above their heads, making the children jump, and Charlotte whimpered. As the eldest, she'd been trying to protect the two younger, but she was only a lass of twelve years.

"'Tis another pirate dropping from my tainted stew,"

Tessa said. "If they eat a large portion and follow it with spirits, they will fall asleep before their body starts to purge, possibly choking them. If they take a small enough portion, they'll be awake while their bowels and stomachs try to get rid of the herbs."

"He must have eaten a lot," Grace said, pointing to Hubert.

"I hope they don't ever wake," Bann said, wiping a hand across his mouth as if he still tasted bile. He sat on the end of the bed away from Hubert.

Eagan laid his hand comfortingly onto the lad's thin shoulder. He could feel shivers and pulled the end of the blanket not trapped under the unconscious man around Bann. This horror would either make him bitter and pull into himself or make him stronger and ready to battle as a man. He leaned to his ear. "We will battle on, something they don't expect. We've already escaped from below." The boy looked up at him and nodded, a bit of strength in his eyes.

Eagan's gaze locked with Tessa's. There was determination in the set of her shoulders and courage even if her lifelong dream of a loving father was crumbling beneath her.

"We can do this," she said. "We will get off this ship."

Her firm stare told him clearly, and he gave a brief nod. They would get off this ship. Neither of them would allow the children to be tortured and sold. They would all die if they must, but they would be off this floating Hell.

The hard crack of boots landing down the corridor as if someone had jumped down the ladder made them all look to her door. Tessa began to wave her arms and mouthed "hide."

Grace and Bann scooted under the small bed, and Tessa yanked the edge of the quilt to block the space.

Hard clacking of boot heels sounded louder until it stopped outside her door.

Rap. Rap. Rap. "Daughter." Jandeau's voice cleaved

through the wooden planks.

Eagan had his sgian dubh out but ushered a shaking Charlotte behind the privacy screen. He lifted the screen, setting it to look flattened against the wall, the thin wooden slats and fabric leaning over them where he held the shaking girl against his chest. "Not a sound, Charlotte," he whispered and felt her hide her face against his tunic.

If the children and Tessa weren't in there, he'd attack the pirate captain, but he couldn't when failing meant they'd be taken. Nay. He would have to keep his temper and Charlotte from giving them away.

Jandeau threw the door open so hard it banged against the wall, and he strode inside, his gaze piercing Tessa. She took a step back in the face of his fury. But then the accusation that Tessa was expecting froze on his open mouth when he saw his crewman lying face down on Tessa's rumpled bed, his legs dangling off.

She tried to control the rapid beating of her heart so she could mold her voice into concerned annoyance. "He..." She indicated Hubert with an open hand. "He came in to ask me if I was hungry and then just"—she indicated the prone body—"fell over."

Jandeau scowled, his dark expression sliding from Hubert to Tessa. Sia hissed from her corner, and Tessa prayed she wouldn't give any hiders away. Overhead another thump made Tessa startle. Jandeau's gaze lifted to the ceiling. "Why are my men suddenly falling over, Claudette? Some of them puking and shiting themselves?"

Because I drugged them. It was right on the tip of her tongue as if her father had some magic to compel her to spit out a truth that would see her stripped naked and tied to a mast.

Tessa swallowed down the confession and shook her head. "I don't know, Father. I can examine them to see if they've taken ill. I learned some curing from my mother." She made herself look at Hubert. "Although, it could be from too much drink. Perhaps they celebrated surviving the storm."

Jandeau turned to the door, his fist snapping forward. *Crack!* Tessa jumped, her hand flying to her chest, an instinctual reaction to protect her heart. Jandeau yanked his fist back from the wall where the hard planks were cracked. Blood trickled from his knuckles, but he dropped his arm as if he didn't care, as if pain was such a part of his life that he didn't even wince nor avoid it.

He pivoted back to her. "I'll tell you what I think. I think my daughter somehow poisoned my men."

Her eyes widened but then her brows came together. "How would I do that and why?"

He strode to her satchel on the table. The room was so small, too small to hide four people for long. Grabbing the bottom, Jandeau upended her bag, sending all her jars and packets of herbs flying across the room. They hit the floor, one rolling under the bed. One jar hit her legs with such force, Tessa thought she might have a bruise through her petticoats.

"I've been locked in my cabin," she said. "And those are herbs for curing."

"Hubert," Jandeau growled, but the man didn't move. His mouth was open, and drool began to trickle out onto the bedspread. "He's too soft. He let you into the galley yesterday and aided you."

"Hubert?" She opened her mouth in bafflement and then looked at the sprawled man. "Why would I drug a man helping me?" She tried desperately to slow her rapid breaths. "Couldn't someone else in your crew have access, courage, and a desire for mutiny?"

She imagined herself small and timid, hoping he would believe it. She used to pretend to be slight and invisible when she'd had to traverse the French court, trying to avoid ensnarement. It had worked then, but her father wasn't an inebriated, easily fooled courtier.

He stared at her with black eyes, shiny orbs like those of a rat in the dark. His teeth, in his tanned, weathered face, looked just as sharp. His upper lip curled back. "There's no time for this," he said. "You'll start with reviving Hubert and then come above to revive the others. I'll wake the second rotation to set sail." His voice showed that she had no other option but to obey.

He turned to the door and then swung back around to her. "Make certain, daughter, that you truly are thankful for my benevolence. Any contrary action will result in discipline. No one gets away with mutiny on my ship."

She swallowed hard.

"Do you understand, Claudette?"

"Oui, mon père," she said, her tongue so dry it tried to stick to the roof of her mouth.

As soon as the door closed and clicked with a key, Eagan moved the privy screen away and led Charlotte out. The girl's face was stained with tears. Eagan flipped up the blanket and silently ushered the two little ones out from the bed. They all stood without saying a word, just looking at each other.

Tessa wanted nothing other than to run into Eagan's arms. She knew he'd hug her, support her, but to succeed in this mad plan to escape, they both needed to be strong. They had to work together.

Tessa went to Hubert, shaking him. "Wake up."

"Nay, Mum, I didn't let the pigs in the house," he murmured, his words fading off and ending with a small groan as vomit erupted from his mouth to spread across the quilt.

Sia hopped down from the bookshelf onto the bed. Her pink nose sniffed toward Hubert from several feet away. She sneezed and hopped up to perch on his back.

At least Jandeau didn't seem to think Hubert was helping her. If she must leave him behind, he could continue being a crewman on the *Bourreau*.

She looked up at the hatch above her where the sky had lost its pitch darkness. Was dawn already breaking? They needed to move quickly.

Eagan motioned for them all to gather closely, away from the hatch above. He spoke into their little circle. "I tied my rowboat to the stern…to the back of the ship." He pointed at the back wall of the cabin.

"Hubert said 'tis still there," Tessa said.

Eagan nodded. "With the men unwell and the shadows still thick, we'll sneak as quietly as possible to the back and climb down the rope there."

"Climb down a rope?" Charlotte's voice was a whispered squeak.

"I'll go first," Eagan said, "and catch ye if ye fall."

"I might fall," Bann said. His eyes were large, but Tessa saw a shine to them that signified fever. The boy knew he was weak.

"And I'll catch ye, too."

"I'll go last," Tessa said. She touched Grace's face. "Can you take Sia if I put her in my satchel and loop it over your head?"

The girl's eyes widened even more, but she nodded. Tessa scooped the cat off Hubert, who twitched slightly. Sia meowed but allowed Tessa to lower her back end into the satchel, which she helped to put over Grace's slim frame.

"Even if she scratches me, I won't let her get away." Grace's voice twisted Tessa's heart. It was her fault they were here. If her father hadn't returned to Wolf Isle a second time he wouldn't have found them. If Tessa hadn't befriended the Macquaries, they wouldn't have protected her the day of the picnic, making her father have to return during the night. She would do anything she could to get them back to the safety of Wolf Isle.

"I'll carry Bann," Tessa said, glancing at the feverish boy who'd sat back down on the bed, far from Hubert.

"I'll take him if he's too heavy," Eagan said.

Tessa shook her head and then took a big inhale. "We need your sword arms free." She picked Bann up, and he wrapped his arms around her neck. "Let's find that boat," she said, meeting Eagan's eyes.

They were hard, watchful, but softened when he looked at her. In two silent steps, he reached her, his fingers going under her chin. Despite Bann between them, Eagan leaned in to kiss her lips. The warmth and tenderness felt like a promise, and Tessa wanted to cling to it.

He pulled back gently, and they stared at one another. They didn't say anything because it was all right there in their gazes. They would do this together. She blinked back a swell of tears and nodded once, exhaling. She handed him the key from her pocket, shifting Bann over her hip.

Eagan peeked into the corridor, nodded to them to follow, and moved before her to lead the way while she guarded the rear of the line, keeping the children between them. They walked on light feet to the ascending ladder.

Dearest God, help us escape.

Eagan climbed and looked over the edge of the hatch to the deck, the toes of his boots balancing on the ladder rung. Tessa's heart pounded a rapid staccato as she waited. His hand beckoned them to follow. The girls climbed up first. Tessa set Bann on the ladder rungs as high as she could. Eagan helped him climb the rest of the way up from above. Tessa followed into the fresh breeze. Dawn was creeping closer, reducing the inky shadows as the horizon lightened.

Bann held Tessa's hand weakly as they followed Eagan in a crouched position behind the crates that had been stacked toward the stern. Angry voices came from the front of the ship, floating back to them.

"Rouse the men."

"Some of them have fouled themselves, Captain."

"They can hoist sails covered in vomit and shite."

Remaining crouched, they moved from crate to crate and shadow to shadow toward the back of the ship. The absence of moving crewmen was a blessing. Thank God, she'd gotten the herb formula into the stew. This would be impossible with a full contingent of sailors about.

The ship creaked, and the water lapped against the hull as the last bit of the storm's temper calmed. Grace clutched Sia in the bag against her chest, and Charlotte hurried after Eagan. Bann tripped, and Tessa caught him from hitting the deck, lifting him again. Bann's hot little body barely held onto her stooped frame. Her back muscles screamed but she moved as low as possible, trying to keep them hidden amongst the crates.

Tessa kept her eyes on Eagan's form, all predatory muscles contained in his clothing. The smell of decaying seaweed tainted the salt air, indicating the tide was low and they were indeed near land. Choppy waves still splashed against the hull. In a large ship, it was hardly noticed, but the dinghy would toss. A nauseous stomach was the very least of Tessa's worries at present. *Together.* They *would* succeed together.

They made it to the rail off the back, and Tessa's heart leaped when Eagan looked over and then nodded to her. The dinghy was still there.

She came alongside him, lowering Bann to the deck. Eagan found her hand in the shadows, and the warmth of it, the gentle squeeze funneled strength through her, allowing her to breathe. This would work. They would climb down and row away from the *Bourreau* before the sick crew noticed in the dimness of pre-dawn light. But climbing down a rope with a boy over one shoulder wouldn't be possible. *Mon Dieu.* Bann would have to climb down on his own unless Eagan could carry him.

A soft gasp made her spin around. Charlotte, clutching her hands, and Grace, holding Sia, stared into the darkness, their backs against the rail. Her father's words reached Tessa before he stepped out of the shadows, his boots falling with soft tread.

"Stealing cargo is mutiny, daughter." Jandeau's bulk emerged from the shadows like a wraith taking on human form. "Disloyalty is punished."

Breath deserted Tessa despite her heart pounding, demanding more. Eagan stepped before her, blocking her.

"And…" Jandeau drew out with a surprised lilt of pleasure, "you brought me a Macquarie pup." His voice hardened. "The one you've been spreading your legs for."

"Do ye feel all-powerful, Jandeau," Eagan asked, "because ye can overpower the young and those physically weaker than ye?" Eagan gently pushed Tessa toward the rope.

Jandeau shrugged like he hadn't a care. "Does not the lion hunt the weakest of the herd? I merely profit off the hunt like a lion feeding his pride."

"'Tis the lioness who hunts," Tessa said, "not the lazy lion." Where had those words come from? The strength to show courage when shaking must be from Eagan and their imperative need. Tessa pulled Grace and Charlotte to the rail. "Climb down," she whispered to them.

"There's a bit of a hiss from my meek daughter," Jandeau said. "I knew it was in you, just like it was in your mother. I tolerated it in her because I was young and foolish and thought I was in love. But now I'm wise and know how far to break you, daughter, to rid you of your obstinance."

She'd taunt him to kill her before he let him break her. The knowledge of that thrummed through Tessa. "Wise? You are a selfish monster who preys on the world."

Eagan stood tall before Jandeau, still blocking her. "Yer fight is with the Macquaries. Let them leave, and ye can try to break me."

Mon Dieu. Tessa's fingers curled into Eagan's tunic. Her father would torture him, cut parts off, until he begged for death. Just the thought of the pain and humiliation wrought upon the man who'd come to save her, who'd taught her that passion was more than a practiced art, who'd shown her what family really meant… Tears welled out of her eyes, but she blinked them rapidly away.

"He wants me," she whispered behind Eagan. "Jump over and save the children."

Eagan didn't respond, only kept his gaze on Jandeau.

Jandeau advanced slowly. *Tsk*. "I will break all of you. I think my daughter watching me dismember you, Macquarie, will show her what happens to my enemies. But I'll still have to punish her for poisoning my crew. And here I thought I would make you a cook, Claudette. Since you can't be trusted, I'll have to come up with another job for you, perhaps making you a plaything for my abused crew."

Eagan's hand slid behind his back to her, and he pushed her away from him. Without saying a word, he was begging her to throw herself over the side of the ship. She could almost hear him shouting inside his head. *Save the children. Save yourself. Go.*

But she wouldn't leave him again. She'd done it once, bending to her father's will.

"Why do ye want Wolf Isle anyway?" Eagan asked. They stood beside some stacked crates, which partially blocked the children.

Tessa bent to Grace. "Climb down the rope to the boat."

"Sia?" The girl hugged the bag with Sia's head sticking out. The cat's eyes were wide with fright.

"Go." Tessa took the bag, freeing the girl of her burden.

Tessa tried to put the bag around her shoulder, but the cat jumped out, running off. *No!* She almost called the cat, but there was no use. She'd run and hide, and Jandeau was standing before them. Grief yanked Tessa's heart. Had she lost the cat forever?

"The isle would be perfect for my king if he chooses to attack England," Jandeau said. "I explored it when I picked up Rebecca. 'Tis good to keep the monarchy happy when I bend all his maritime rules."

"The Macleans won't allow it," Eagan said.

"I know you are trying to stall with your questions," Jandeau said and drew out a pistol. "Time to start your punishment." Without another word, Jandeau aimed straight at Eagan. And fired.

"No!" Tessa yelled as Eagan's body flew backward from the hit, throwing him against the rail. "Mon Dieu! My love!"

"Ship! Ship to starboard!" A voice came from high above in the rigging. "There's a ship coming upon us, Captain!"

Grace was almost down the rope, her feet dangling over the bobbing dinghy. Charlotte screamed as two brawny crewmen rushed to the rail and grabbed her arms from the rope, hauling her back aboard. Jandeau strode to stand before Tessa while Bann clung to her leg.

"Bring the Macquarie pup," Jandeau called to two more men heading their way.

"No!" Tessa screamed again.

Her gaze met Eagan's. There was no fear in his face, just fury and regret.

Before her father could drag her away, Tessa lunged

toward Eagan at the rail. "I love you," she said and pushed with all her might against his chest.

Eagan fell backward over the rail. He disappeared, and Tessa closed her eyes tight, the sound of a huge splash covering the one sob she allowed herself.

Chapter Twenty-One

"Let go of me!" Charlotte screamed, kicking out at the two men who outweighed her four times over.

"Not a chance, la fille."

"Father, please," Tessa called, bending to pick Bann up. He nestled his face into the space between her neck and shoulder, his body limp.

The two men who'd been coming for Eagan leaned over the side. "La petite fille is clinging to the rowboat. I don't see the Scotsman." He turned back, disappointment on his rough features. "He's dead and sinking."

The proclamation tightened through Tessa's stomach. *Eagan. No. Please be alive.*

The other man grinned at Tessa. "But we have your daughter, Captain." He leered at her as if anticipating how Jandeau would punish her. He rubbed his mouth, his skin pale. "My friends are all puking or shiting themselves because of you."

Jandeau hauled her up against his hard frame. The smell of perfume and sweat assailed her, making all the hairs on her body stand high. Her stomach heaved. She breathed the salt breeze, trying to keep from vomiting.

"Give up the lad," Jandeau said near her ear, and a crewman pulled Bann from her arms. The boy looked panic stricken and couldn't catch his breath. He was still weak with fever and had no fight in his slim arms.

"Shall we go after the girl below?" one sailor asked, looking over the edge.

"Leave her," Jandeau said; the rumble of his voice would fuel Tessa's nightmares. "My daughter and I have a meeting to attend. Bring the other two."

Her father's hand was an iron manacle around Tessa's wrist, and he strode toward the front of the ship. She trotted to keep from stumbling and being dragged, her heart pounding as she tried to keep the tears from coming. Was Eagan dead?

When they reached the starboard side, hope shot up through Tessa. A ship nearly as large as her father's galleon pulled closer, the sails being lowered to slow it. The shadows had lightened with the coming dawn, and the dark-colored sails made the ship hard to spot. She'd seen them before lowered and tied at the Macquarie Clan's port on Wolf Isle. 'Twas a Macquarie ship!

Before her father could do anything to stop her, Tessa cupped her mouth with her free hand. "Eagan's been shot! He's in the sea!"

Jandeau whipped her around, and she squelched a cry at the pain in her shoulder, the joint ridiculously vulnerable. She stared out at the ship, the rising sun glinting across the shining brass against the black sails like a cat's eyes in candle flame.

Jandeau bent to speak close to her ear. "I have unfinished business with all the Macquaries. Thanks to you, daughter, they've come to me and will die."

Tessa inhaled through her nose to calm herself. She

strained her eyes to see if anyone was trying to get to Eagan. Had they heard her? Her gaze moved from person to person until she recognized someone. Eliza, Beck's wife, stood along the side, a crossbow perched in her arms.

"Ah, Cherie, Eliza," Jandeau yelled across. "You've come to visit."

"You depraved, stinking whoremonger," Eliza called back. "We've come to rescue the children you stole and Tessa."

"My daughter," Jandeau indicated her, "is named Claudette Tempest Lemaire. Her whore of a mother called her Tessa Ainsworth."

A commotion made several crewmen of the Macquaries' ship run toward the port. Tessa's gaze followed them, and she squinted to see a head above the waterline, one arm holding a rope. "Eagan," she whispered, but shouted it in her heart. He wasn't sinking to the cold, dark bottom of the sea.

Two Macquarie brothers, the stoic leader Adam and dark-haired Callum, dove over the side of the ship. Surfacing, Callum came up next to Eagan while Adam stroked toward the rowboat where Grace sat, desperately trying to use the oars that were as large as her.

Crack! Tessa jumped, and Charlotte yelped at the pistol's discharge. A ringing sound shot through her ears, muting the sound of the wind. One of the pirate crew had fired at Eagan. He was exposed against the ship as he tried to climb with one arm, Callum under him. Suddenly, even with two heavy Highlanders hanging on the rope, it was pulled upward quickly, the two Macquaries holding on with their legs and arms. First Eagan and then Callum were lifted over the side by many hands.

"Dieu merci," Tessa murmured, her eyes shutting briefly, but opening to see Adam pulling the rowboat across from the water. Grace was lying completely flat in the hull while Adam dragged her around the back of the ship to the other side so there'd be no clear shot as the child was raised. Grace and Eagan had made it.

The world lightened, and Tessa could see Eagan's drenched frame as he stood at the rail, Drostan and another of their crew working on the gunshot in his shoulder. Eagan's face was taut, his brows bent in fury and focus. She knew he wished he was still there to help her, Charlotte, and Bann, but what could he do? He'd have just been another piece for Jandeau to use to bargain with or torture for his amusement.

"He didn't die after all, daughter," Jandeau whispered at her ear. "It seems he will continue to hurt as he watches you sail away from him."

She didn't reply, and he straightened, signaling to his men. "No matter, Macquaries. I have what I wanted." He pulled Tessa against him as if giving her a hug. "Plus two extra." The crewmen pushed Charlotte toward the rail, Bann holding onto her skirts.

Adam Macquarie came to stand beside Eagan, both of them now without their tunics as dry ones were brought. But Drostan was busy wrapping Eagan's large shoulder. Men on either side of Eliza and Adam held muskets trained on the few crewmen along the deck. Beck was arguing with Eliza.

"Don't shoot," was all Tessa could make out. If they started shooting, then others would follow, and Charlotte and Bann could be hit. Did they notice the missing pirates?

"Release Charlotte and Bann of the Macquarie Clan," Adam pronounced, his voice like thunder. "And Claudette Tempest Ainsworth."

"Mon Dieu," Jandeau called across. "You would wrench apart a father and daughter just when they've been reunited." She could feel the thrum of her father's voice against her back since he held her so tightly. His lies made her spine itch with cold.

He made it sound like Tessa had longed to be with him. Well, hadn't she? She'd dreamed of her father returning all her life, and when he did in France, she thought he was her golden savior. She'd watched for him daily from Wolf Isle, hoping and praying to see his ship on the horizon.

She shook her head, but Jandeau's other hand clasped the back of her neck and pinched it like a vise. She grimaced. Could Eagan see her features? If he saw her in pain, he might act irrationally. She concentrated on keeping her face smooth.

Jandeau's mouth dipped back to her ear, and she cringed, trying to move away from his hot breath, but she couldn't. "Tell them you wish to stay with me."

"Eagan knows I want nothing to do with you."

Instead of anger, he chuckled. "Oh, but you said you loved me when I came for you, Claudette. You dined with me and pretended to be an obedient child." He tsked. "Girls are so inconsistent."

"I despise what you really are, now that I know it to be fully true. A pirate and cruel stealer of children. I so wanted to believe otherwise." Her voice came with the strength of conviction. She would not let herself live under his thumb.

"You've forgotten commander, wealthy businessman, and your father." The talons on her nape loosened, and he stroked her cheek with the back of his hand. "Your blood runs thick with me. If a Macquarie wants you, 'tis only because they want to punish me. They'd have no other use for you, la fille."

It was a lie. Eagan knew she was Jandeau's daughter and still came to rescue her, risking his life to sneak onboard. *He came for the children.* A little voice slithered through her mind. But he'd forgiven her for not believing him. Hadn't he?

"My daughter came with me willingly," Jandeau called across. "She is mine again, and I will see to her comforts."

And torture.

"'Tis a delusion," Eagan called back. "And ye're mad if ye think Tessa wishes to stay with ye."

Off to the right, Tessa saw Grace peeking over the rail of the ship. She was wrapped in a wool blanket.

"Tell them, Claudette," Jandeau spoke in her ear, and she imagined she felt spittle coming with the words.

"Kill me here then, for I won't lie." She'd rather die than leave with Jandeau, but her desire to live, to touch Eagan again, to tell him what she'd realized when he was shot, all of that made her quake where she stood. She hated Jandeau even more for making her act weak. She closed her eyes, tipping her chin higher. "Slice my throat then."

"Stubborn," he murmured. He pulled her tighter around the waist until she almost couldn't breathe. "I'll let the others go if you tell them you want to stay with me."

She twisted, catching sight of his face. "You'll let them go over to their ship? Charlotte and Bann?"

"Oui. I swear it."

Adam was yelling more demands over as Tessa's mind whirled. Her hand came up over Jandeau's arm to rest on her mother's crushed golden locket under her bodice. It sat above the valley of her breasts, and her fingers traced the birdcage outline.

Her mother, too, had tried to escape from the life she'd been left to endure without a husband. She'd felt trapped like the bird in the cage, a golden cage at court. Rebecca had done everything she could to keep her daughter safe, tying herself to powerful men even though it led to her death. Now Tessa was trying to keep these young souls safe. A tear slipped from her eye. Like her mother, she would give up her freedom and happiness, her very life, to save these innocent children.

"Say it," Jandeau hissed in her ear, "and the children go free right now."

Tessa stared at him instead of looking across. "I wish to

stay with my father."

"Louder," he said, pushing her shoulder so hard she spun to face Eagan where he stood across from her. "Claudette has something to tell you. A change of heart it seems."

She cleared her throat against the tightness. No matter what she said, Eagan would know the truth anyway. "My father will send the children across to you, but I wish to stay."

"Stay where?" Jandeau prompted quietly. "Say it."

The sight of Eagan across from her turned watery as tears swelled in her eyes. She let them fall freely but didn't acknowledge them. *He knows I'm lying.* She wanted to jump over and swim to him. Swim to him or drown. Anything rather than stay here tortured by the man who was supposed to rescue and love her as his flesh and blood daughter.

"Say it!" Jandeau hissed, his fingers biting into her arm while his other arm squeezed around her middle.

"I wish to stay with my father here on his ship," she called out. *Mon Dieu!*

Eagan stared back. "I will follow ye across the globe. I won't let ye leave me. I cannot. We can marry." Adam pulled his arm, his lips moving rapidly, but the sound didn't carry. Eagan yanked his arm out of his eldest brother's grasp. "I'll follow ye to the end of the earth, Tessa."

Jandeau stiffened behind her. "A Macquarie pup demands to marry my daughter." His hand slid down from under her breasts to sit over Tessa's abdomen. The caress felt incestuous. Tessa choked back the bile rising in her as his lips brushed her ear. "Mon Dieu. Could you, by chance, be carrying a Macquarie bastard, daughter?"

...

Eagan's hand curled so tightly around the rail of the *Calypso* that his fingers ached along with the throbbing in his shoulder where they'd left the shot. There was no time to remove the embedded ball. His teeth clenched as he stared across the water to the *Bourreau*. Foking Jandeau held Tessa before him like a shield, knowing that they didn't dare fire or shoot at him with her there.

"He's whispering things into her ear," Adam said next to him.

"Threats obviously," Callum said on the other side.

Eagan kept his gaze on her. "He's making her lie. If we leave her, he'll torture her and let his men at her."

"Bloody vicious devil," Callum said.

Drostan pointed. "Fok, that's Sia climbing the rigging."

"The cat ran when Tessa took her from Grace," Eagan said.

"If she ducks," Eliza said, still holding her crossbow steady and aimed, "I can shoot him right through the skull." She spoke of Jandeau of course, the man who'd killed her parents, stolen her baby brother, and pursued her for years. Every minute or so she lowered the bow to relax her muscles, but then she raised and aimed quickly again.

"If I yell 'duck' across, Jandeau won't allow her to," Eagan said without taking his eyes off Tessa. "He's got her around the waist and maybe the back of her neck." She kept grimacing as if he were hurting her, and her eyes glistened in the rising sun as if they swam with tears. He'd never seen Tessa cry, and it tore at him.

"She's saying something," Eliza said.

"Take Charlotte and Bann, too, but…I will stay with my father." Tessa's gaze remained tethered to Eagan's. "I never cared for you, Eagan Macquarie. I am…nothing but a whore and belong with my father. 'Tis his blood and that of my whoring mother that run through me. I'm not pregnant, so leave me here. Take the children."

Even though he knew she was repeating what Jandeau

told her to say, her words, said in her lyrical voice rocked through Eagan. *She told me she loves me.* He'd heard it as he went over the side of the ship. Even the freezing water and pain of the shot couldn't wipe it from his mind.

"He's telling her what to say," Adam said.

"She doesn't mean any of it, brother," Drostan said.

"I know." Eagan met her gaze, trying to pass strength to her across the water. He hated that he'd left her there. If anything worse happened to her, it would haunt him forever.

Callum cursed again. "She's sacrificing herself for the children."

Eagan knew all of this. "I'm not leaving her."

"She might be with child, and that's why Jandeau wants her so badly," Callum said. "He knows a bastard will doom our clan."

"Pregnant or not, I'm not leaving her with him," Eagan said. "She'll kill herself rather than be with him."

"Do we have a deal, Chief Macquarie?" Jandeau said, and his gaze rose slightly higher to the upper deck where Beck had returned to keep his crew ready. "Captain Macquarie? Claudette, my daughter, who is legally mine, stays with me in exchange for these two? That's a good price. I could get a high sum for the virgin girl and the boy." Jandeau shrugged. "If he survives the fever weakening him."

Behind Eagan, Grace cried softly, one of the crewmen by her side. "Bann is ill with fever," Eagan said. "Tessa gave him some feverfew."

"Tessa has potions with her?" Adam asked.

"She did but then used most of it to poison the crew," Eagan said, his mind still partially paralyzed by watching Tessa suffer.

"Most of the crew is poisoned?" Beck asked, coming up behind him.

"Mother Grissell says plants can work better than

steel in some cases," Grace said. "Many of the pirates are unconscious or sick."

"That's why there are only"—Callum counted in a whisper—"eight of them at the rail."

"Hubert ate the stew, too, and passed out on Tessa's bed," Grace continued.

"Hubert?" Beck asked.

"He's a pirate Tessa convinced to help us," Eagan said, his words coming faster. "Most of the pirates are poisoned. We need to act."

Tessa's dark hair moved in the wind, reminding him of the thick branches of the willow tree in Gylin's bailey. It matched Jandeau's dark hair, but that's where their similarities ended. It didn't matter what blood ran in her. Tessa was a courageous, kind, beautiful woman. *Daingead.* He wouldn't let her go. He couldn't.

"Do we have a deal?" Jandeau yelled across. "Leave me and my daughter alone, and we will leave you and Wolf Isle alone."

"Lies," Callum murmured. "Everything that comes out of his foul mouth is a lie."

"Aye," Adam called back. "Send the children over."

Eagan didn't question his older brother. He would get the children back before attacking. With the possibility of Tessa being pregnant with a Macquarie child, his brother would never let her leave. Eagan was thankful he and Tessa had slept together. If they hadn't, he'd still go after her, but with the curse pressuring his brothers, he knew they'd help. Maybe they'd help even without the curse hanging like an ax over their necks.

"Row the boat back, and I'll have them climb down," Jandeau said.

"And Sia, my cat," Tessa yelled. "She must go, too."

Jandeau's face contorted, and he spoke to her. Eagan

couldn't hear him, but Tessa faced them, and her words carried. "I can climb up and retrieve her."

"He's not letting her get the cat," Drostan said, his voice hard. "Sia climbs everything, and she never comes down without someone offering up their body for her to cling onto with her pointy claws."

Beck called down to his two crewmen who'd entered the dinghy after Grace was handed out, and they began to row back across while the line of Macquarie crewmen held muskets and bows ready to fire. *Bloody hell!* Tessa was right in the crossfire.

"Don't shoot," Eagan said down the line at the *Calypso's* rail.

"Unless they must," Callum added.

Jandeau said something and the brutes holding Charlotte and Bann pushed them down the rail toward a rope ladder that was being thrown over. It was an eight-to-ten-foot drop to the water, and the impact if one of them fell into the icy water would deliver a dangerous shock. He knew personally how it stole one's breath.

Eagan heard Tessa calling to Sia even though Jandeau still held her before him at the rail.

"The cat won't come to calling," Drostan said, frustration heavy in his voice. He called out, "Send one of yer crew up the mast so the cat can come down. It will cry up there and drive ye mad otherwise."

Jandeau said something, and a wiry man ran over to the main mast, climbing quickly up the tall pole. Meanwhile, Charlotte was helping Bann climb down before her on the ladder that kept turning, almost throwing them off it into the sea.

"Wait for the cat," Drostan yelled out to the men in the dinghy. "Lia will be distraught if she's left."

"How are we getting Tessa off?" Eagan said, his voice

low.

"We'll attack as soon as the children are safely on the *Calypso*," Adam said and looked at Beck. "'Tis yer ship. Whenever ye say, we attack with cannon and muskets."

"We could hit Tessa," Eagan said.

"She doesn't look chained to Jandeau," Drostan said. Lia had been chained to the pirate captain and then to a cannonball to make her sink if she tried to leap overboard. "She won't sink if she jumps."

"I'll start swimming as soon as the first blast hits them," Eagan said and looked to his second oldest brother, Beck. "Hit away from her for the first round."

"Ye only have one working arm," Adam said. "I'll go."

Eliza snorted, lowering her bow to watch, her eyes raised up the mast. "The cat is feisty and likes French pirates as little as we do."

The man had reached the top and stretched out over the yard that would hold the main sail out if it were unfurled. His colorful curses filtered down while Sia hissed from her spot near the end of his reach.

"Sia!" Tessa called out uselessly.

As if deciding to live, the cat trotted forward along the wooden arm and leaped, hissing, onto the man's face. Eagan could almost feel the sharp prickles that erupted over the pirate's forehead and chin as the fuzzy stomach pressed over his mouth and nose. One of his arms flew off the ladder, and he almost fell to the deck below. His cries of surprise were muffled with the cat's stomach pressed against his mouth. "Get it off! Merde!"

"Descendre, you buffoon," Jandeau called.

The man pushed the cat up his face to his head, Sia scratching him, and the man cursed. It looked like he had a cap on his head made from a cat's hide. Ears back, the cat looked feral and ready to bite. It hissed as the man climbed quickly down the mast.

The crewman strode over to Jandeau. "This cat's a devil!"

Eagan could see the red slashes on the man's cheeks and eyebrows. Blood dripped from one of them, leaving a trail into his dark, unkempt beard.

"I'd throw it to the sharks," the crewman said.

As if she understood, if not the words, then the threat in his hard tone, Sia leaped. They all stood rapt along the *Calypso's* rail as the cat landed, not on Tessa but on Jandeau's face.

Chapter Twenty-Two

Jandeau's arm dropped from Tessa's waist as Sia landed, claws extended. The rough release threw Tessa off balance for a second. Her gaze slid around as if time had stopped. Charlotte and Bann were being rowed across to the *Calypso*; there were only a handful of her father's men standing on the deck, their muskets forgotten with the spectacle, and Sia attached to her father's furious face.

Twenty-four tiny needles from her six toes on each foot poked and slid lines down Jandeau's swarthy skin.

"Bloody beast!" her father yelled, raising his talon-like fingers to grab her.

Tessa reached out, pulling Sia from Jandeau before he could reach her. "Sia!" she yelled, and the cat turned to cling to her bodice. Her sweet face was frantic with terror, ears flattened and eyes wide.

Without any thought except an instinctual need to flee, Tessa clung to the cat and dashed to the rail.

"Bloody foking cat!" Jandeau yelled. "I'm going to skin you alive."

Tessa's steps took her right up to the gunwale. Sia clung to her so Tessa held her with only one hand and used the other to steady herself as she threw a leg up and over the rail.

"Grab her!"

Her father's voice made Tessa throw herself off, releasing into the open air, her whole body curling inward around Sia. The shock of the icy water knocked the air from Tessa's lungs, and her petticoats flew up over her head. Even though dawn had broken, the darkness of the fabric blocked all light.

She was caught in her own, heavy clothes. She let go of Sia to use both hands, pushing the fabric out of her way as bubbles rushed out of her mouth.

Tessa kicked against the pull of the sea, her legs growing numb at the cold embrace that tried to pull her down. Salt burned up her nose, and she clawed at the freezing water. The surface was above her somewhere. *Kick! Kick!* She pushed with her hands against the cloth and the water. *Swim! Up! Up! Up!*

The need for air made her long to open her mouth. But if she did, if she sucked in the sea, she would forever be part of it. Her water-filled body would be dragged down into the frigid blackness below her like into the open maw of some great, icy beast.

She fought harder, kicking and pulling against the water with her arms, and saw a light above. *The surface!* As her face broke through, she gasped for precious air. She spat and coughed, her face skimming the surface for Sia.

Boom! Cannon fire heralded the splintering of wood behind her. *Boom!* And then in front of her. Debris rained down, but she fought against the numbing water trying to drag her back under.

"Tessa!" Eagan's voice called, and her gaze snapped toward the *Calypso*. Eagan pointed at a man, swimming toward her. It was Eagan's brother, Adam. Tessa's heart pounded, her body starting to go slack with relief and numbness.

Another man's head popped up, and he lifted something up out of the water. The cat climbed up the man's face to the top of his head as if he were an island in an icy sea. Drostan swore, probably at the cat's piercing claws. Sia was thin with her fur wet against her body, and she arched her back as Drostan swam back to the *Calypso* with a drenched cat as a hat.

Tessa's legs had grown numb, and she couldn't tell if they were moving. Her body began to sink again, and she tried to use her arms to paddle her way higher on the surface.

"Eagan will put me to the rack if I let ye drown," Adam said. "Relax. 'Tis easier for me to pull ye if ye're on yer back."

She coughed against the salt water that kept trying to throw itself down her throat and maneuvered her body behind Adam. "I...I didn't mean to...bring Jandeau to your family," she said between gasps for air. "I didn't mean to endanger Eagan."

Adam swam, one arm around her neck. "He was going to leave us," he said. "I found his packed things."

Water kept sloshing into her ears, and men yelled overhead, but Tessa fought to hear Eagan's brother.

"Ye've kept him here, Tessa," Adam said. She couldn't see him as she stared up at the looming Macquarie ship as pistol fire erupted. "I thank ye for that and for flushing out Jandeau." His words, coming with his big huffs of breath, sounded sincere. He didn't hate her for bringing her father to Wolf Isle.

Boom! Cannon fire exploded, sending wood from the front of the Macquarie ship into the air. *Boom! Boom! Boom!* The Macquaries retaliated.

Tessa kicked as best she could, but the combination of heavy petticoats and numb legs made her efforts as useless as using a rock to paddle a rowboat. She held her breath against the choppy water splashing in her face, the briny taste almost like cold blood. As they neared the ship, she could hear shouting above, but the cannons had stopped pounding.

When they met the bobbing wooden hull, Tessa felt arms grabbing her, and she was pulled upward. The cold fingers of the sea seemed to cling, furious that it had lost its victim. Too exhausted to help, Tessa went limp, letting whoever was lifting her do their task.

"Eagan," she murmured, realizing he was there, helping to bring her aboard.

"I'm here, Tessa," he said, the sound of his voice washing over her as he pulled her freezing, soaked body up against his chest. The heat penetrated her, and the feeling of protection and strength encircling her nearly made her sob with relief.

"Get her into the captain's quarters." Eagan's voice sliced out of the void that was wrapping around Tessa. "Eliza, help her out of those clothes and into something dry and warm."

"But Jandeau," Eliza said, her voice surly. "He's getting away."

"We have children on board," came another man's voice. And I don't want to lose the *Calypso* again." Tessa thought it sounded like Beck, Eliza's husband and the captain.

"Jandeau doesn't seem ready to give up his ship, either," Callum said. "He's heading out to sea."

"'Tis his third *Bourreau*."

"Yer safe now," Eagan said as he helped her walk away from the rail. "I won't let Jandeau harm ye again."

But how could he possibly promise that when her father still lived?

...

"I've sent word to Captain Wentworth of the English Navy,"

Adam said. "He's looking for Jandeau, too, for killing his brother and sister-in-law."

"My brother, Edward, sails with Wentworth and seeks revenge as much as I do," Eliza said. Despite her cold tone, she patted the back of her two-year-old son whom she held against one shoulder. She dipped in a rhythm meant to put the lad to sleep, although his blue eyes were wide open, watching everyone.

'Twas a family meeting in the great hall of Gylin Castle. Eagan, Adam, and Drostan had soaked in warm baths to pull the cold from their bones, and Lark and Anna had helped Tessa to do the same. Now Tessa rested in Eagan's large bed above with Charlotte, Grace, and Bann, while Sia roamed the room and the two wolfhounds stood alert, seeming to guard them. Despite the fright and cold sea, the cat seemed as hearty as usual.

"Did ye see Jandeau's face when Adam made it to the *Calypso* with Tessa?" Callum asked.

"He was furious," Eagan said, still wishing he could have been the one to dive in after her. His arm, shot extracted, was cleaned, stitched, and packed with a poultice, and Lark was pouring bitter concoctions down his throat every hour to fend off infection.

"He retreated to fight another day," Beck said. "With most of his crew unconscious, he knew he couldn't win against us."

"His gaze wouldn't leave Tessa," Eagan said. "He's coming back for her."

"Good," Eliza said, "I'm going to cut his—"

"Let's wait a few more years to scar our lad with his mama's bloody details about dismemberment," Beck said, pulling Richard out of her arms while continuing the gentle rhythm of bobbing up and down.

Eliza slid her thumb across the chubby cheek of her son

and smiled at him. "Our Richard will be the fiercest captain on the seas with the most courageous and golden heart." The bairn smiled back at her, reaching to tug a curl that hung along her face.

"If Tessa carries a Macquarie child, Jandeau will be back immediately," Callum said, and they all looked at Eagan.

He exhaled and gave a small shake of his head. "I don't know if she does or not."

Callum crossed his arms over his chest. "If the tree starts to lose leaves—"

"Foking hell, I hate that bloody tree," Eagan said, frustration heavy in his voice. He shoved his hands through his hair, ready to pull it out.

"We all do," Lark said from her seat at the table.

"We'll all move away if it starts to die again," Anna said, cradling her daughter, Elizabeth, against her shoulder.

The five brothers looked at her. "Not unless I'm dead," Adam said.

"And me," Beck followed.

Callum and Drostan nodded together.

Eagan looked at Anna. "'Tis a bit more than merely a piece of land to us."

"Foolish arses," Aunt Ida said, sounding like her old grumpy self.

Rabbie stood next to her. "Ye got to understand, Ida, we men fight for our land. And this land is Macquarie land. 'Tis in our blood."

"You're a MacDougall," Ida said, "not a Macquarie."

"I pledged my loyalty to John Macquarie," Rabbie said, crossing his arms. "Makes me a Macquarie."

Eagan didn't know if he agreed with his brothers. He loved his clan, his brothers, and their growing families. But life was more important than land to Eagan, and if pressed to save their children and wives, his brothers would agree with him. As it was, Eagan had been ready to leave his clan and Wolf Isle anyway.

He rubbed a hand down his face. His bag was still packed, waiting for him to take it up and strike out on his own. Bloody hell, so much had happened since he'd left it beside the door of his bedchamber.

"We should fortify the coast," Eagan said, "in case Jandeau returns here. He made landfall on Grissell's side of the isle before. And no one's there right now." Grissell, who was too weak to live on her own, had remained at the castle to help care for her returned children.

"Drostan and I will organize groups to patrol the coastline," Callum said.

"I'll finish the repairs to *Calypso's* forward deck," Beck said, "and sail her around near Drostan's cabin on the northeast side of Wolf Isle. It will be ready to strike if the *Bourreau* comes around."

"And I'll send word to Cullen and Tor," Adam said, "although, I think they're already at sea."

Lark rested both palms on the table. "We should put everyone in Ormaig and the surrounding homesteads on alert. 'Tis a small community, so strangers will stand out immediately."

Eagan trailed his gaze across them all. "Thank ye for yer efforts."

Eliza quirked one side of her smile higher. "'Tis obvious you love her, so if you lose her, you'll be impossible to live with."

Emotion poured through him like warm honey. He smiled, relief and gratitude overflowing inside him. He did love Tessa. Watching her sacrifice herself to rescue the children only deepened the strength of his love. She was everything opposite of her bitter, angry, evil father.

"I do love her," Eagan said, his words soft. "And when

she wakes, I'll ask her to wed."

"I'm awake." Tessa's voice rang out clear and even.

Eagan turned to see her standing in the archway leading to the stairs. She wore a simple pale and dark blue ensemble, that followed the inward curves of her waist over her hips. Her hair had been cleaned and brushed to fall in soft waves around her face. Her cheeks were red-hued with health. She was beautiful with her dark hair and fine, smooth features. The blue in her costume brought out the color in her eyes framed by dark lashes.

She met his gaze, a smile bending her soft lips. "I love you, too, Eagan Macquarie."

Eagan's heart jumped in his chest, and his smile widened.

Grissell stood beside her holding onto her arm.

"What are you doing out of bed, Grissell?" Ida asked.

"She came to see me and said I should come below," Tessa said, but her gaze remained on Eagan. "That she thought things were happening that involved me."

Eagan strode over to Tessa, wanting to snatch her up in his arms, but he couldn't knock the old woman aside. Or could he? Gently of course.

But Aunt Ida, apparently reading the situation in his rapid steps, came up beside Grissell, taking her other arm and leading her to the side.

Tessa gasped with a laugh as Eagan lifted her with only one arm to press her to him and spin her around. He set her down and kissed her, his hand cupping her jaw gently. "Thank the Lord I have ye back." Eagan let all the gratitude in his heart bleed out in the words. "And I will never let ye go."

Her laughter had that musical quality that reminded him of her singing. "I will have trouble getting dressed if you don't let go occasionally."

His brow went up, and he bent near her ear. "Then ye'll have to stay naked in my arms."

She chuckled.

Eagan inhaled, growing serious, as he let her back up. "Claudette Tempest Ainsworth, will ye wed me and spend the rest of my days as my wife and love?"

No one made a noise, not even the fussy bairns. She nodded, her smile bright. "Of course, Eagan Macquarie. I pledge myself to you for the rest of my days."

Rabbie slapped his hands together, making Ida jump and scowl at him. "That's basically a wedding right there," he said, his thick eyebrows raising with glee. "Oaths taken before witnesses. Ye're married."

Eagan's heart felt full to bursting, and he pulled Tessa against him, kissing her. She opened under him as if she hungered for him like he did for her.

"Let's make it official before the willow tree," Adam said.

With a frustrated groan, Eagan rested his forehead against Tessa's. "They want to make certain the tree *hears*."

Tessa shook her head. "Macquaries are a strange lot."

"They're cursed," Ida said. "That would make even the Pope strange." She frowned at Grissell, who was still on her arm. "And now finally," Ida said, "we will see Wilyam Macquarie's sins washed away."

The old woman neither agreed nor disagreed with Ida but let her lead her across the hall.

"Right now," Adam said. "Outside." He almost sounded giddy with the thought of finally breaking the curse that had plagued their clan for a century.

"Without a priest?" Lark asked.

"Sure," Beck said. "Before the tree. We can get a priest next week but the two need to marry right away, just in case."

In case Jandeau stole Tessa away again? Eagan's body clenched. He leaned to Tessa's ear. "He won't get close to ye."

She looked up at him, her smile faded away. "My father is still alive?"

Eagan nodded. "He sailed off, and we brought ye and the children home to Wolf Isle."

Her face remained tight. "I don't know yet if I'm with child, but either way, I fear he won't let me go," she whispered. A slight shudder ran through her as he rubbed up and down her arm. "Even if I'm married."

Then I'll kill him, he thought but didn't say it. Tessa had longed for a father but had received a monster instead. Her heart must be broken. Eagan kissed the top of her head. *I promise to heal it.*

Sia trotted down the stairs and into the great hall. "Oh, sweet Sia," Lia said from afar. "Did Charlotte let you out of Eagan's room?" Drostan put his arms around her as if she would forget her terrible reaction to cats and run to pick her up. "I know," Lia said, patting his arm.

The cat walked between them all on her way to the doorway leading to the bailey. "Follow the puss," Rabbie said, waving his arms to get them moving. "Go say the words before the tree, and then one of ye needs to pole the ferry over to Mull to get Father Thomas to make it a Godly union."

"So then this is what?" Ida asked, "a pagan union?"

"Woman," Rabbie said, "ye sure make it hard to like ye."

"Maybe I don't want you to like me," Ida said, her hand flapping up and down at him. "With that scruffy hair and stains on your tunic."

Rabbie looked down and pulled his shirt outward to see the marks that looked like apple tart. "'Tis better than bloodstains."

Ida rolled her eyes and continued to hold a silent Grissell up as they walked slowly toward the door arm in arm. They all followed.

The morning fog descended inside the walls surrounding the bailey. The cool temperature had the bite of winter in it. Eagan kept his good arm around Tessa as they walked.

He saw her fingering the golden birdcage still on a chain around her neck. "It didn't break away from ye in the sea."

Tessa clutched the golden locket lying on her chest. "Jandeau smashed it."

"We'll have it fixed."

She gave him a small smile and squeezed his hand that she held. "And I will put a likeness of you inside." Eagan kissed her gently on the lips.

"Very well now," Rabbie said, "we be all out here before the willow. Say yer pledges."

Eagan looked down into her eyes. "Tessa, I pledge to love, respect, and protect ye for all my life. I will be true to ye always."

Tessa smiled up at him, holding both his hands. "Eagan, I pledge to love, respect, and protect you for all my life. I will be true to you always."

They both smiled brightly at her reciprocated words. A small cheer rose in the bailey from his brothers, their wives, and the older children who'd run out of the castle to witness the union.

"Is the curse broken?" Ida asked.

Eagan tucked Tessa against his side, and they all turned to look at the ancient willow as if the green leaves would suddenly turn yellow like they should at this time of year. The wind blew the whip-like limbs about, the green leaves on them the same as they'd been.

"Maybe they will start turning color in the next day or so," Lark said, her daughter, Hannah, on her hip. "Falling to the ground like from any normal tree in autumn."

"Can I touch it then, Mama?" her five-year-old son asked, his hands outstretched.

Adam scooped up the lad. "Not until we deem it safe."

"I can touch it again," Drostan said, but Lia held tight to his arm.

"Let's not right now," she said.

"But I did before," Drostan said. "Once touched I'm unable to father a child." He took a step away from her.

"That part of the curse may not be true," Lia said, drawing out the last word with a little twist of her lips.

Drostan turned on the balls of his feet to face her, his boots crunching on the pebbles. His mouth dropped open, his eyes widening. "Are ye…?"

Lia nodded, her hands going to her abdomen. "I think so." It had been two years since they'd wed, and no child had been conceived yet. They both had decided that they would adopt when the opportunity came.

Drostan whooped, lifting her off the ground in a hug and twirling them both around as more cheers erupted in the bailey.

"Curse or not," Eagan called out, "the Macquarie Clan is growing."

Lark stuck her finger into Adam's chest. "Curses are only real when people believe in them."

"Well," Adam said, setting his son down. "I believe this curse is broken." He kissed her and looked out at all of them. "We've learned about love, things Wilyam Macquarie never did." Adam grinned at Lark. "Like love can come from unexpected proposals."

She nodded. "And true love can heal a lifetime of old hurts."

Beck pulled Eliza closer, taking their son from her. "Love means respecting each other's differences and not expecting another to be something she's not." Eliza pulled his face down for a kiss while their son tugged on her hair.

Callum turned Anna in a circle, and she wove under his arm. "Love means never abandoning your partner no matter how difficult the circumstances."

"And trusting one another with each other's secrets,"

Drostan said, capturing Lia's face between his two hands for a kiss.

Eagan's heart swelled with happiness, and he looked from his brothers to Tessa. "And it means being loyal to one's love even if their family is…a bit…"

"Vicious, murdering, lying," she finished.

He chuckled, his brows going up. "Aye, even if their family is all that."

Clap. Clap. Clap.

The cracking sound made everyone turn toward the gate. Eagan's hand moved straight to his sword as his gaze rose to the top of the wall. Instead of the two usual guards in the gatehouse tower, another figure stood dark and mocking.

"The Macquarie pups have found love," Claude Jandeau said and continued his cracking, slow applause. "Bravo." All around the wall, pirates rose, some adding to the slow, stark clapping while others held muskets primed and aimed at the people in the bailey. The entire Macquarie Clan was surrounded.

Chapter Twenty-Three

The sentimental warmth that had spread through Tessa's body drained as if she'd been struck mortally, leaving cold dread in the emptiness.

Claude Jandeau continued to clap slowly with each hard thump of his boot as he stepped down the stairs from the guard tower. The children screamed, running for their parents. The Macquarie brothers and Rabbie pushed the women and children behind their backs, forming a circle around them.

Men from Jandeau's ship stood at stations along the wall holding muskets aimed at them.

Tessa stood between Lark and Lia, their arms pressed against one another while the children crowded into the very center at her back. They clung to each other, fidgeting and trying to keep the youngest ones quiet and still. Tessa's heart thumped hard, and 'twas difficult to draw breath. But she forced an inhale and turned to face the children. A soft ribbon of song came from her.

"Hush les enfants, be strong and brave…" She translated

the short French song into English. Little eyes stared up at her, transfixed and settled for the moment. She let the song run out and turned back.

Rabbie tried to keep Ida behind him, and she smacked his arms to let her see. Grissell had moved into the shade of the willow tree as if its whipping boughs would guard her, away from the pirates' target.

"What do ye want, Jandeau?" Adam called. All the brothers had their swords out, but they would do little at this distance against muskets.

"I've come for my daughter, and I'll also take your isle and maybe your wives and children if you give me any trouble."

"Ye have come to die then," Eagan said, his words commanding and dark.

"You're not in a position to threaten, Macquarie pup." Jandeau motioned to the men around the wall. "As you can see, my men have recovered from your poisonous concoction, la fille." He peered between the broad shoulders standing sentry before Tessa to meet her gaze. He *tsk*ed. "My daughter has a cruelness in her." He grinned. "Your knowledge could be of help to me."

Tessa followed him with her gaze while Jandeau walked around their circle, out of reach of the Macquarie swords. If they lunged, no doubt one of his men would put a shot through the Macquarie's face. Jandeau acted like he was in complete control of the situation, and it seemed he was.

Jandeau glanced at the willow tree and Grissell standing beneath. "So the crone still lives. I thought she'd died and was in the ground already." He turned away, not bothered by the limbs blowing around, grazing his head and back like a lover's fingers.

From along the wall, one of the Macquarie guards must have broken through his restraints. He yanked off his gag and lunged for one of the pirates, but the large man snarled, lifted him, and threw him over the side. Tessa and Lark gasped as he hit the ground with a thud. He was most likely dead.

Hannah, who was only one year old, cried, and Lark bounced her up and down, trying to soothe her.

"I could order them to shoot all Macquarie men," Jandeau said, pointing around their tight circle. "Then we will take your women and children to use or sell. He moved his head left to right as if weighing his choices, as if he weren't talking about rape and slavery. "The old women will die of course." He met Eagan's gaze. "But, really, I want my daughter. Claudette, come to me and save your Wolf Isle friends."

"You promised that before and still took the children," she called out from the inner circle.

Jandeau shrugged. "You don't have a choice but to hope my offer is true now."

"I'm not with child," Tessa said even though she still hadn't gotten her courses.

Eagan's hand reached behind him, finding hers to hold. "And we just married, so even if she was with my child, it wouldn't be a bastard."

Jandeau clicked his tongue. "A shame that." One of the willow limbs must have tickled his neck, because he yanked it hard, breaking it away from the tree and tossing it. "But I will still take my daughter."

"She's wed now," Eagan said, moving around the circle so he could stare at Jandeau where he stood by the tree. "Ye have no legal control over her anymore."

Jandeau laughed. "Since when do I care about legalities? Non. I will take my daughter and anything else of yours. Compensation for two ships and countless crew you've cost me."

"How did ye even get in here?" Beck asked.

Jandeau's hand flipped around. "'Twas dark and yer village is guarded by aging, easily fooled pirates, eh. You will find a number of them incapacitated."

Eliza cursed, and Tessa remembered that many of those ex-pirates were her family.

"Shhh, Hannah," five-year-old John whispered to his baby sister. "Da will kill the bad men."

Terror bloomed inside Tessa. The whole Macquarie Clan would be killed because her father wouldn't relinquish his hold on her. How could she allow that? Even if she remained hiding here behind them, once Eagan and his family were killed, Jandeau would still drag her back onto his ship, the children thrown into that dank, dark cell in the hull. Would Jandeau's men find Charlotte, Grace, and Bann up in Eagan's room? Barging in to grab them out of sleep into terror? They'd shoot the two wolfhounds too.

Bang! Tessa jumped, and the children screamed inside their tight circle of mothers. Tessa looked out to see one of the men on the wall aiming outside the bailey where an agonizing groan sounded. The crewman yelled down. "And any more of you trying to sneak up on us will be shot, too." He quickly set about reloading his musket while six other pirates aimed directly toward their huddled group and two others glanced over the wall.

"Word is out, Jandeau," Adam yelled, facing out even though Jandeau stood behind their circle. "The whole village will be coming to attack yer men."

"You will die before they can get inside," Jandeau said. "You and your wives and children. Unless you send Claudette out to me."

Tessa looked at each of the pirates, her gaze stopping on Hubert. He hadn't been stripped and devoid of his tongue. Perhaps he'd been saved by eating her potion. Would Hubert fire at the Macquaries to further show his loyalty to Jandeau?

"Come out here, daughter," Jandeau called. "Or I order my men to start shooting."

Eagan squeezed her hand as if to tell her not to step out. "I must," she whispered.

"Nay," he whispered back.

"You'll save me again."

"Bloody hell, he will hide ye away."

"On the count of three, ma fille, your friends and your man will die. Une, deux—"

"Arrêt! Stop!" Tessa yelled and yanked her hand from Eagan's.

"Nay, Tessa!" he shouted, the words like thunder.

There was no getting through the wall of Macquarie brothers with their powerful arms and shoulders in the way. Tessa crouched and threw herself between the space formed by their legs and scrambled out of the protective circle. "Don't shoot them. Leave them unharmed," she yelled, running to her father where he stood at the edge of the willow's reach. "And I will go with you. I will..." She wet her dry lips and pushed the words out: "I will stay with you."

"Nay!" Eagan roared, but his brothers held him back, their gazes raised to the muskets ready to fire if any of them approached Jandeau.

Jandeau grabbed her to him, his arm curling around her middle like he'd held her on his ship. Once again it felt indecent. Was that an erection against her backside? Did power inflame his passions? Cruelty? The thought made her nearly vomit.

...

Eagan watched Tessa blanch to a sickly pale. Life seemed to drain out of her as her father held her against him. She looked like a tortured plaything he refused to give up. She wouldn't remain alive for long in his care. If he didn't abuse the life out of her, she'd find a way to take her own life.

Heart pounding, Eagan fought his brothers to rush at the pirate. His insides were raw and twisted.

"They'll shoot ye," Adam rasped, his arm wrapped around Eagan's good shoulder.

Callum's hands were like vises around Eagan's waist. "'Tis what he wants. Ye run at him, and his men will start shooting. Once we are fallen, they will shoot everyone else."

A whimper sounded from inside the circle, and one of the mothers tried to soothe the frightened children. Turmoil and fury roiled inside Eagan. "Take me," he yelled. "Ye can torture me however ye want, but leave her here, and leave my family alone."

"Fok," Drostan whispered, but Eagan ignored him and whatever else his brothers were saying. His entire focus was on Tessa's face. Tears ran down her cheeks, and she closed her eyes as if willing herself to disappear or die there on the spot.

Jandeau scoffed. "'Tis an uneven trade. A lovely woman, my own daughter, for a Macquarie pup. Non." The monster slid the back of his finger up Tessa's neck to her cheek as if he were her lover instead of her father. Jandeau looked back out at Eagan, his gaze sliding amongst all the Macquarie brothers. "Now offer me Wolf Isle along with your life, and I might consider your offer."

Behind Jandeau, something moved underneath the dancing branches of the willow tree. *Grissell.* She stood near the trunk, her bent frame straightening as if she shirked off a cloak of years from her shoulders. She wrapped her hands around the dagger that had been stuck in the tree for a century, the dagger no one had been able to draw out, the dagger that still bled with the curse.

The old woman had been barely able to walk. Drostan had been the last Macquarie to try to draw the dagger out of the tree. Even with his muscular strength, it hadn't moved.

And yet...

"Holy God," Beck whispered.

Off to the side, Rabbie passed the sign of the cross before him, and Aunt Ida actually held onto the old man's shoulder as she stared.

In silence, Grissell slid the dagger from the tree as if the willow had been merely holding it for her. She turned, and with three strides that seemed as strong as a woman's half her age, Grissell reached Jandeau's back. The willow branches seemed to gather around her, hiding her from the pirates with the muskets. The limbs moved in a frenzied fashion, making it hard to see her from the sides.

Hands clasped around the dagger's hilt, Grissell raised it over her head and plunged it down into the pirate's back, under his left shoulder. If the man had a heart, it was skewered.

Jandeau's face contorted with a mix of pain and bewilderment. His arm dropped from Tessa, and he spun, trying to reach the protruding dagger.

Crack! A musket went off. Adam and Callum released Eagan as they turned to shield their families, pushing them down to the ground. Eagan rushed toward Tessa. Two more muskets went off, and Eagan grabbed Tessa to him, dropping them both to the ground to cover her with his body.

"Tessa. Oh God, Tessa," he said, holding her.

"Eagan!" The panic in her voice made him squeeze her tighter. "You're bleeding!"

The warmth of the blood caught his attention seconds before the sting of the shot registered in his other shoulder. Daingead! Two shots in less than two days.

Eagan lifted his face to Jandeau's shouts. The limbs of the willow tree whipped across the pirate's face, slashing it hard enough to leave lines of blood. Grissell had stepped back under the tree, watching the pirate thrash as blood poured from his slashed heart.

Shouts along the wall continued, along with a few blasts from muskets. Jandeau dropped to his knees, and Grissell walked back to stand tall before him. "An appropriate sacrifice," she said, and spat.

From Eagan's position on the ground, covering Tessa as she desperately tried to stop the blood pouring from his shoulder, Eagan watched Captain Claude Jandeau Lemaire release his final fetid breath.

Chapter Twenty-Four

Tessa pressed her hand against Eagan's arm where warm blood wet her palm, staining his tunic bright red. "You're shot, Eagan. Let me up." She pushed against his chest. The man was heavy. Had he lost consciousness?

"They're still shooting."

She yanked the sash he wore on his belt. "Lie flat. Now!" She put all the authority she could muster into her voice.

The tight circle of Macquaries had dispersed, and Tessa saw Hubert on the wall throwing a musket to Callum on the ground before running along the wall to a crewman leaning over it, dead. Had Hubert shot him? Surprising his crewmates and picking them off as they fired down into the bailey?

Tessa yanked Eagan's tunic up, but she couldn't reach the source of the blood because it was in his upper shoulder. "We have to stop the bleeding right now."

He lay back, his eyes closed. The look made it hard for her to swallow, but the medical training she'd learned from her mother helped her keep moving.

"'Tis just a graze," Eagan said, but his face had paled.

"If by graze, you mean a lead ball lodged in your upper arm, then oui, 'tis just grazed." Her words shot out with sarcasm, and she saw him smile. "Shot in both shoulders. Mon Dieu."

Eagan watched the red of the sun behind his closed eyes. "Not the best way to start a marriage."

She tied the rag as tightly around his arm as she could while his jaw tightened, but he never cried out. The gunfire had ceased, and Tessa stood, yelling. "Eagan's been shot. Again."

Lark and Anna ran toward her as well as Ida.

"Lady Claudette," Hubert yelled, his hands raised as Beck and Drostan came toward him along the wall. "Tell them I'm for you, milady. I shot me own men to save you."

"We know," Beck said.

Drostan carried a musket as he came toward Hubert on the other side. "Put yer bloody hands down."

"He helped me on the *Bourreau*," she said and turned back to Eagan. Adam had come over, lifting him off the ground with a grunt. Callum quickly helped by pushing upward under Eagan's arse as they carried him.

"'Tis in the other shoulder, above the heart. No organs hit there," Eagan said, but all the blood made Tessa worry.

The cluster of women and children trotted after Adam and Callum as they carried their brother into the castle, laying him down on the long wooden table. "Are you hurt, Tessa?" Anna asked, inspecting her light blue gown.

Tessa glanced down at the red smeared across it. "No. 'Tis Eagan's blood."

"I have a lot," he said softly. "Enough to spare."

"Ye already lost enough yesterday," Drostan said.

Tessa looked at a wide-eyed maid who stood in the archway. "We need hot water, whisky, pliers, needle, thread, rags, and a lit candle." She leaned into him. "I might have been nearly unconscious on the ship when you were shot the first time, but I'm fully awake now. And I know what to do."

"Lark and I will help her," Anna said. "Come along, Jane." The two ran off to fetch supplies.

Eagan opened his eyes. "I love ye, Tessa." The truth of his love shone in his blue eyes.

"I love you, too." She leaned in to kiss him gently. "Just stay alive."

He held her gaze. "That's my plan."

With Adam's help, they cut his tunic off. The musket ball was fished out of Eagan's shoulder, and Lark quickly stitched it internally when Tessa's hands were shaking too much. It hadn't hit a major blood vessel. The wound was cleaned and packed like the one in the other shoulder.

Callum, Beck, and Drostan jogged back into the hall, carrying muskets. "Eagan?" Callum asked, his face tight.

"All sewn up," Dora said from the cluster of little children near the hearth.

"Thank God," Drostan murmured as the brothers surrounded the table.

"We moved the dead outside the wall," Callum said.

Beck spoke to the room. "That sturdy little man, Hubert, is planning the *Bourreau* takeover with Eliza's men from the village. They used to battle Jandeau and buried one of their own this past week when Jandeau abducted Tessa and the children."

Eagan's eyes were fastened to Tessa's bright gaze. Adam cleared his throat. "Tessa is ready to beat Death off with a stick if it comes near ye, brother."

"I know every tincture, poultice, and tonic to keep the grave away," she said, touching his face, although her hand still shook slightly.

Eagan closed his eyes but kept his smile. "I'm bloody tired."

Callum let out a breath. "Ye deserve a rest. Ye saved yer

bride and broke the curse by loving her."

"Where is Grissell?" Tessa asked.

"Left when we opened the gates." Rabbie's voice came from the entryway. "She walked off with the six-toed cat and her two white cats. But she handed me this." He held the dagger between his thumb and finger as if it was tainted. Even out of the tree, the ancient weapon still sent a shiver through Tessa.

Drostan nodded to the dagger. "Do ye think Grissell could have pulled it out at any time?"

"Nay," Adam said and laid his hand over Eagan's uninjured forearm. "It took the breaking of the curse to release it from the willow. Good job, little brother."

Eagan frowned, his eyes still closed. "Ye know I'm taller than all of ye."

Callum snorted. "Not right now, ye aren't."

Rabbie released the dagger. It clanked onto the wooden floor, and he picked up a tankard, raising it. "Here's to the end of the Macquarie curse!"

The sound of steel sliding filled the room as the four brothers unsheathed their long swords, holding them high into the air. Eagan opened his eyes to see them raised on all sides.

"Here's to the end of that bastard, Jandeau!" Callum yelled, and the whole room roared, including Bann, Grace, and Charlotte who had come downstairs.

The noise echoed in the room from all those mouths, and Eagan smiled up at Tessa. Charlotte, Grace, and a much healthier Bann ran over to hug her there next to Eagan, unaware of the deadly nightmare that could have befallen them. The two wolfhounds loped beside them, having been trapped above and safe with the three.

"Here's to Eagan finally falling in love!" Beck yelled out, and another roar rose and fell like a ferocious wave followed by giggles from the children even though some of them covered their ears. Lark and Anna's other sisters from the village ran into the room from outside. The gathering was quickly growing into a celebration.

Tessa broke free of the children to lean over her Highland love. His pallor was subsiding, and his eyes were clear. He smiled up at her. Placing a palm on his cheek, she leaned down, her words only for him. "No matter what storms come our way..." She kissed his lips. "No matter what, we will ride the tempest out together."

"Aye, Tessa lass." His smile turned into a seductive leer. "I will ride my Tempest all night long."

Her smiling mouth dropped open before turning wicked. She kissed him before leaning into his ear. "We will see who does the riding and who does the groaning on his back while you heal both arms, husband."

They were nose to nose. "Creativity is the key," he said, and she leaned back in for a kiss full of promise, passion, and most definitely love.

Six Months Later

Eagan presented his arm to Tessa, and they entered Gylin's great hall. She took it gingerly out of habit, but he laid his other hand over hers. "They don't pain me anymore," he said of his healed bullet wounds. He'd worked over the winter with Adam to strengthen both shoulders and arms again.

"Thank God they've healed well," she said.

Tessa wore a new rose-hued gown made of soft wool. The color brought out the healthy glow in her cheeks. Half her luxurious sable-colored hair was pulled up and woven into braids that circled her head like a crown while the rest fell in waves past her shoulders.

He leaned into her. "Ye're gorgeous, lass."

She smiled but turned her gaze toward the room full of people. "There's no time for you to be pulling me into a dark corner, so keep your honeyed words to yourself until *after* dinner."

He chuckled. "But 'tis true. Ye're truly lovely." Truth was that his vigorous bride pulled *him* into dark corners as much as he pulled her.

She smiled, and his heart clenched with gratitude that they'd survived against the odds and were together.

"Tessa!" Grace called, running over to them to twirl in her new petticoat. "Look what Mistress Ida sewed for me. Charlotte, too. And Bann has a new waistcoat." She pointed over to where Bann showed Ida Macquarie how well he played a game, catching a ball on a string into the attached little cup. Aunt Ida looked ten years younger since coming to Wolf Isle to live, mostly because she now smiled.

"'Tis quite bonny," Eagan said, and Tessa agreed.

The girl curtsied and ran back over to Charlotte, who was talking to Dora and Kat Montgomerie. The Macquarie family was all gathering for the Beltane meal after the all-day festival. The youngest children had fallen asleep by the fire, after the full day of running in the spring fields. The wolfhounds slept near them, guarding their small charges.

A second long table had been brought in and cloths covered both where pewter plates were set with goblets, eating daggers, and napkins. Bunches of spring buttercups and bluebells lay in ribbon-tied bunches down the center of the table. A cheery fire blazed in the hearth that kept them warm against the chill of a spring night in the Highlands.

"I think that's all of us," Lark called and started pointing out where couples could sit, the children mixed in with them. Rabbie, who had taken to trimming his beard and keeping himself washed, held out a chair for Aunt Ida. The woman gave him a narrow-eyed glare but smiled when she turned toward the table, letting him help push her chair in.

Kofi, Eliza's friend and cook for the castle, had created a feast. Maids brought out platters of meats, seasoned early greens, warm bread, fresh butter and jarred jams, and candied fruits. The grass was growing greener and lush on Wolf Isle, the berry bushes full of flowers, the gardens sprouting like never before, and the new beehives were thriving. The willow tree had lost its fall leaves and new buds had formed along the thin limbs. It was as if a veil had been lifted from the isle. Or a curse.

Adam stood. "Quiet down," he said. The murmuring and light laughter faded slowly.

Lark stood next to him, and he nodded to her. She brandished a bouquet of green above her head. "This is sorrel," she said, her smile mischievous. "When I came to Wolf Isle five years ago, I brought this, thinking I would be making a stew for my new husband. Little did I know that I had also married into a cursed clan with four unruly brothers."

Deep laughter rumbled through the hall.

"There were dirty dishes and tankards scattered along the table." Lark pointed upward. "Birds roosted in the rafters, and Callum and Drostan were wrestling on the floor."

"I won," Callum said.

Drostan snorted with a shake of his head. "Not how I remember it."

"I had to check my brothers' fingernails," Lark continued, "and remind them not to fight."

"Even though they did, and we were nearly banned from Mull," Adam said.

"I seem to remember you joining in," Lark said, looking pointedly at her husband. But then she waved her hand and looked back along the table. "But look at you all now. Clean..." She flapped a hand across the table. "Even Rabbie."

He grinned at her and showed his dirt-free fingernails around the table. Everyone laughed.

"He certainly smells a lot better," Beck said.

"Aunt Ida likes fresh-smelling things," Eagan said, earning him a glare from both his aunt and Rabbie, but everyone knew they were growing close.

"And our clan is increasing," Lark said, indicating

everyone filling the hall. "Gylin Castle is no longer dark, dirty, and lonely. 'Tis full of life now, thanks to you all."

Eagan raised his goblet filled with wine. "Huzzah!"

"Huzzah!" everyone answered, even the children who were awake, holding their small cups of spiced juice.

Next to Eagan, Tessa stood. "Thank you to Ida Macquarie for taking over the children's home with the passing of the amazing woman who truly saved us." They all murmured and smiled at Ida, and Tessa continued. "I raise my cup to Grissell Macquarie, the wisest and fiercest protector I've ever known."

They raised their cups quietly in solemn remembrance. After stabbing Jandeau in the heart, she'd walked back to her cottage, sat before her fire, closed her eyes, and died with her two white cats in her lap. Records found in her cottage noted her birth year and lineage. Grissell's great-grandmother had placed the original curse on Wilyam Macquarie and his clan. She was the daughter of the bairn cut free from her hanged mother, Elspet, and she'd used the last of her strength to save the Macquarie Clan. Her final age was ninety-seven years.

Eagan had moved into Tessa's cottage, and they were building onto it. Then he could be right there to help his aunt with anything she needed, although Rabbie stopped by every morning now.

They'd all moved out of Gylin Castle except for Lark and Adam and their children. Drostan and Lia were expecting their first bairn in the summer. Beck and Eliza, with the help of the men from Ormaig Village, had taken over the *Bourreau* and turned over the remaining pirates to Eliza's father, Captain Wentworth of the English Navy. The Macquaries had renamed the *Bourreau* the *Grissell* and were refurbishing it.

Eagan's other brothers were raising their cups to their wives, and Eagan held his goblet high, smiling at Tessa. "How did I get so lucky as to lure a lass like ye to me?"

She sat back down and kissed him. "Who says you lured me? I believe I'm the siren."

Eagan chuckled, setting his cup down to take Tessa into his arms. With the sounds of laughter and merriment filling the great hall of Gylin Castle, he kissed her. Once cold and alone, his life and his entire family were now filled with the greatest blessing of all: love.

Acknowledgments

I can't believe we've broken the curse of Wolf Isle! Thank you, dear readers, for following these five wonderful Macquarie brothers and the women who stole their hearts. Without you I would have no one to cheer with me about the end of Captain Jandeau. Thank you for loving happily-ever-afters as much as I do!

Thank you to my agent, Kevan Lyon, who has kept me sane for 12+ years and continues to help me navigate the deep waters of publishing. And to Alethea Spiridon, my amazing editor who keeps me going, is always kind, and makes my stories so much richer.

Also…

At the end of each of my books, I ask that you, my awesome readers, please remind yourselves of the whispered symptoms of ovarian cancer. I am now an eleven-year survivor, one of the lucky ones. Please don't rely on luck. If you experience any of these symptoms consistently for three weeks or more, go see your GYN.

- **Bloating**
- **Eating less and feeling full faster**
- **Abdominal pain**
- **Trouble with your bladder**

Other symptoms may include indigestion, back pain, pain with intercourse, constipation, fatigue, and menstrual irregularities.

About the Author

Heather McCollum is a *USA Today* and *Publishers Weekly* bestselling author of historical romance full of adventure and touched with spice. Brawny Highlanders with golden hearts and fiery heroines are her favorites. She has over twenty-five romance novels published and is the 2022 Winner of the National Excellence in Romance Fiction Award.

When she's not creating vibrant characters and magical adventures on the page, she's roaring her own battle cry in the war against ovarian cancer. Ms. McCollum slew the cancer beast and resides with her very own Highland hero, a rescued golden retriever, and three kids in the wilds of suburbia on the mid-Atlantic coast. For more information about Ms. McCollum, please visit www.HeatherMcCollum.com.

Don't miss the rest of the Brothers of Wolf Isle series...

THE HIGHLANDER'S UNEXPECTED PROPOSAL
THE HIGHLANDER'S PIRATE LASS
THE HIGHLANDER'S TUDOR LASS
THE HIGHLANDER'S SECRET AVENGER

Also by Heather McCollum...

THE HIGHLANDER'S WILD FLAME

SONS OF SINCLAIR SERIES

HIGHLAND CONQUEST
HIGHLAND WARRIOR
HIGHLAND JUSTICE
HIGHLAND BEAST
HIGHLAND SURRENDER

HIGHLAND ISLES SERIES

THE BEAST OF AROS CASTLE
THE ROGUE OF ISLAY ISLE
THE WOLF OF KISIMUL CASTLE
THE DEVIL OF DUNAKIN CASTLE

HIGHLAND HEARTS SERIES

CAPTURED HEART
TANGLED HEARTS
CRIMSON HEART

Discover more historical romance from Entangled...

A Highland Rogue to Ruin
a Highland Handfasts novel by E. Elizabeth Watson

Tormund MacLeod only wants vengeance for his brother's murder. But the Lughnasadh festival offers many distractions—including a fair and bonny masked vixen whose touch disarms him. Lady Brighde MacDonald might understand her brother's overprotectiveness—but what she needs is the reckless freedom in the arms of a Highlander. Only too late, they both recognize that they're enemies. Now their tryst could mean war. And Tormund hides a long-buried secret that could destroy both clans.

The Highlander's Enchantress
a novel by Violetta Rand

If her cruel and domineering father were to be believed, Kali Bane is the worst of women. Defiant. Independent. When she refuses to wed, her father bans her to the McKay clan in the Highlands, warning them that she's a witch. Here she is little more than a hostage, kept from sight from almost all but Adam McKay, the laird's son. The longer she remains imprisoned in the McKay tower, the more Kali and Adam realize there are other forces at play. They're both pieces in a silent, terrible game that could destroy everyone they've ever loved...including each other.

Printed in Great Britain
by Amazon